MURDER IN A CORNISH ALEHOUSE

MURDER IN A CORNISH ALEHOUSE

A Mistress Jaffrey Mystery

Kathy Lynn Emerson

This first world edition published 2016
in Great Britain and 2017 in the USA by
SEVERN HOUSE PUBLISHERS LTD of
19 Cedar Road, Sutton, Surrey, England, SM2 5DA.
Trade paperback edition first published
in Great Britain and the USA 2017 by
SEVERN HOUSE PUBLISHERS LTD

British Library Cataloguing in Publication Data
A CIP catalogue record for this title is available from the British Library.

ISBN-13: 978-0-7278-8676-7 (cased)
ISBN-13: 978-1-84751-779-1 (trade paper)
ISBN-13: 978-1-78010-848-3 (e-book)

This is a work of fiction. Names, characters, places and incidents
are either the product of the author's imagination or are used fictitiously.
Except where actual historical events and characters are being described
for the storyline of this novel, all situations in this publication are
fictitious and any resemblance to actual persons, living or dead,
business establishments, events or locales is purely coincidental.

All Severn House titles are printed on acid-free paper.

Severn House Publishers support the Forest Stewardship Council™ [FSC™],
the leading international forest certification organisation.
All our titles that are printed on FSC certified paper carry the FSC logo.

Typeset by Palimpsest Book Production Ltd.,
Falkirk, Stirlingshire, Scotland.
Printed and bound in Great Britain by
TJ International, Padstow, Cornwall.

ONE

14 May 1584

Sir Walter Pendennis, a justice of the peace for Cornwall, knew the kiddlywink in Boscastle – an alehouse with a few beds for travelers – for the haunt of pirates and smugglers. Bound by an agreement between himself and Alexander Trewinard, he turned a blind eye to these activities. In return, the alehouse keeper provided him with intelligence, some of which Walter passed on to an agent of Queen Elizabeth's principal secretary and spymaster, Sir Francis Walsingham. Matters of purely local interest, he kept to himself.

It had been some time since the two men last met in person. Walter noted the changes in Trewinard without remarking upon them. The alehouse keeper's once bright red hair had faded and become sparse. What Walter knew to be fair skin was deeply tanned, as if he had gone to sea himself, rather than remaining ashore as a receiver of contraband. Trewinard's features, always rough-hewn, also appeared more gaunt than Walter remembered.

Of greater concern was Trewinard's reluctance to meet his eyes.

'You sent for me for a reason,' Walter said.

Trewinard heaved a deep sigh, his manner that of an elderly man.

Walter frowned. Trewinard was five or six years his junior and Walter had seen but fifty-five winters. It might be true that most people regarded anyone above the age of fifty-six as old, but there were plenty of men, and women, too, who lived to be eighty or ninety. No one milestone inevitably led to a decline in health or limited what remained of a man's lifespan.

He spared a moment's thought to the fact that his own hair, once sand-colored, had begun to thin by the time he was in his mid-thirties. For the last ten years or more, only a fringe had decorated his pate. In every other respect, however, he was as fit as ever he'd been. His muscles were strong, his reflexes sharp. He took exercise daily, both walking and riding, and he practiced on a regular basis with a variety of weapons. He was as deadly with a pistol as he was with a bow and arrow or a sword and dagger.

Trewinard cleared his throat. 'You will have heard of the death of Sir John Killigrew.'

Walter nodded. Killigrew had been a fellow justice of the peace, captain of one of the queen's castles on the south coast of Cornwall, and the head of the queen's commission on piracy for Cornwall. He had died a bit more than two months earlier, on the fifth of March. Walter had traveled to Arwennack, at the mouth of the river Fal, for his funeral.

Now that he thought about it, he was surprised that Alexander Trewinard had not been present on that occasion. Sir John's mother – still living and like to reach one hundred – had been a Trewinard before her marriage. The alehouse keeper, he assumed, was kin to her.

Saying nothing, Walter waited for the other man to come to the point. It was so quiet in the alehouse that he could hear the raucous cries of gulls flying over the harbor. The tang of salt air drifted in through the open window, mixing with the ever-present smells of spilt ale and beer, fish, sweat, and wet dog. For no readily apparent reason, Trewinard let a shaggy-coated cur – a friendly dog, but useless – have the run of his establishment.

The alehouse keeper drank deeply from a wooden vessel known as a black jack. Having drained it, he stared morosely into the dregs. 'You will know already what happened last summer off the coast of Dorset. Forty-three pirates were captured. Seven of their captains were executed.'

Walter nodded. It had been the first serious attempt on the part of the queen's government to put an end to the widespread piracy that plagued their island nation. Trewinard's reference to Sir John Killigrew now made sense. The Killigrews in general, and Sir John in particular, had done far more than turn a blind eye to such criminal acts.

'There's something strange afoot, Pendennis. Something that

could change things for every man jack of us. I hear whispers that the crews were pardoned on condition that they enter the queen's service.'

Granting pardons to lesser offenders was not uncommon. Recruiting them seemed odd. It was possible, Walter supposed, though for choice he'd not put his trust in a reformed brigand. He studied his companion. He had never seen Trewinard so shaken. The other man was not just nervous, constantly glancing over his shoulder. He was afraid.

Walter quaffed his ale, savoring the sweet, thick drink while he studied their surroundings. He could discern nothing alarming. Trewinard's wife, a big, buxom woman, waited on two men seated at the other table. That they were dressed for travel suggested that they were strangers.

As he watched, Morwen Trewinard refilled their earthenware cups from her jug, exchanging pleasantries with them as she did so. She laughed at something one of them said – a rich, earthy sound – and tapped the fellow none-too-gently on the ear with the flat of her hand.

'Thee'rt a gookoo!' she chided him, using the local dialect to call him a fool for thinking he could tempt her to misbehave.

Despite her words, there was a distinct sway to her ample hips as she walked away. She carried her jug to the window. Just outside, more alehouse patrons lounged on a bench set against the wall. This ale bench was a popular spot for local folk to gather, since beer bought out of doors was cheaper than that consumed by the fire. The servants Walter had brought with him lingered there in company with two or three other men.

He turned his attention back to Trewinard. 'Why is this recruitment cause for concern?' The question was intended to prod the alehouse keeper into revealing the reason he'd wanted Walter to come to him in Boscastle.

'An army of pirates? It is not to be thought of!'

'A navy, I should think. And as it is only a rumor—'

'Truth,' Trewinard insisted. 'But others know far more than I do.'

'Give me a name.'

Trewinard clutched his empty black jack with both hands, but when his wife started toward them with her jug, he waved her away.

Her scowl was thunderous.

Walter glanced past her to the other table. Neither man seated there appeared to be paying attention to anything other than his ale.

Trewinard took another uneasy look around before he leaned closer. 'Talk to Diggory Pyper.'

'Sampson Pyper's lad?' Walter did not trouble to hide his amazement. The Pypers were a prominent merchant family in Launceston. Wealthy enough to style himself a gentleman, old Sampson also owned land at Tresmarrow and Liskeard. 'What does young Diggory have to do with pirates?'

'He is lately made captain of his own ship. Those who know him say he means to take over where Captain Piers left off.'

Walter did not care for the sound of that. John Piers had been one of the most notorious of the Cornish pirates. His execution some two years earlier should have served as a warning to those who contemplated going 'on the account'.

'Can you arrange a meeting?' he asked aloud.

'I have a wife and children, Pendennis. I'd as soon not sign my own death warrant.'

'If I have not once clapped you in gaol in all the years we've done business together, Trewinard, I am not likely to do so now.'

The alehouse keeper sent him a sickly smile. 'You are not the one I fear. I have told you all I can, mayhap more than I should have.' He stood so abruptly that the stool he'd been sitting on tipped over with a crash.

Walter rose, making a placating gesture. 'There must be something more—'

'A good journey home to you, Sir Walter,' Trewinard said in a loud, carrying voice. Under his breath, he added, 'Ke war gamm!'

The phrase, in Cornish, meant 'leave me alone'.

To oblige his host, Walter left the alehouse and rode away, but he was deeply troubled. A merchant's son turned pirate? Pirates fighting for the Crown? Both revelations had surprised him, but neither seemed sufficient reason for the alehouse keeper to fear for his life.

TWO

11 June 1584 – 12 June 1584

A blissful smile on her face, Rosamond Jaffrey lay curled against her husband's side, using his arm for a pillow as they drifted into sleep. Sated, well content with her lot, she closed her eyes and counted her blessings.

She knew she was not a beautiful woman, having inherited her father's narrow face and high forehead, but Rob insisted that her features were most pleasing to him, especially her long, dark brown hair, at present unbound and tangled, and what he termed her 'sparkling and mischievous' dark eyes. She suspected he waxed poetic with that description, but she believed him when he said that he would never love anyone else as well as he loved her. After all, they had grown up together. He knew her flaws better than anyone and accepted what most men would not, that she would never be an ordinary, biddable female.

Two months had passed since their life together began anew. In that time, not a single ripple of discord had surfaced to mar their happiness. Untroubled by what the future might hold, confident that they would face any adversity together, Rosamond slept deeply and without stirring until first cock crow.

She was wide awake in time to hear the lark sing.

Despite the popular belief that there were dangers lurking in the night air, Rosamond preferred to sleep with her windows open . . . unless the wind was blowing the scent of the tanneries her way. She had gone to bed with the casement flung wide and the richly brocaded bed hangings drawn back as far as they would go. The moon had been nearly at the full and a warm, rose-scented summer breeze had caressed them while they coupled and afterward as they slumbered.

Rosamond turned her head far enough to see the tower room grow ever brighter as the sun's pale gold rays streamed in to illuminate the chamber and pick out its rich furnishings – wardrobe chests, stools with embroidered cushions, and a table with a chair drawn up to it – and the hastily discarded clothing, both hers and his, scattered on the floor.

Far too comfortable to think of rising, she returned to her original position. With her face only inches away from her husband's, she had a clear view of pale skin, light brownish-gray hair, and ears that were just a bit too big for his head. She could also see the slight scarring left by the burns he had suffered the previous year. There were more scars elsewhere on his body, but he had been fortunate. He had survived and regained his health and his strength. He was whole again, and he was hers.

She ran a proprietary hand over his well-muscled bare left shoulder and saw his lips curve into a smile. It was followed almost at once by a wince. At the same time, his right shoulder twitched. She could scarce fail to notice, since she was still pressed tight against it.

'Oh,' she said, and sat up. Rob had spent the entire night with her weight pinning him to the feather bed. 'Has it gone numb? Can you feel anything at all?'

He grinned at her.

She returned his suggestive look with a glare and scrambled backward until she was off the bed with her bare feet firmly planted on the night-chilled floor tiles. 'In your *arm*!'

He flexed his fingers while bending and unbending his elbow. 'Pins and needles. All will be well in a moment.'

It hurt her to have caused him even that much pain. She had been selfish . . . again.

Once she had mumbled her way through a hasty morning prayer, she collected her shift and began to dress. As she did so, she chided herself for her carelessness. She had been working diligently since Rob's return to put his comfort ahead of her own, or at least on equal footing, but it was not easy to change the habits of a lifetime. She had been pampered as a child, no doubt to make up for what her foster mother saw as the deficiencies in her parents' care of her.

Even when she had bitten the hand that fed her, she had been rewarded. Through a series of legal machinations, she had been granted complete control of her inheritance, an almost unheard of indulgence for any woman, let alone one who had a husband. Solely because she'd asked it of him, Rob had surrendered his right to claim her fortune for himself. This was no small sacrifice. Under the law, everything a wife possessed was supposed to become her husband's when they married. In defiance of this rule, it all belonged to her, even the house. Rob had naught to call his own save what she gave him. She tried to be generous, but she found it difficult to share after managing the entire estate on her own for such a long time.

She resolved to do better. Turning toward him, a bright smile on her face, she blinked in surprise when she realized that he was already half dressed.

'Shall I call for Melka?' he asked.

'I would rather you serve as my tiring maid.'

'Why not? Did I not do a most excellent job of getting you out of that clothing?'

'Dressing a woman is not as simple a matter as undressing her.'

'Ah, a challenge!' He scooped up random garments as he approached.

With much laughter, and only a few amorous detours, they succeeded in assuming their clothing. Only Rosamond's hair remained untended. She had just begun to run a comb through the snarled locks when the faint sound of hooves striking cobblestones reached her ears.

Rob noticed her sudden stillness. 'What's amiss?'

'Someone has just ridden into the courtyard, and in some haste, too.'

'I will go down.'

'Not without me!'

Stuffing her hair into a net, Rosamond pinned the haphazard result into sufficient order to satisfy propriety and followed Rob from their bedchamber, through what she called her privy chamber, and on into the gallery. From there they had only to descend the main staircase of Willow House to reach the hall.

By the time they set foot on the ground floor, Charles, Rosamond's mute manservant, had opened the heavy wooden door that led to the courtyard to admit their early-morning visitor. Rosamond recognized Jacob Littleton at once, even though it had been a long time since she had last seen the old man. Jacob had been manservant to Sir Walter Pendennis, Rosamond's step-father, and had later taken the position of steward at Priory House, Sir Walter's home in Cornwall. For the past few years, he had occupied Sir Walter's lodgings in Blackfriars, preferring the bustle of London to the remoteness of the West Country.

Jacob was a small, nondescript fellow, his only distinctive feature the bushy eyebrows that were as white as what little was left of his hair. He plucked off his high-crowned, narrow-brimmed hat and held it to his chest, almost obscuring the dark velvet trim on his plain cloth doublet. Above a small white ruff, his face was a mask of misery.

Rosamond's breath caught and her left hand went to her throat. With her right she reached for Rob's arm. 'Jacob! What is wrong?'

'I bring evil tidings, Mistress Rosamond.' He had to clear his throat before he could continue. 'Word reached me an hour since, in a letter from your mother. Sir Walter is dead.'

Rosamond had been braced for bad news, but this announce-ment had her sagging against her husband, her eyes filling with tears. Rob guided her to a chair and went to fetch the bottle of aqua vitae she kept in a nearby cupboard. Now that his message had been delivered, Jacob appeared to be on the verge of collapse.

Rob poured the potent libation into two cups, pressing one into his wife's hands before taking the other to Jacob. He steered the older man to a bench and urged him to sit.

'It is not possible,' Rosamond murmured. 'Sir Walter is too vital, too vivid a personality to be suddenly dead.'

She shook her head as if to clear it, well aware there were flaws in her argument. The plague came every summer to carry off hundreds of victims. Gaol fever decimated not only the popu-lations of prisons, but judges and justices and lawyers, as well. Sir Walter was . . . had been . . . a justice of the peace in Cornwall.

'How?' Her question came out as a whisper. She repeated it in a louder voice.

Jacob started and stared at her. 'Did I not say? A fall from his horse. A terrible accident. He struck his head on a rock and died instantly.'

'At least he did not suffer,' Rob said.

Rosamond appreciated the attempt to soothe with comforting words, but they did nothing to lessen her grief. A dull ache throbbed at the base of her skull. She prided herself on her ability to cope with whatever came her way, but of a sudden all she wanted was to lock herself in her study at the top of the tower and mourn in private.

For the three years she had, most reluctantly, resided at Priory House at the insistence of her mother, Sir Walter Pendennis had been a kind and loving father to her. Now that it was too late, she wished she had made her peace with him. Even if she and her mother had remained estranged, she should have tried to reconcile with Sir Walter.

'If only I had been able to mend the rift between us,' she whispered. 'I never had any quarrel with my stepfather.'

Rob opened his mouth and closed it again when she sent him a quelling look. He did not need to remind her that Sir Walter had supported his wife when she attempted to arrange Rosamond's wedding to a 'suitable' young member of the gentry, or that her stepfather had been as angry as everyone else in both their families when he was told of their runaway marriage. That Rosamond had chosen her own husband was bad enough, but Rob was the son of a housekeeper and an estate steward, making their union a shocking misalliance. Even a yeoman farmer might have been seen as a more suitable match.

Revived by the aqua vitae, Jacob began to speak in a low voice. 'The funeral took place two days after his death. The Inquisition Post Mortem was a week later. In his will, Sir Walter most generously left me the lease to his lodgings in Blackfriars. Everything else, save for the widow's third, goes to his son, Benet – your half-brother, Mistress Rosamond.'

Rosamond nodded to show she was aware of the boy's existence, even though she had never met him. He was eight or nine years old, she recalled, far too young to be left fatherless.

'There is cause there for concern,' Jacob continued. 'The boy is now a ward of the Crown. The Court of Wards will sell his wardship to the highest bidder, who will then take charge of young Benet, and his inheritance, until he reaches the age of twenty-one. Benet's guardian will also have the right to arrange his marriage. Lady Pendennis writes that she fears she does not have the wherewithal to purchase her son's wardship for herself.'

Rosamond had been staring at her hands and the untouched

cup they held. Now her head snapped up. Her cheeks were still damp with tears, but her eyes narrowed and her lips flattened into a thin, hard line. *There* was the truth of the matter – had it not been for her son, Eleanor Pendennis would never have written to Jacob at all. He, as well as Rosamond and Rob, would have been left to hear of Sir Walter's sudden passing by chance.

The moment Rosamond reached that conclusion, all the reasons behind the rift with her mother rushed into her mind. Eleanor Pendennis was a grasping, greedy creature and always had been. She had never cared about her daughter's welfare, and it was doubtful she cared about her son's. Her only interest in the boy was his inheritance, and she was angling to use Rosamond's wealth to keep control of it.

Rob had no difficulty guessing her thoughts. 'No matter what your mother's intent,' he reminded her, 'the boy is kin.'

'I know that.' She heard the defensiveness in her voice and moderated her tone. 'The Court of Wards must not be allowed to give his keeping to a stranger.'

She glanced at Jacob. The old man knew better than anyone how unfit his old master's widow was to be anyone's guardian. Eleanor had borne Rosamond out of wedlock and coerced the baby's father's wife, Lady Appleton, into supporting them. Then, when Rosamond was but three years old, Eleanor had left her behind in England while she accompanied her newly-acquired husband, Sir Walter, to live abroad. Jacob had gone with them. Years had passed before they returned to England, years during which Rosamond shed copious tears and spent far too many long, sleepless nights wondering what she had done to make her mother abandon her.

Rob had borne witness to Rosamond's suffering. He had been a child himself at the time, but he had told her since how his heart had gone out to the lonely little girl she had been. Indeed, he claimed he had lost his heart to her entirely, even at that young age.

'What must we do to secure Benet's wardship?' she asked.

'Hire a lawyer,' Jacob advised, 'and solicit support from any powerful friends you may have.'

'I authorize you to undertake the matter on my behalf.'

'Your husband—'

'Will accompany me to Cornwall.'

Both men gaped at her.

'What is the use in going there now?' Rob asked. 'We will not be welcome.'

'How else am I to determine if it is in young Benet's best interest to remain in his mother's care?'

'Sir Walter always hoped you would be reconciled with Lady Pendennis.' Jacob's expression gave nothing away.

Rosamond suspected he spoke out of misplaced loyalty, keeping his true opinion to himself. 'I do not think that is possible. Mayhap, if Sir Walter was still alive, he could have used his diplomatic skills to negotiate a truce, but without his calming presence, I do much doubt there is any hope that she will forgive me for marrying Rob. For my part, I will never apologize for thwarting her plans, not when the result is the greatest happiness I have ever known. We will make preparations today and set out on the morrow.'

'It is a journey of nearly two weeks' duration,' Jacob reminded her. 'If you must go, then first take the time to make proper arrangements.'

Anxious as she was to settle matters and return home again, Rosamond saw the good sense in his advice. If she was to be absent from Willow House for more than a month, she must leave detailed instructions for the servants. Nor could she neglect the other properties she owned. Then, too, there was the matter of Watling, her cat. There would be certain difficulties if she simply abandoned him for such a long period of time.

'We must hire outriders,' Rob said, 'and we will need a baggage cart.'

Rosamond repressed a sigh and accepted the inevitable. They would need more than a day to settle everything. She did not suppose a short delay in leaving London would make any great difference in the grand scheme of things.

'This is Friday,' she said. 'We will leave at dawn on Tuesday.'

This time, no one argued with her.

THREE

15 June 1584

On the evening before they were to leave for Cornwall, Rob Jaffrey took the ferry across the Thames from Bermondsey to London to visit the headquarters of the Muscovy Company. He was not a member, but by virtue of his sojourn in Russia the previous year, he was always welcome as a guest. He had only to be accompanied by someone who was affiliated with the merchants who held the monopoly on trade with the tsar's domains.

So it was that he shared a wooden bench with Toby Wharton, some ten years his senior and decades more worldly wise. It had been Wharton's employer, the wealthy London man, Nick Baldwin, who had made it possible for Rob to go adventuring rather than remaining at Christ's College, Cambridge to complete his studies. He was not sorry he'd taken advantage of the opportunity, even though it had led him into unforeseen dangers.

After his return to England, he had applied himself with diligence to earning his degree. It had been awarded to him on Palm Sunday, the twelfth day of April. In the two months since, he had given much thought to his future. He had come to the conclusion that he was not cut out to pursue any of the careers for which his university education had prepared him. He had no interest in becoming a lawyer, a doctor, or a clergyman. He had too great an interest in the wider world. Nick Baldwin had offered him the wherewithal to pursue an alternative and he had seized it. Now he had only to work up the courage to tell Rosamond what he had done.

Balancing a half-empty pewter tankard on one knee, Wharton fished with his free hand for the small box that was always on his person. Removing it from inside his doublet, he opened it with a practiced flick of his thumbnail and plucked out one of the whole cloves it contained. When he'd popped it into his mouth, he chewed gently for a minute or two before tucking it between teeth and cheek. Then he offered the box to his companion.

Rob shook his head and took another swallow of ale instead. Wharton claimed he could make one clove last an entire day. Although the taste was pleasant enough – stronger than nutmeg and similar to cinnamon, but not so hot – Rob had never understood why his friend wanted to keep that flavor on his tongue.

Loud voices and louder laughter flowed around them, making conversation difficult, but Rob was content to listen to what others had to say. By this means, he learned a great deal, not just about ships and trade, but also of politics. The members of the Muscovy Company were the first to hear that the tsar, universally known as Ivan the Terrible, was dead. He had died on the eighteenth of March. Within a day, the English ambassador in Moscow, Sir Jerome Bowes, had been clapped in prison by the new tsar.

It took months for a letter to make the journey from Moscow to London, close to two by sea and nearly six if it was sent overland. Some messages never arrived at all. The most recent information indicated that Bowes had been freed and would return home with the Muscovy fleet. If they enjoyed smooth sailing, those ships were expected to reach Gravesend before the end of the month.

Rob was curious what other passengers might be on board, but not sufficiently so to delay the journey to Cornwall. For an entirely different reason, he'd have preferred to remain longer in London, but there was no help for it. His wife needed him at her side. Rosamond might be convinced that she could accomplish anything she set out to do on her own, but it was his equally firm belief that two heads were always better than one. He thanked the good Lord that there were men he could trust, Wharton and Baldwin in particular, to act for him in his absence.

Wharton nudged him with a sharp elbow to the ribs. 'There's Carleill. Pity about his expedition.'

They were not the only ones to notice Christopher Carleill's entrance. Several members of the Muscovy Company at once made their way to his side.

Carleill was a heavy-set, rawboned man, although he was shorter than most. His skin had been darkened and weathered by

the sun, and in slop-hose and a russet shirt he could pass with
ease for one of his own able-bodied seamen, right down to the
eyepatch. His sound seafaring instincts made members of his
crew respect him and obey his orders without question. Even
more significantly, they did so without complaint. To his advantage, Carleill also possessed the manners and bearing of a
gentleman. On this occasion he was dressed like one in a peascod-
bellied doublet, a starched white ruff, and a stylish hat with a
jaunty red plume.

Rob had first met the captain when he was on his way to
Muscovy. He had begun the voyage as a passenger on Nick
Baldwin's ship, the *Winifred*. Carleill, aboard the *Tiger*, had been
ordered by Queen Elizabeth to escort the merchant fleet from
London to St Nicholas, the port at the mouth of the Dvina where
the Muscovy Company had their base. Partway through the journey,
Rob and several other passengers had been rowed to the *Tiger* to
be briefed on the threat posed to the fleet by Danish pirates.

Back in England, Captain Carleill had spent the past year
seeking backers for his proposal to send a fleet of ships to explore
the coast of the Americas. They were to search for likely sites
for a plantation – a permanent English colony in the New World.
Unfortunately, a competing expedition had been mounted by one
of the queen's favorites, Sir Walter Raleigh. The previous month,
word had reached London that two barks under Raleigh's auspices
had set sail from Plymouth. Speculation, accompanied by wagers
both large and small, placed them anywhere from the Isles of
Scilly, becalmed by unfavorable winds, to the lands claimed by
Spain on the far side of the Atlantic Ocean.

Rob would gladly have offered Carleill a ship for his expedition, had he owned one at the time, just as he'd have been tempted
to sail west with her as a passenger. His desire to visit lands he'd
only read about was a powerful force within him. The only desire
he felt more strongly was to remain close to his wife.

Given Raleigh's triumph, Rob expected Carleill to be in low
spirits. Instead, he made himself amenable to all and sundry. He
was an affable fellow, witty in his conversation as any courtier.
Despite his popularity, it was not long before he noticed Rob.
Instant recognition flared in his one good eye and he at once
began to thread his way toward him through the press of bodies.

Reaching his goal took some little time. Carleill could scarce advance more than a step or two without encountering someone who wished to speak with him. Wharton was just asking Rob if he expected to remain long in Cornwall when Carleill hove into port.

A broad grin spread over the captain's face as he clapped Rob on the shoulder. 'I did not realize you had family in the West Country, Jaffrey.' The heartiness of his greeting suggested that this intelligence pleased him in some obscure way.

Rob slid sideways, making room on the bench. 'My wife's mother is the widow of Sir Walter Pendennis, who died not long ago. We leave for Priory House, near Launceston, on the morrow.'

Carleill offered condolences. Then he surprised Rob by revealing that he knew a great deal about the purchase Rob had made shortly before learning of Sir Walter's death. Without giving Rob the opportunity to ask his advice, he changed the subject yet again by remarking that he would soon be leaving London to head west himself.

'I have business in Ireland,' he confided, 'but it may require dealings with the Cornish, as well. I could use eyes and ears in that vicinity.'

Rob did not hesitate. 'I am at your service, Captain. Only say the word.'

'I'll hold you to that, lad.' Carleill rose, once again clapping Rob on the shoulder, and moved on to speak with someone else.

A snort from Wharton's direction had Rob turning his way and narrowing his eyes at the other man. His friend had the knack, one Rob envied, of being able to lift one pale eyebrow in an unspoken question. He did so now, putting Rob on the defensive.

'I owe him my life,' he reminded the other man. 'Without Carleill, the fleet would never have reached Muscovy in safety.'

Wharton smoothed his bushy yellow beard with one hand and looked thoughtful. 'That may be, but you must ask yourself why Captain Carleill has an interest in the part of Cornwall you intend to visit. Priory House is not on the coast, nor is Launceston a seaport.'

With a sinking feeling in the pit of his stomach, Rob searched for an acceptable explanation and found none. In time, mayhap, he could be of service to Carleill, but during their visit to Sir Walter's manor? He did much doubt it.

Wharton shook his head and contrived to look disappointed. His eyes twinkled with suppressed laughter. 'And here I thought you were a clever lad, you being a scholar and all. I warrant the need for eyes and ears in Cornwall has more to do with Carleill's stepfather than with his own interests.'

Rob instinctively braced for a blow. 'His stepfather?'

'Aye. Did you not know? Carleill's mother was Sir Francis Walsingham's first wife.'

This news sent Rob's mind reeling. Walsingham, the queen's Principal Secretary, was also her spymaster and a man Rob had vowed to avoid at all costs. Twice now, he and Rosamond had become entangled in the dangerous webs Walsingham spun. The last thing he wanted was to be caught in another.

Stifling a groan, Rob drained his tankard and called for another. He told himself that the Christopher Carleill he had known on shipboard was no spy. He and Rosamond were in no danger of becoming caught up in another of Walsingham's intrigues.

And if he consumed enough ale, he reasoned, he might begin to believe it.

FOUR

Advance. Retreat
  Advance. Retreat.
  Glide. Turn.

Rosamond executed the dance-like steps with graceful precision despite wearing heavy skirts held as wide as any at Queen Elizabeth's court by the undergarment known as a wheel farthingale. Since there might be times of crisis when her movements were restricted by similar garments, she practiced while wearing them. A wise woman learned how to overcome her disadvantages.

Advance. Retreat.
Advance. Retreat.
Glide. Spin. Stab!

The dagger in her right hand slid smoothly through leather and straw before imbedding itself in the heart of the man-sized bag suspended from the ceiling of the gallery at Willow House. It struck within an inch of the spot where its twin was already lodged.

'Hah!'

Her cry of triumph went unheard by anyone but the cat, Watling, who had been watching from a cushion on a window seat. The large gray and white striped feline stared at her with unblinking green eyes. Then, with the supreme rudeness only a cat could manage, his mouth opened wide in a yawn.

Rosamond laughed. When she had retrieved her daggers, she crossed to the window to scratch him behind his one good ear. The other was crimped, damaged in a long-ago battle for supremacy with another of his species.

Although she was accustomed to the sight, this evening it made her frown, reminding her all too strongly of the injuries that scarred Rob's body. He'd gone off adventuring, as so many young men did, and had nearly lost his life. Now she feared he was about to do something equally foolish.

'What is he plotting?' she asked the cat.

Ever since she'd made the decision to go to Cornwall, Rob had been behaving strangely. He'd spent much of his time, including this last evening before their departure, at the head-quarters of the Muscovy Company in London.

'I do not mind that he has his own friends,' she said aloud, 'but why choose those men in particular? That the old tsar is dead does not make Muscovy a safe place for Englishmen.'

She had no desire to make a return visit to that distant land, and had thought Rob was of the same mind. Had her assumption been wrong? Was their recent happiness an illusion? Did he mean to leave her at his first opportunity and sail off to new adventures?

What made matters worse for Rosamond was that she understood the lure of exploration and discovery, the desire to see and experience new things. She was as curious about the world as her husband was, but as a woman she had far fewer opportunities to indulge that curiosity.

Abruptly, she stood and returned to her exercises. She had

repeated the movements of her deadly pavane dozens of times during the past hour, honing her skill, training her muscles to obey without conscious command. Now she reached for the new lynx-lined cloak she had left draped over a chair and flung it around her shoulders. The hem was weighted. Should anyone ask, this had been done to make it hang correctly, but the reality was even more practical. As any skilled swordsman knew, a cloak could be used as a weapon.

It could also conceal one. Rosamond sheathed one of her daggers in a purpose-sewn pocket on the inside of the cloak. The other blade customarily lodged in her right boot, but it was difficult to reach her foot when she was wearing a farthingale and voluminous skirts. The process of extracting that blade from its sheath was neither smooth nor unobtrusive. Returning it was just as difficult, frustrating her to the point where she had been tempted to hack the interfering fabric to bits. Better in future to suspend the second weapon from her waist, she decided, in place of her pomander ball or feather fan, but for the nonce she kept it in her hand.

During the earlier session, she had concentrated on stabbing with precision while wearing bulky, tightly laced clothing. Now she strode to the far end of the gallery to practice throwing her knives. She lifted a portrait of the queen from the wall and set it out of the way. Behind it lay a much-scarred wood panel.

The same knives she had just used for stabbing were balanced for throwing. The boot blade in her hand flew through the air to imbed itself in the wainscoting with an audible thump. It was followed a moment later by the second knife. Rosamond's aim was true, pleasing her, but there had been a moment's delay before the second blade slid free of the pocket inside the cloak. Even such a brief hesitation might prove fatal if she found herself face-to-face with a deadly enemy.

Mindful of her need to increase the speed with which she could draw that dagger, she repeated the exercise and again encountered an infinitesimal check in the smooth movement of her weapon. The situation was not as dire as the struggle to reach her boot sheath had been, but the source of the problem was the same – too much fabric in her way.

Annoyed, Rosamond flung the cloak knife for the third time

without her usual care. It went wildly astray, the blade nicking the edge of a picture frame before tumbling to the floor. Wincing, she swore under her breath and went to examine the dagger for damage. She was angry with herself for giving in to that burst of temper. Strong emotion of any kind gave one's opponent the advantage. So said Master Rocco Bonetti, the finest teacher of swordplay in all of England.

Rosamond had twice visited the school Bonetti had set up in Blackfriars. For a fee, spectators were allowed to watch his classes in rapier and dagger fighting from a gallery. Rosamond had also acquired and read instruction manuals on using bladed weapons. Her collection included books written in several languages. None of them discussed fighting with knives alone, but they all stressed the importance of remaining calm during an armed encounter. The ability to think clearly while under attack was as important as honing one's skill with a blade.

With that in mind, Rosamond decided it would be best to abandon her practice session for the nonce. She retrieved her knives and carefully rehung the portrait. She did not look forward to the next part of the process. For some reason beyond her ken, blades became contaminated when they touched human flesh. The brush of a fingertip was enough to launch the process of corrosion. That meant she must clean, sharpen, and oil her knives after every use.

She started to return to Watling's window seat, meaning to sit beside him while she worked, but she had forgotten that she was still wearing the wheel farthingale. With a low sound of disgust, she changed direction. She could not take her ease on any ordinary bench, stool, or chair, only on a maid-of-honor stool, purpose-built to accommodate skirts that stuck out a foot in every direction. She could not even extract herself from the hideous contraption without help. The flat top of the cartwheel, above whalebone hoops covered with silk, was made of canvas with a hole for the waist. It had been dropped over her head by Melka, her tiring maid, and attached in place with tapes. When properly adjusted, it tilted up behind her and dipped downward in front in a singularly cumbersome fashion.

'Melka!' Rosamond shouted as she swept out of the gallery, through her privy chamber and into the bedchamber she shared

with Rob. It was empty and in darkness until she lit several
candles with the taper she had brought with her from the gallery.
'Melka, where are you?'

She was annoyed to find she was winded and perspiring. She
blamed the restrictive clothing as she dabbed with the back of
her gloved hand at the thin sheen of sweat beading her forehead,
knocking her elaborate headdress askew in the process. With a
soft curse, she tugged at it until it came free and flung it to the
floor. If she had to wear something on her head, she much
preferred a simple French hood, or better yet, a plain coif.

While she waited for Melka to appear, Rosamond's gaze drifted
toward the north-facing window. A few steps took her close
enough to glimpse the moonlit landscape beyond.

Willow House stood some little distance from the Thames – a
blessing, as it meant the inhabitants were not subjected to the
foul smells of the river. Rosamond could see over the chimneys
of Bermondsey to glimpse bits of water and the close-packed
rooftops of the city beyond. Off to the right stood the tall, white-
washed walls of the Tower of London – prison, fortress, and
royal residence all in one. She avoided looking that way. She
had been partly responsible for the capture of one of the prisoners
currently housed there. He had been sentenced to be hanged,
drawn, and quartered for treason, a horrific death she found
difficult to contemplate.

The headquarters of the Muscovy Company also lay in that
direction. Abruptly, Rosamond closed and barred the shutters.
She turned away to find Melka watching her.

The Polish-born maidservant, a short, stocky woman with gray
hair, held a stack of freshly-laundered shifts, chemises, and men's
shirts. She took her time packing them into the traveling trunks.
When she closed both lids, it was with resounding thumps that
made Rosamond wince.

This was a bad sign.

Since Melka had known Rosamond as a child, she enjoyed
certain liberties that no other servant in the household shared.
She could be counted upon to put her mistress's wellbeing first,
but in return she felt free to make her opinions known. Fortunately,
she preferred to express both approval and disapproval in her
native tongue, which none save Rosamond could understand.

'Help me out of this torture device, Melka, I beg of you, and remind me never to accept an invitation to visit the queen if it means I must endure hours of confinement in such an absurd suit of clothes. I would rather be lashed to a stake and have rotten cabbages thrown at my head!'

Muttering to herself, Melka set to work on the laces. As she undid them, Rosamond gave silent thanks to the good Lord above that her customary attire was constructed along much simpler lines. No one in Bermondsey thought twice about seeing a woman wearing a best gown that was twenty years out of fashion. Even to attend church, Rosamond felt no need to wear more than a bum roll underneath her favorite fawn-colored silk skirt.

Both bum roll and skirt were already packed for the journey to the West Country, along with a matching bodice that buttoned up the front. In common with the other garments she was taking, they were clothes she could put on and take off without assistance if she had to. Because Melka's presence would slow them down, Rosamond had decided against taking her with them.

In a matter of minutes, Rosamond was free of bodice, kirtle, sleeves, whalebone, and canvas. In her shift, she seated herself on the edge of the bed to clean, sharpen, and oil her knives. Melka continued to grumble, but since she did not articulate any specific complaint, Rosamond ignored her.

A short time later, the tiring maid startled her by speaking in English. 'Take book?'

Melka had picked up Rob's copy of *A Briefe and Summarie Discourse upon the Intended Voyage to the Hintermost Parts of America*, the proposal Captain Christopher Carleill had written to convince investors to participate in a scheme to explore the lands across the Atlantic Ocean. Rob had found the contents fascinating, even going so far as to read long sections aloud to his wife.

Rosamond was perfectly capable of reading the book for herself, if she'd cared to!

A sharp pain made her cry out. She had nicked her finger with the dagger she'd been oiling. Yet another warning, she thought, not to be ruled by strong emotion. She set the blade aside to inspect the damage. A single drop of blood beaded up, then another.

Melka appeared at her side with a cloth and one of Lady Appleton's healing salves. Rosamond resigned herself to being tended to and afterward made no objection when Melka added Carleill's book to the traveling trunk that contained Rob's belongings.

While her maid finished packing, Rosamond wiped excess oil off the first dagger and started work on the second. Despite her best efforts to focus only on the task at hand, she found her thoughts returning to the matter that troubled her most.

Rob had been seduced by the excitement and adventure of foreign travel once before, when he had made that fateful journey to Muscovy. That left her wary of his fascination with Carleill's expedition. Was it possible that Rob planned to *join* the expedition? Was that why he had decided not to pursue a career in the law, the path his mother had urged him to take?

Rosamond replaced the boot dagger in its sheath and put the other blade away in her everyday cloak. She stoppered the bottle of special oil, cutting off its faint but not unpleasant smell, and returned it to a wooden box before handing it to Melka to pack.

The hour grew late.

Melka finished her tasks and left the bedchamber. Rosamond snuffed all but one candle and got into bed, but she was unable to fall asleep. Although they were to leave at dawn, Rob had not yet returned from London.

She told herself not to be selfish. It was unfair of her to want to keep him always at her side. She should be glad he had companions in London, especially since his closest friend, Andrew, was still at Cambridge.

She rolled over, closed her eyes, and immediately began to worry that something had happened to her husband. What if he had hired an unscrupulous link boy to light his way from Muscovy House to the nearest place where he could hire a wherry to take him across the river? It was not unheard of for a wicked lad to lead a man straight into the clutches of a band of robbers. Was Rob even now lying in some alley, beaten and bloody?

By the time another hour had passed, concern had turned to irritation. Rob had no business making her fret like this. He should have been home by now, snug in this bed beside her. He was inconsiderate and thoughtless and a great deal of trouble.

Mayhap she would have been happier had he never come back into her life at all!

She told herself that she had been on her own for a long time. Why should it matter if her husband preferred the company of his friends to that of his wife? Let him sail the seas with Captain Carleill, if that was what he wanted!

The thought of being left behind made her heart ache. By the time she finally succumbed to sleep, her cheeks were damp with tears.

FIVE

16 June 1584

D awn came far too early. Eyes burning and temples pounding, Rob sloshed cold water onto his face. It did little to help his condition. His head felt as if it was stuffed with wool, functioning only well enough to warn him that it would not be wise to break his fast with bread and ale, as Rosamond had. Under the circumstances, an empty stomach seemed wiser.

He delayed entering the courtyard. The servants were making an inordinate amount of noise as they loaded traveling trunks and provisions into a cart and saddled horses. Then there was a commotion of some sort. When a shrill voice rose to an intolerable level, he clapped his hands over his ears.

Rosamond stormed back inside. She ignored her husband to advance on Toby Wharton, who had come home with Rob in the wee hours of the morning. 'You will have to take charge of Watling,' she informed him.

Wharton, whose bloodshot eyes suggested he was also feeling the effects of overindulgence in drink, paled and sputtered a protest. Rosamond paid no attention.

A wail that would put a banshee to shame made both men wince. A moment later, Melka carried in the source of the sound. Watling, confined in a large wicker cage, expressed his displeasure with a series of ear-splitting howls. Blood welled up from a dozen scratches on Melka's hands, ample evidence that the cat had fought hard against being confined.

'That noise is the reason he cannot remain here,' Rosamond said, still addressing Wharton. 'He does not like me to leave him for an extended period of time. During my first long absence, while you and Rob were in Muscovy, he kept up such a continual racket that no one at Willow House could hear themselves think, let alone sleep at night. Even otherwise loyal retainers threatened to abandon the premises.'

Rob frowned, trying to make sense of this development. The cat had accepted temporary caretakers in the past, but only Rob himself, Melka, or Nick Baldwin. Baldwin had come to the rescue on that earlier occasion, taking charge of the animal for the duration. Rob had thought Melka would be looking after Watling while they were in Cornwall. Instead, she thrust the cage into Wharton's arms and stepped away, a triumphant gleam in her small, wide-spaced eyes.

Watling continued to yowl, adding the occasional growl and hiss for variety. Wharton held the cage as far away from himself as he could manage, all too aware that there was ample room between the bars for a paw tipped with razor sharp claws to dart out and inflict serious damage.

'Fare well, my darling,' Rosamond said to the cat. 'Toby will deliver you to your old friend Nick and I will return for you as soon as may be.' She reached out as if to stroke Watling's head before a closer look at his arched back and puffed tail made her think better of the impulse.

As soon as Wharton left with the cat, Rob followed his wife and her maid into the courtyard. The pair of burly henchmen who served Rosamond as guards and outriders were already mounted. They were brothers, Luke and John, hired for their strength and for their ability to keep their mouths shut. They were men of limited intelligence but indisputable loyalty. Rosamond paid them well to make certain of it. In common with all of her servants, they took orders from Rob only because he was married to their mistress.

For reasons beyond his ken, it appeared that Melka was to accompany them to Cornwall. She clambered, unaided, into the cart that held their baggage.

The change in plans surprised Rob. He knew that Rosamond had intended to leave Melka in charge of both Willow House and Watling during their absence. In the ordinary way of things, it took a powerful argument to change her mind. A glance at her set expression warned him not to ask questions.

Braced for a jolt that would exacerbate his aching head, Rob put one foot in the stirrup and swung himself into his saddle. He gave silent thanks that his stomach was no longer queasy. It should have been after all the ale he'd consumed at Muscovy House. Perhaps, he decided, it was just as well that Rosamond was not speaking to him this morning.

He would need all his wits about him when he made his confession.

SIX

18 June 1584

Although Rosamond was impatient to arrive in Cornwall, she knew all too well that excessive haste led to carelessness. Long journeys were dangerous for even the most cautious of travelers. The roads, often in such poor condition that riding along them was akin to running a gauntlet, were also haunted by vagabonds, footpads, and masterless men on the lookout for victims they could set upon and rob. Rosamond was obliged to think of her cattle, too. If one of the horses came up lame, it would mean an even longer delay.

They had reached Staines the first day and Hartfordbridge the second. On this, the third morning of the journey, Melka abandoned her perch atop their baggage to ride on a pillion behind Charles. This obliged her to sit sideways and cling to his waist for balance. Since Charles was mute, he had no choice but to bear this added responsibility in stoic silence, but Rosamond did not think he minded having Melka's arms wrapped around him. She felt certain that if he had strong objections, he would have found a way to communicate his displeasure.

As for herself, Rosamond disdained the pillion. It was nearly as uncomfortable and unstable as riding in the cart. Her true preference would have been to ride astride wearing male attire. She had been dissuaded from this plan by common sense. The road to Cornwall might not be the most traveled in the realm, but it was a major east-west route across England. A proper gentlewoman did not disguise her gender, or show off her legs in public. Given the possibility that she might have to vie for the custody of her young half-brother, she would be ill-advised to make a spectacle of herself.

Instead she rode using a sidesaddle that required her to hook one knee over a pommel in order to stay in place. This, too, was a precarious and unnatural position, but at least she had her own horse and was able to face forward.

The only sounds were the rustle of leaves from the trees on either side of the road and the clop of hooves on hard-packed earth. Luke rode ahead of their small party with Rosamond and Rob riding side by side just behind him. Charles and Melka and the baggage cart, its horse on a lead, came next, with John bringing up the rear.

Rosamond had scarce spoken two words to her husband since leaving Bermondsey, at first because she was wroth with him for staying out so late the night before their departure and then because he seemed lost in his own dark thoughts and disinclined to speak with her. The first two nights on the road had been spent apart, in inns where female travelers slept in one chamber and males in another.

The longer this unnatural silence continued, the more difficult it was to break. As they left Hartfordbridge to ride in the direction of Basingstoke, Rosamond's thoughts turned, as they so often had since Jacob brought the news of Sir Walter's death, to memories of her stepfather.

She found herself recalling the first time she had ventured into his private study at Priory House. She had been bold, helping herself to the books he'd left atop his flat-topped traveling chest. They had been far too advanced for her – the illustrated edition of Vitruvius, one of the volumes of Sebastiano Serlio, Vredeman de Vries's *Architectura*, and John Shute's *The First and Chief Grounds of Architecture*. Much later, she had learned that

Sir Walter had helped Shute with his research. As young men, they had traveled together through the Italian city states.

At first, her stepfather had been curt with her. He'd informed her that he was busy and demanded to know what it was she wanted. She'd made herself look as pitiful as possible and answered with a question of her own: 'Why are people always too busy to spend time with me?'

Reluctant sympathy for her plight had turned Sir Walter gallant. For the next little while, he had given her his full attention and he'd agreed to her request that he tutor her in French. Even at that young age, she'd had a talent for languages. Thanks to Melka, she'd already been passing fluent in Polish.

Another memory erased the smile from Rosamond's face. If she was not mistaken, it had been on that same occasion, when she had expressed a wish for siblings, that Sir Walter had admitted that he would like to have a son. Now, because her stepfather had died before his time, she was the one who would have to save the legacy he'd left behind for Benet.

'Ros? Is aught wrong?'

Rob's question pulled her out of her reverie with a start. 'It is nothing. Just a passing thought.'

'A grim one from the look on your face.'

She scowled at him. 'I was thinking of my brother.'

'Poor lad. No doubt he was close to his father. Sir Walter was the sort of man who would spend time with his child.'

'He was good to me. His attention very nearly made up for Mother's neglect.' Rosamond's lips curved into a rueful half smile. 'For a long time I wanted nothing more than to have my mother back, but when she did reappear in my life, I'd have given a fortune to send her away again.'

She had wrenched Rosamond away from the foster mother she had come to love and call 'Mama'. Lady Appleton, Rosamond's father's widow, had taken a lonely child into her life and into her heart and raised her to think for herself.

Rosamond reached across the short distance between their horses to touch her husband's forearm. 'Do you think Mother loves Benet? That is what I want most for him – as much love as I received from Mama.'

'I doubt Lady Pendennis knows what love is.'

Rosamond sighed. 'It might be best to purchase his wardship myself.'

The suggestion brought a look of consternation into Rob's face. 'Do you intend to bring him home with us?'

She frowned at that. She'd had little to do with children and she liked the household at Willow House the way it was. 'I could ask Mama to take him in.'

'Would you burden her with raising yet another young child? Surely he is old enough to be sent away to a proper school.'

'He'd find little affection there!'

He conceded her point with a shrug. 'Mayhap you should discover what *he* wants before you make a decision. For all you know, he loves Lady Pendennis and wants to remain at Priory House.'

'And for all I know,' Rosamond admitted, 'he is an entirely unlovable child, like to drive us both mad should we bring him to live at Willow House.'

They shared a moment of silent accord before Rosamond remembered that she was irritated with her husband. Since it was her nature to be blunt, she blurted out a question before she had time to think better of it. 'Did something untoward happen at Muscovy House the night before we left?'

Instead of answering, Rob glanced over his shoulder at Charles and Melka, riding a short distance behind them, and then ahead at Luke.

'It is no good trying to keep secrets from the servants,' Rosamond said.

'I know that better than you do, having grown up as the son of two of Lady Appleton's retainers.'

'Then stop trying to avoid giving me an answer. Why did you stay out so late and drink so much? I have never known you to do either before.'

'I spoke with Christopher Carleill.'

She felt her chest constrict at the mere mention of the captain's name. 'About his expedition?'

Her question seemed to surprise him. 'Did I not tell you? That project had to be abandoned after word arrived that Sir Walter Raleigh's ships were already en route to the New World. The queen will not sanction a second expedition.'

'No, you did not bother to share that news with me.'

Miffed at his oversight, she was tempted to give him a piece of her mind. She held her tongue, reminding herself that Rob had no way of knowing how much she'd disliked his interest in the venture. When a glance at his face showed her a man sunk in gloom, she yielded instead to a natural desire to coax him into a happier frame of mind.

'Mayhap, if Raleigh is successful, more ships will be permitted to set out.'

Rob's expression cleared at the suggestion. 'I will hope for the best. After all, this is not the first time Carleill's scheme suffered a setback. His last attempt to gather a fleet to sail to the Americas was thwarted by the speed with which Sir Humphrey Gilbert organized a competing expedition.'

'And we know how well *that* turned out,' Rosamond said under her breath.

'There are many advantages to trade with the lands on the other side of the Atlantic Ocean.' Rob's face lit with enthusiasm as he expanded on the topic. 'The journey is much shorter than a voyage to Muscovy or the Levant and English ships can sail from ports in England and Ireland at any time of the year, and with favorable winds, too. And for every ten ships that go once a year to Muscovy, twenty can sail to America. Twice. The fishing is as good, and the land can produce pitch, tar, hemp, masts, hides, and furs, all without interference from Danish pirates. If we colonize far enough to the south, the settlers can also plant grapes and olives and produce wax and honey. It is even possible, once the native inhabitants are civilized, that there will be a market in the Americas for English cloth.'

'You paint a vivid picture with words,' Rosamond said, 'but not everyone favors colonization. Moreover, I have heard it said that the cost to plant one hundred settlers in the New World would be over forty thousand pounds. Would it not be better to back a plan to transplant English farmers to Ireland?'

'The Irish appear to object to that idea. It is a rebellious place, scarce safe to inhabit.'

'I should think that the native peoples of the Americas would also object to having their land taken away from them.'

'Colonization was only one of the goals of Carleill's venture.

There was also the possibility of finding a freshwater passage through the northern part of America into the East-Indian Sea – a new trade route that would make investors wealthy overnight.'

Rosamond grimaced. How could she compete with the promise of high adventure?

'Shares in Carleill's undertaking sold for as little as six pounds five shillings,' Rob said. 'A pittance that could have yielded untold riches to those who financed the expedition.'

'Only if the explorers returned. I find myself remembering that Humphrey Gilbert was lost at sea. He left a wife and family behind.'

Rob was silent for so long that Rosamond thought he might not respond. They reached a crossroads and passed through it, heading ever westward.

'Rosamond?' Rob waited until she met his eyes. 'I bought a ship.'

The unexpected announcement left her bereft of speech.

'She's small, only fifty tons, and she is in dry dock at present for repairs to make her seaworthy, but once she's ready and has a crew of eighteen aboard, she'll be capable of sailing anywhere in the world. She's called the *Swallow*, but I intend to rename her. What do you think of the *Rosamond*?'

'I think you are mad.' She narrowed her eyes at him. 'How did you come by the money for such a purchase? No, do not bother to answer. No doubt some usurer was happy to loan it to you on the strength of your connection to me.' Most people assumed that, as her husband, he had control of her fortune.

Rob shocked her by laughing. Any other man would have been furious with her for impugning his honor. 'Your wealth did not come into it, which is why I did not tell you about the *Rosamond* before. Well, part of the reason. You know how much I dislike quarreling with you. It was Nick Baldwin who loaned me enough money to buy and equip her. I will pay him back out of the profits from the first few voyages.'

'You cannot blame me for having doubts about the wisdom of such an investment. Ships do not always return to port with their cargo. They sink. They are captured by pirates. Even if they reach port, the goods they carry do not always survive intact.'

Perishable goods that were exposed to saltwater could easily be ruined, leaving the hapless investor deep in debt.

Rob's enthusiasm was in no way diminished by her words. 'Or, Rosamond, I may be as successful at trade as Master Baldwin has been. Imagine me as a wealthy merchant, mayhap even one who lends money to others.'

In her consternation, she scarce noticed that the horses had come to a halt. 'Is that truly your intent? Or do you mean to go off adventuring and leave me behind?'

'I will not captain her. I am the owner.'

'Merchants sometimes sail on the ships they own.'

He slanted a mischievous look her way. 'If you like, you can invest half the amount of my debt. Then it will be *our* ship. We will both reap the profits, and should I be inclined to sail away on her, you can come with me. Think of it, Ros – we can go anywhere in the world. You like to see new things. You know you do.'

'But I do not enjoy shipboard life. You were not with me on the voyage to Muscovy, and you were still recovering from your injuries for most of the trip home. Seamen are superstitious about having a woman aboard. They blame female passengers for everything from bad weather to spoiled food. Unless you imagine I can successfully pass myself off as a man, my only recourse would be to keep to a cabin.'

'There were parts of the voyage home from Muscovy that were most enjoyable,' Rob reminded her, and used his knees to prod his mount into motion.

The affection in his gaze silenced her. They rode another mile without speaking while she thought through what he had just told her. Only belatedly did it dawn on her that, if he had known for some time that Carleill's expedition to the New World had been abandoned, then that was not the cause of his overindulgence in drink at Muscovy House.

'Is there news of the Muscovy Fleet?' she asked. 'Are there Englishwomen aboard?' She named no names, but two such females had been left behind when she and Rob returned to England. If either one came back, there could be consequences.

'That is not the problem.' Rob's expression turned bleak.

'Then what is?'

'When Carleill heard that I was bound for Cornwall, he suggested that I might do him a small service during our sojourn at Priory House.'

That did not seem too onerous. 'What favor did he ask?'

'He did not specify.'

Rosamond began to see the problem. 'You agreed, not knowing what he intends, based on the strength of your admiration for him?'

'I fear I did.'

'Why fear?'

'Because a short time later, I learned that it is more than likely that he was not asking for himself. I may have committed myself to acting on behalf of Carleill's stepfather.'

Rosamond felt a chill go through her, despite the warmth of the day. 'Tell me the rest.'

'Carleill's late mother was the first wife of Sir Francis Walsingham.'

SEVEN

27 June 1584

In the late morning of the twelfth long, wearying day on the road, a journey enlivened only by bursts of conversation with Rob, some contentious and some not, Rosamond caught her first glimpse of Priory House in nearly ten years. At first the estate did not appear much changed from the last time she had visited. The manor nestled in a narrow but fertile valley where bearded French wheat could be planted on the best soil and rye on the worst. The house itself was surrounded by a wall of light-colored stone that gleamed in the midday sun.

Their party followed the road as it curved in a half circle around the perimeter to reach the gatehouse on the north side. At one time, there had been a south entrance, but it had been walled up. These days, there appeared to be only one way on or off the property.

By lifting herself in the saddle, Rosamond could see over the wall and make out the upper levels of the buildings inside. Once Priory House had been a priory in truth. When she had lived in Cornwall with her mother and Sir Walter, the monks' infirmary and dortor had still been standing. They were gone now. The stone had been used to build another wing onto the main house, giving it the fashionable shape of an E, an architectural homage to the queen.

'You'd best sit down before you fall.' Rob's warning came just as Rosamond caught a glimpse of the pleasure gardens her stepfather had spent so many hours planning. She was glad he had completed them and hoped they had given him many hours of enjoyment.

A sharply barked command to 'Hold!' had them reining in as soon as they reached the gatehouse.

The order was accompanied by the appearance of a pair of mastiffs. The brindled dogs were massive in size. Muscular, with large square heads, their teeth met in a scissors bite. They did not bark, which was all the more disconcerting.

A man armed with an arquebus stepped out of the gatehouse. 'State your names and your business.'

When he tilted his head back to look up at them, recognition stirred at the back of Rosamond's mind. 'Peter? Peter Ludlow?'

'Who are you, mistress, that you know me?'

'I am Lady Pendennis's daughter, Rosamond, and this is my husband, Master Jaffrey.' Excellent rider that she was, she had all she could do to control her skittish mount when the two large canines flanked the horse.

Ludlow's face broke into a grin. 'Do not be alarmed, Mistress Rosamond. Gentle as lambs, they are. They'd hold an intruder at bay by trapping him in a corner, but it is rare that either of them will attack a man.' He set aside the matchlock shoulder gun and reached for the nearest mastiff's collar.

'If you say so.'

Ludlow hauled the first dog away. 'Gorgon here just sits down on top of anyone he thinks should not come in. He's heavier than you are, I wager.'

Rosamond's horse quieted as soon as Ludlow had shut both mastiffs inside the gatehouse, although loud snuffling noises continued behind the closed door. Returning, the gatekeeper squinted up at Rob.

'I remember you, Master Jaffrey. Came here once as a lad, you did. They said you ran away from home to be with Mistress Rosamond.'

Rob's light brownish-gray hair, a color that was responsible for his childhood name of Mole, was not long enough to hide the dull red that crept over his oversized ears. He needed a moment to master the embarrassment aroused by this reminder of his youthful folly. Rosamond hid a smile. At the time, she'd thought Rob's actions passing foolish, but they spoke of his long-standing devotion to her. Looked back upon, his unexpected arrival at Priory House was a fond memory.

'We have come to assist Lady Pendennis,' Rob said when he had recovered himself. 'May we pass?'

'Oh, aye. A moment. Mathy! Come hither!'

A towheaded boy of seven or eight answered his call. After a few whispered words from his father, the lad slipped through the wicket and raced toward the house. Only when he was well on his way did Ludlow unbar and open the main gate to allow Rosamond's party through.

'How is it that a Cornish gatekeeper speaks London English?' Rob asked.

Behind them, Rosamond heard the bar drop back into place with a thump, securing the gate once more. 'Sir Walter required all his servants to ape their betters.'

'To make themselves understood by guests?'

'More likely because my mother refused to learn Cornish or attempt to understand the way local people speak English.'

'It appears your mother also wants ample warning of unexpected visitors,' Rob said.

Rosamond pondered this observation as they followed the long, straight track that ran from the gatehouse to the forecourt. The days of fortified houses protected by moats and drawbridges were long past. Indeed, it was customary for country landowners to offer hospitality to any and all travelers. Ludlow's action in sending his son ahead to warn the house *was* a bit peculiar.

By the time Rosamond and her party dismounted, grooms were waiting to take charge of their horses. At the top of a flight of stairs, an arched entrance led into the screens passage next to the great hall, but the heavy door remained closed and there was no sign of Eleanor Pendennis. Rosamond was about to accost the nearest servant to ask his mistress's whereabouts when the pale-haired lad from the guardhouse reappeared.

He was accompanied by another boy, this one a little taller and likely older. The second lad had wide hazel eyes and a turned up nose, a legacy from his mother.

Their mother.

Rosamond took a tentative step toward the two youngsters, uncertain what to say to her half-brother.

Benet had no such hesitation about approaching her. 'Good day to you,' he said. 'Welcome to Priory House.'

He reached for his cap with his right hand and lifted it, back to front, so as not to leave his hair in disarray. He brought it down along the front of his body, taking great care not to display the lining, since that was deemed uncouth. When he had carried it to waist level, he switched it to his left hand, leaving the right free to make the wide, sweeping gesture that accompanied his bow. This maneuver was executed by placing one foot in back of the other, bending his knees, and inclining his body in Rosamond's direction.

She was charmed by the gesture, but what melted her heart was Benet's sand-colored hair. He had inherited that distinctive shade from his father.

She made an appropriate obeisance in return. 'Good day to you, Benet.'

A puzzled expression came over his face. 'How do you know my name?'

'I know a good deal about you, even though we have never met. You were named for your father's father and you were born eight years and four months ago.'

'Who are you, then?' Benet asked.

It was a voice from the entrance to the house that answered, a voice that carried no hint of welcome, but rather conveyed an abundance of suspicion. 'This, Benet,' said Eleanor Pendennis, 'is Mistress Jaffrey. You need have nothing more to do with her. Her arrival is entirely unwelcome. She will not be staying long.'

EIGHT

The effect of Lady Pendennis's words on her daughter was painful for Rob to watch. Rosamond jerked back as if she had been slapped. He was close enough to see the brief glimmer of tears in her eyes before she gained sufficient self-mastery to hide her feelings.

She was good at that. Too good. People thought her cold when in fact she felt things deeply.

A huge knot formed in Rob's stomach. Had he been another sort of man, he'd have struck back at the person who'd hurt his beloved. It was not only Lady Pendennis's gender that prevented him from doing so, or even her status as a new widow, but rather her infirmity. She leaned heavily on the walking stick she needed to support her twisted lower limbs.

Although Rob knew that Lady Pendennis had borne a son since he'd last seen her, he had expected to find her much as she had been years before – badly crippled as the result of having been run over by a heavily-loaded wagon. During the intervening years, her mobility had clearly improved, but although her wheeled chair appeared to be a thing of the past, she retained the appearance of someone who suffered from chronic pain. The bright midday sun was unkind to her, illuminating every line and hollow of the scars that seamed one side of her face.

Had Lady Pendennis kept a civil tongue in her head, Rob might have felt sorry for this woman who was his mother-in-law, but her suffering, past or present, was a poor excuse for her cruel treatment of her only daughter.

He was not the only one to be appalled and angered by Lady Pendennis's behavior. Unleashing a torrent of Polish, Melka thrust herself forward. Her words were incomprehensible to Rob, but her tone of voice left him in no doubt that she was giving her former mistress a piece of her mind.

It had been Melka who had nursed Lady Pendennis after her accident, staying close to her side for many long years afterward.

She had left Cornwall to become Rosamond's tiring maid only because her mistress had ordered her to do so. Rob and Rosamond had not been living together at the time this 'gift' of a tiring maid arrived, but Rob knew that Rosamond had realized at once that Melka had been sent to spy on her. She'd been amused by her mother's presumption and had set herself the task of winning the Polish woman's loyalty. She had succeeded surpassing well.

Driven back by Melka's sharp-tongued lecture, Lady Pendennis tottered a bit as she retreated. The short, stocky maidservant followed her until they were both swallowed up by the shadows just inside the door. The diatribe continued, muted, from within.

Rob went to his wife, sliding one arm around her waist and leaning in close enough to whisper in her ear. 'We need not stay here. We have time to return to Launceston before nightfall.'

A grim smile answered him. 'I did not expect to be welcomed with open arms, but no matter what our reception is, we must stay long enough to sort out Benet's future.'

Mathy, Peter Ludlow's son, had fled toward the safety of the gatehouse, but Benet stood his ground. Rob could not help but notice how closely the boy resembled his mother. That made him wonder if what was at the heart of Lady Pendennis's treatment of her daughter might be Rosamond's strong physical resemblance to her late father. Anyone who had known Sir Robert Appleton could immediately recognize his features in Rosamond's face.

Before her marriage to Sir Walter, Rosamond's mother had loved Sir Robert enough to live with him in sin and bear his illegitimate daughter, but when he had abandoned her, that love had soured. She had been obliged to raise Rosamond on her own for the first few years of her little girl's life.

Rosamond's father had been devious, dishonest, and disloyal to both wife and mistress. While it was true that Rosamond did not share her father's worst traits, Sir Robert had gifted his progeny with his intelligence and his facility for languages. Now that Rob thought about it, her ability to pick locks and her skill with a knife might also be part of his legacy.

Setting aside speculation, he turned his attention to the boy. 'Benet, do you know who this gentlewoman is?'

'Her name is Mistress Jaffrey, sir.'

'That is true. I am Robert Jaffrey and she is my wife, but she is also your half-sister – your mother's daughter.'

'I did not know I *had* a sister!' Benet's brow furrowed in confusion. If the look in his eyes was anything to go by, he was suspicious of Rob's claim.

Rob lowered himself to one knee, bringing himself eye-to-eye with the boy. 'Her Christian name is Rosamond. She is much older than you are and lives near London but she is indeed your sister. It was your father's hope that you two would one day know each other and become friends.'

Benet continued to look doubtful, but he led them through the great hall to the parlor where his mother was already ensconced at the head of the table and dinner was about to be served. Since the boy customarily ate with his tutor, he left them there.

Although Lady Pendennis scowled at Rob and Rosamond, she did not order her servants to evict them. Rob suspected that was because Melka stood just behind her chair, whispering in her ear. They took seats as far away from their reluctant hostess as possible.

The meal passed with excruciating slowness. The very air seemed charged with tension. Even if Rosamond had been prepared to make amends, no reconciliation seemed likely as long as Eleanor seethed with such cold, quiet fury.

While they ate, Rob wondered about the two others dining with them. A young woman, by her clothing an upper servant of some sort, kept her head down and said nothing. She appeared to be no older than fifteen or sixteen. The man was in his prime and similarly well dressed. At a guess he was either the Priory House steward or had been Sir Walter's secretary. He, too, avoided meeting Rob's eyes.

'Do you know either of them?' Rob whispered to his wife.

Rosamond shook her head and concentrated on the food, which was both plentiful and well prepared. As the last course, servants carried in platters of cheese and fruit. As soon as they left, Lady Pendennis cleared her throat.

'I had intended that Jacob handle my business in London on his own, but since Melka informs me that he chose instead to ask for your help, I suppose I must accept your presence, daughter, and that of your husband, and tell you that I am much beholden to you for your generosity on Benet's behalf.'

So, Rob thought, she had not anticipated that Jacob would

need Rosamond's financial assistance in obtaining the wardship. Had she expected the faithful old retainer to sell the property Sir Walter had bequeathed him to raise the money? Foolish of her if she had. As for her grudging attempt to be conciliatory, at best she seemed to offer a temporary truce.

'The boy should not go to strangers,' Rosamond said. 'For Sir Walter's sake, if not for yours, I intend to do everything in my power to prevent that from happening.'

'We are sorry for your loss,' Rob said. 'Your husband was a good man, taken before his time by a tragic accident.'

Lady Pendennis fixed him with a piercing look. 'If you mean that, you can do Benet one other service while you are here.'

Rob was careful not to make any hasty promises until he knew more. 'What is it you would have me do?'

'Find and punish the man responsible for my husband's death,' said Lady Pendennis. 'Walter did not die in an accidental fall from a horse. He was murdered.'

NINE

Shock kept Rosamond motionless and silent for the first crucial moments after her mother's astonishing announcement. Eleanor had time to exit the parlor by a door near her chair. Only the slow pace necessitated by her damaged lower limbs kept her from ascending the stairs that led to her bedchamber before being overtaken by her daughter.

'Explain yourself!' Rosamond's voice came out as a fishwife's screech. To make such a claim was bad enough, but to leave without offering proof of it was beyond the pale.

The look Eleanor bestowed upon her was cold enough to cause chilblains. 'I should have thought my words were self-explanatory.'

'Provide details, then. Why do you think Sir Walter's death was murder?'

'I do not *think* it. I *know* it.' She continued up the stairs, trailing the faint aroma of sweet marjoram, her favorite perfume.

Rosamond seized her mother's arm, startled to feel little more than fabric and bone beneath her fingers. For the first time, she took a hard look at her mother's face. Fine lines had etched themselves into her skin. Although only a little of her hair was visible beneath her coif, the dark brown color Rosamond remembered had turned a dull and lifeless gray.

'If you have seen your fill, I would retire.'

'Are you ill?'

'I am tired.' Abruptly, Eleanor sat down on the stairs.

When she glanced over Rosamond's shoulder, her mouth twisted into an expression of displeasure. Everyone who had dined with them, and the servants, too, crowded into the passage.

Rosamond gestured toward a nearby door. If she remembered aright, Sir Walter's study lay beyond. 'I will keep out anyone you do not wish to be privy to your reasoning, Mother, but since all these people bore witness to your accusation, it might be best to keep them close until you have explained yourself.'

'Carnsey and Audrey are already privy to my observations. They know, too, how little attention the coroner paid to them.'

Rosamond frowned at her mother's peevish tone of voice but also because a coroner, of all people, should have been glad to entertain the suspicion of foul play. He was required to convene an inquest into any sudden death, but for accident or self-murder, he received no remuneration. In a case of homicide, he was entitled to thirteen shillings and fourpence, once the murderer was identified and his property had been seized by the Crown.

'Carnsey?' Rob asked. 'Audrey?'

The man who had dined with them stepped forward. 'Ulick Carnsey, at your service,' he said with a lopsided smile. 'I was Sir Walter's secretary and general dogsbody.'

He was perhaps thirty, Rosamond reckoned, with a wiry build and dark complexion. Although he had spoken only a few words, his accent told her he'd been well educated.

Melka and the young woman – Audrey – took charge of Eleanor, guiding her into the study and settling her in the Glastonbury chair that had been Sir Walter's favorite place to sit and think. The room had a musty smell, as if its windows had not been opened since Sir Walter's death. Rosamond remedied that, reminded as she did so that this chamber projected from the center portion of the house, giving it a fine view in three directions. Sir Walter's study provided an excellent vantage point from which to watch the arrival of visitors. So, she realized, did her mother's solar, located directly above.

Rosamond turned away from the window to find that the girl, Audrey, had come up behind her.

'I am Audrey Gravitt, Mistress Jaffrey, companion to your lady mother.'

Her low, pleasant voice was steady but she betrayed her nervousness by the way her fingers clenched and unclenched in the dull red wool folds of her skirt. She was slim and hazel-eyed with reddish-brown hair – not unattractive, but no beauty, either. Rosamond could not help but notice her accent.

'You are not a Cornishwoman.'

The girl took a step back, as if she expected to have her ears boxed. 'I came here from Westmorland.'

'Are you a kinswoman, then?'

Westmorland was the northern county where Eleanor had been born. Rosamond had never met any of her relatives from that side of the family. Her mother had long been estranged from them. The rift, Rosamond felt certain, had come about when Eleanor ran off with Rosamond's father.

Before Audrey could answer the question, Eleanor interrupted. 'If you wish to hear what I have to say, Rosamond, sit down and listen.'

Petulant, imperious, Eleanor waited impatiently for her daughter to do her bidding. Her fingers drummed on the arm of her chair until Rosamond perched atop the flat-topped traveling chest in front of the arras showing *The Judgment of Paris*.

Rob came to sit beside her, lending silent support. The others ranged themselves around the room. Carnsey leaned negligently against a valuable carved and painted panel that had been taken from a church during the Dissolution. Audrey seated herself on a stool near the windows while Melka continued to stand sentry at Eleanor's elbow.

'It is a wife's duty to prepare her husband's body for burial.' Eleanor's words were clipped and her voice devoid of emotion. 'That is how I came to notice suspicious bruises and other marks.' She held up a hand to prevent Rosamond from interrupting. 'You will say they were the result of the fall that killed him, but the wound here –' she touched her brow – 'could only have come from a rock. It struck him hard enough to cause him to fall from his horse, mayhap hard enough to kill him outright. That is why he died. Murder, not accident. He was attacked.'

'He was alone when he died,' Carnsey said. 'No one saw what happened. Only after his horse returned without him did we send searchers to look for him. He had been dead for some hours before he was found.'

'Where?' Rosamond asked.

Carnsey described a remote area of the estate. 'There was no reason he should not have gone there alone. He did so every year to examine the summer pasture before moving the horses, oxen, colts, and kine to higher ground.'

That meant anyone at Priory House might have known where he was going that day. But a murderous ambush? Rosamond could not imagine anything so unlikely. 'A thrown rock seems an uncertain way to kill a man.'

'It worked for David when he slew Goliath,' Rob said.

For the first time, Eleanor looked with approval upon her daughter's husband. 'That is what I tried to tell the coroner. He would not listen. No one took me seriously, and I was not prepared to tell strangers what I will now confide to you. You know already that Walter was an intelligence gatherer as well as a diplomat. What you are likely unaware of is that he continued to send regular reports to Sir Francis Walsingham after we settled here in Cornwall. He dispatched the last one only days before he died, shortly after he returned from a visit to Boscastle to meet with one of his informers.'

Rosamond bit back a curse. She had known her stepfather's history. He had sometimes talked of those early days to her, and of his later appointments as Queen Elizabeth's representative in Poland, Sweden, and Bavaria. He had been a gifted storyteller. She had never been certain how much he embellished the tales he told her, but she had always assumed that he gave up spying when he retired to Cornwall. To all appearances, he had lived the life of a simple country gentleman.

'Did he go to Boscastle alone?' Rob asked.

'Carnsey was with him,' Eleanor said, 'and one of the grooms.'

'Sir Walter met with an alehouse keeper named Alexander

Trewinard.' Carnsey shrugged. 'I did not overhear their conversation, nor do I know the content of Sir Walter's last message to Sir Francis Walsingham.'

Rosamond sent him a sharp look. 'I thought you said you were his secretary.'

'Some correspondence he handled himself, Mistress Jaffrey.'

She turned back to her mother, her mind full of questions, but one look at Eleanor's haggard face and drooping body stayed her tongue. Eleanor had not been lying about her need to rest. Resigned to postponing her interrogation until the morrow, Rosamond instead suggested that Melka and Audrey help the exhausted woman to her bedchamber. After Eleanor had slept, they would talk again.

Carnsey followed the women out.

'Did you believe her?' Rob asked when they were alone.

'I am not convinced Sir Walter was murdered.'

'And his association with Walsingham?'

Rosamond sighed. 'That, I do not *want* to believe.'

TEN

28 June 1584

I t was with a heavy heart that Rob Jaffrey entered the library at Priory House. This large, pleasant room was located in the same wing of the house as the guest chambers where he and Rosamond were lodged. Sweet-scented rushes covered the floor and the walls were hung with brightly colored maps. Chests held books and papers while two small tables, a desk, and several chairs completed the furnishings.

Rob was uncertain where to begin. Both Lady Pendennis and the secretary, Ulick Carnsey, had said that Sir Walter corresponded with Walsingham, but would Rosamond's stepfather have kept copies of his letters? He started his search with the papers on the desk.

A full day had passed since their arrival at Priory House and

Lady Pendennis's demand that they investigate her husband's murder. In the interim, Rob and Rosamond had questioned all the members of the household. It had been an exercise in futility. Everyone had been cooperative, but no one had been able to add to their knowledge.

Sir Walter had gone out on horseback, a common occurrence, and the horse had returned without its rider. After a search, the body had been found and brought home. The girl, Audrey, had confirmed Lady Pendennis's description of her husband's wounds, but that was little help. How could anyone tell, hours afterward, if a rock had been in the air or on the ground when it came in contact with Sir Walter's skull?

Interrogating the servants had taken all the previous afternoon and evening. As today was Sunday, everyone had been obliged by law to attend church services in the morning. The local clergyman was inoffensive but long-winded. Afterward, Rosamond had intended to talk to her mother again, but Melka had thwarted that plan. Fierce as any guard dog, she kept everyone away from Lady Pendennis during church services. As soon as they returned from church, she hustled her former mistress straight to her chamber and into bed. She insisted that her lady was ill and must not be disturbed.

Muttering under her breath, Rosamond also absented herself from dinner, going off to search Sir Walter's study instead. Rob had taken time to eat before he tackled the library and so far the only records he had found related to running the estate. The few letters were from other Cornish gentlemen, including Sir Walter's brother Tristram.

Rob had just begun to peruse a note wondering if Sir Walter meant to attend the fair to be held at Bodmin in August, when he heard the door creak open. Benet peered around the edge. As soon as he realized that Rob had seen him, he came the rest of the way into the room.

'This is my father's library.'

'Yes, it is. I am trying to find something he left behind.'

'What?' The boy came closer.

'I wish I knew.' He considered Benet's presence with the jaundiced eye of one not far removed from the rigors of university life. 'What have you done with your tutor?'

Rob had not been impressed with the fellow, Sutton by name, an Oxford scholar past his prime. He was worthy enough, but somewhat long in the tooth to deal with a lad of Benet's years. He had professed to know nothing at all about Sir Walter's last days. Sutton kept himself to himself, or so he claimed.

'He takes a nap after every meal.' Benet's manner was matter-of-fact. 'He falls asleep in his chair.'

The boy's attention shifted to the globe that held pride of place in a corner between two of the windows. Moving to stand beside it, he ran one finger along the deep gouge that marred a section of what was labeled the Western Sea. These days, it was more commonly called the Atlantic Ocean.

'Father said a girl did this. Do you suppose that was my sister?'

'It would not surprise me in the least to learn that it was.' His wife still had a temper, although she controlled it much better now than she had when she'd been Benet's age.

When the boy wandered over to the maps on the walls, Rob rose and went to stand beside him. Pride of place in the display had been given to Master Mercator's rendering of the world. Hand colored, with a patterned border, it was made up of more than a dozen separate sheets of copperplate engraving and had been mounted on a length of canvas more than four feet in height and six in length. It was a magnificent work of art, and alleged to be one of the most accurate representations of known geography. Mercator had also made an attempt to show the unknown regions of the world. Charting the New World was a matter that involved much guesswork.

Benet moved on to a smaller map of Spanish origin. 'Do you want to see where my parents traveled?' In turn, he pointed out each of Sir Walter's postings. 'And here is where my mother was when she was crippled.' He jabbed a finger into the dot on the map that was Augsburg. 'She wanted Father to be appointed ambassador to France, but he never was. He lived in Paris once and he said that was enough. He was only a secretary then, just as Master Carnsey is now.'

Only a secretary? Rob doubted it, just as he doubted that Sir Walter had been more than a simple intelligence gatherer in the old days. If the stories his parents and Rosamond's foster mother told were true, Sir Walter had once commanded a spy network of his own. Sir Robert Appleton, who had also gathered intelligence for the Crown, had reported to him.

'Where have you traveled?' the boy asked.

'I will show you, but not on one of these maps.' He led Benet back to the globe, spinning it until North Cape, where the Barents Sea began, was at the top. 'When you are here, on a sailing ship, the northern sky is like a clear mirror and there is no night at all, not as we know it. There is only the continual brightness of the sun reflected by an endless sea.'

'No night?' Benet sent him a doubtful look. 'How can that be?'

'How, I know not, but I witnessed for myself this absence of darkness. At the midnight hour, the ship's mast casts a longer shadow on the water and a smudge of gold shows in an otherwise silver world. The sun there is silver in color, you see, not gold like our English sun. That was the only sign that it was night. I can still remember how tired my eyes became from staring at the empty sea and sky. There were times when I longed for darkness with well nigh painful intensity.'

'I would like to stay up all night,' Benet said, 'especially if it was bright enough to see everything around me.'

'Some sights are worth seeing.' Rob could not claim to have witnessed them all himself, but he was not averse to repeating stories he had heard from others. 'There was once a most spectacular rainbow off the coast of Norway.' He indicated that land on the globe.

'Rainbows are nothing special. They often appear after a hard rain.'

'This one was a half circle, such as we see here in England after a storm, but both ends were turned upward.'

Benet remained unimpressed.

'Mayhap you would have enjoyed an encounter with the Maleleand, although I do much doubt it. That is an enormous whirlpool in the sea between Röst and Lofoten. It makes such a terrible noise that it can shake the iron handles on the doors of houses on an island ten miles distant.'

'You are making that up!'

'Indeed, I am not. I swear it on my mother's honor!'

'Did you see it for yourself?'

'I admit I did not, but the story comes from a most reliable source.'

'I think someone was cozening you with a wild tale, just as you are attempting to cozen me.'

Rob chuckled. 'It is possible, my young skeptic. Let me tell you, then, of something I did see with mine own eyes. As far north as we sailed, we encountered great heaps of ice rising out of the sea. What shows above the water is enormous, but much more lies out of sight below the waves. More than one ship has come to grief from sailing too close to one of those behemoths.'

'Was that the greatest danger you faced once you left England?' Benet asked.

The question catapulted Rob into the past. In his mind's eye, he saw the filthy cell in the Moscow prison where he had been held. That was not an experience he intended to share with anyone, let alone a young boy. Even Rosamond did not know all the grisly details. When Toby Wharton had freed him from that harsh captivity, Rob had made him swear that he would never tell Rosamond how close he had come to dying.

'Sir?' Benet prompted him.

Recalled to the boy's interest in his long, arduous sea journey from England to Muscovy, Rob settled for a tale of the fleet's encounter with the King of Denmark's pirates. 'We had one of the queen's warships with us as an escort,' he said after he had told Benet about earlier sightings and of how the pirates had chased another merchant convoy halfway back to England.

'When they saw the ordnance mounted on the *Tiger*,' he said, concluding the tale, 'they turned tail and fled.'

'There was no battle?' Disappointment brought a frown to Benet's face.

'Men die in battle. This was the best possible outcome.'

'But it is not very exciting.'

'Then I will tell you something that was. Do you know what a whale is?

'It is a giant sea creature. There is a picture on one of my father's maps. Come see.'

Together they studied the painted detail. The artist had exaggerated the fearsomeness of the beast, but not by much.

'Imagine dozens of these great monsters, some as many as sixty feet long, all gathered together for their time of engendering.'

Benet sent him a blank look.

For a moment, Rob was at a loss. Explaining this was a father's task, but Benet had no father. He cleared his throat. 'Like all creatures, a whale seeks its mate. These huge beasts were not, in truth, much interested in our puny ships. The males were too intent upon attracting the attention of the females, but it was this love play that was so dangerous to us. Water surged up as they cavorted, threatening to swamp the smallest vessels. We sailed out of range with as much speed as we could muster.'

'Did you encounter other strange animals on your journey?' The tale of the whales, like that of the pirates, had clearly disappointed him.

Rob tried to recall what he had been like at Benet's age. Bloodthirsty, he suspected. Most boys were. 'When we made port in St Nicholas, our principal port in Muscovy, I saw multitudes of seals. The sight surprised me. I had heard that these creatures were massacred in great numbers every spring, and this was only a few months later. They are bludgeoned to death because their bodies are a source of train-oil, one of the most profitable commodities merchants in Russia ship home to England.'

'Did you bludgeon the ones you saw?'

'No, I did not.' He searched his memory for a sighting that might please Benet better. 'Later, as we sailed along the Dvina river on our way to Moscow, I saw a bear that was white as snow.'

'Did you kill it?'

Rob shook his head, fighting a smile. It seemed he was destined to be a great disappointment to his young brother-in-law. 'I left the killing to others, but we had many fine furs in our cargo when I sailed home again.'

In truth, when he'd first arrived in St Nicholas, all he'd cared about was setting foot on solid ground again. It was a primitive place, but it boasted some forty wooden houses and one of them had been set aside for the use of the English factor.

Once again, a memory came back to him with potent force. It had been an uncommon hot day when they arrived, far warmer than any July in England. When Rob had seen a man walking stark naked down the wooden street, he'd attributed this strange behavior to the excessive heat. A more experienced member of the Muscovy Company had been quick to disabuse him of that notion. It seemed that dicing was endemic in St Nicholas, as was heavy drinking. The man he'd seen had gambled away everything he owned, including the clothes on his back.

A tug on his sleeve brought Rob back to the present. 'Does Muscovy have a queen as we do?'

'It is ruled by a tsar – that's Russian for emperor.'

'Did you meet him?'

'Thankfully, I did not.'

But that gave him an idea. He proceeded to regale the boy with the tales he'd heard about Ivan the Terrible. The late tsar had deserved his name. The stories would curl the hair of those older and wiser, but they were mother's milk to a lad of eight. Details of the gruesome torture of a physician named Bomelius filled Benet with delight.

'That is better than any of Master Foxe's stories.' Benet indicated the copy of John Foxe's *Book of Martyrs* on a nearby shelf.

Rob grimaced. He had never cared for Foxe's work. The fellow took too much delight in detailing the horrors of life under Queen Mary and King Philip. In those days, Catholics had persecuted Protestants. Now, under Mary's Protestant half-sister Elizabeth, Catholics were the ones who were fined, arrested, tortured, and executed. *Conform and live. Stay true to your convictions and die a martyr.* It seemed to Rob that the only difference between then and now was that the Church of Rome had made saints of its martyrs.

'Do you have a favorite story?' he asked Benet.

Benet shook his head. 'It was Father's book. He consulted it often. But once he let me read the story of Agnes Prest because she was from Cornwall. She was born in Nortcott in the parish of Boyton but she went to work as a servant in Exeter – that's in Devon – and that is where she was converted to the New Religion. Then later, she returned to Cornwall and married a farmer, but he was a papist, so she left him and their children and supported herself by spinning. That is when her husband reported her to the authorities because it was against the law not to be a papist when Queen Mary was queen.'

'And then what happened?' Rob removed Foxe's book from the shelf and opened it to the frontispiece. Since it was one of the most popular books in England, it had been through many printings. This was the most recent edition, published the previous year.

'Goodwife Prest was imprisoned in Launceston for three months and tried at the Launceston Assizes and then she was sent to Devon and the Bishop of Exeter condemned her to death because she spoke out against the mass and refused to recant. She was burnt at the stake outside the walls of Exeter.'

And that explained why she was in *The Book of Martyrs*. Rob opened Foxe's book to the written account and discovered that the boy had done an excellent job of summarizing.

Then he looked closer. There were faint marks under some of the letters.

He consulted it often, Benet had said. It appeared he had, at that.

Here was proof, if he had needed it, that Sir Walter had still been involved in intelligence gathering. He had written to Sir Francis Walsingham using a code and the key to it was this book. Instead of each word, Sir Walter would have written three numbers – the page, the line, and how many words one must count in from the left-hand margin to find that word. Unless one knew what book he had used, the code was unbreakable.

Unaware of the role he had played in Rob's discovery, Benet began to chatter about his horse, a gift from his parents. Rob closed the book and returned it to the shelf, dividing his attention between Rosamond's half-brother and the dilemma he now faced.

If Sir Walter *had* been murdered, then it appeared that Lady Pendennis's conclusion was correct. Something he had discovered while engaged in espionage had led to his death.

ELEVEN

Just past midnight, 29 June 1584

The soft sound of Rob's breathing soothed Rosamond, but sleep remained elusive. Troubling thoughts kept her mind too active to rest.

If Sir Walter's death *was* a case of murder and had its roots in her stepfather's service to Walsingham, then finding his killer might well be impossible. And yet, despite the likelihood of failure, she was resolved to make the effort. To begin their investigation, she and Rob planned to travel to Boscastle to question Alexander Trewinard.

Rosamond had to admit that she was glad of an excuse to leave Priory House. Her mother's illness – if she *was* ill – cast a pall over the entire household. Once she'd taken to her bed after church, she had refused to admit anyone but Melka and Audrey to her chamber.

Rosamond sighed and rolled onto her back to stare into the darkness above her head. Melka had intended all along to stay in Cornwall. Rosamond did not know why it had taken her so long to realize that the reason her tiring maid had insisted upon accompanying them had more to do with loyalty to her old mistress than with concern for her current employer. Melka had been Eleanor's servant first. She had left her native Poland in the household of Ambassador Pendennis and afterward had accompanied Eleanor to Sweden, Bavaria, and several of the German city states. She had been the one who cared for Eleanor when Rosamond's mother was trampled by horses and run over by the heavy wagon they were pulling.

The injuries had been so severe – a broken hip, a broken leg, horrible bruises and deep cuts, and a dislocated shoulder – that everyone had expected Eleanor to die within a fortnight. When she had surprised them by surviving, her physicians had predicted that she would never walk again. Those prognostications, too, had been proven wrong. Despite Rosamond's acrimonious relationship with her mother, she had to admire the strength of will it had taken for Eleanor to overcome such enormous odds.

Determination was a trait Rosamond had inherited. She told herself that stubbornness was not a *bad* attribute to possess, especially if one looked upon it as being dedicated rather than pig-headed.

Rosamond squirmed, trying to find a more comfortable position. She pounded her pillow into a different shape, but that did little to help, nor did taking deep, calming breaths.

Since she had, as usual, left both bed hangings and shutters open wide, her gaze strayed to the window. Mild summer air flowed into the bedchamber, carrying with it the quiet sounds of the countryside. An owl hooted. A breeze stirred the leaves on nearby trees. In these, Rosamond heard nothing untoward, but of a sudden she had the feeling that something was not quite right. After a moment, she realized what it was. On this moonless night, someone had lit a lantern or a torch. She could see it flickering.

The stable lay in that direction. The obvious explanation was that one of the horses required attention. A mare about to foal? A case of the bots? For neither did she need to get out of bed.

She dozed, and the next thing she knew, she was jolted awake by the sound of hooves striking cobblestones. *Not again!* she thought as she sat up, clutching the sheet to her bosom. She stared at the window. For a moment, she was back in Bermondsey on the morning Jacob brought word of Sir Walter's death.

Rosamond strained to hear, wondering if she'd been dreaming. Had she imagined a horse? No – now she could make out voices, faint but real, at an hour when no honest soul should have been stirring. She slid out of bed and felt her way to the window. Although there was no light behind her to give away her presence, she took care not to show herself when she looked out.

She had not been mistaken. A lantern hung at the entrance to the stable showed her the shapes of two men and one horse. She had always had excellent night vision and recognized the taller of the men as Gryffyn, one of the Priory House grooms. She and Rob had spent some considerable time questioning him, since he was the one who had accompanied Sir Walter and Ulick Carnsey on that last trip to Boscastle.

There was something familiar about the other fellow, too. Squinting, she stared harder. She bit back a gasp when the object of her attention turned his head.

As if he'd heard that faint sound, Henry Leveson's gaze swept over the lower level of Rosamond's wing of the house, surveying the buttery, pantry, and kitchen on the ground floor. Finding them dark and quiet, all but deserted until the first scullion awoke before dawn to stir the fires, he looked up. He seemed to stare straight at Rosamond's open window, but after a moment, apparently having seen nothing to alarm him, he turned away. The two men entered the stable, taking the lantern and the horse with them.

Rosamond lost no time locating a loose-bodied gown and flinging it over her head. She delayed long enough to light a candle and place it in a dark lantern, adjusting the shutters so that only a glimmer showed, then set off along the narrow passage just outside her lodgings.

It did not occur to her to wake her husband. She had nothing to fear from the men in the stables.

The passage led to a flight of stairs. Down one level, the door to her right gave access to the household's service rooms. The one in front of her opened into an herb garden. Moving swiftly, she ignored the bite of the gravel on the path beneath her bare feet. The crunch at each step sounded loud in the stillness of the night, but she felt certain the men inside the stable would not be able to hear her approach.

At the stable door, Rosamond paused to listen. Muffled voices accompanied the creak of leather – a saddle being removed from a horse. Other sounds suggested the horse was being fed and watered. Closing her lantern fully, Rosamond slipped into the shadows at the side of the building. She would wait until Leveson came out and then accost him.

If he came out.

What if she had miscalculated? He must have carried some official authorization or he'd not have been permitted past the gatehouse. That suggested urgency. But what if he was waiting for a more reasonable hour to wake the house and in the meantime meant to bed down with the grooms? She fidgeted and finally crept closer to the open stable door.

Only the smallest of sounds – the rattle of a displaced pebble – alerted her to a presence behind her. She whirled, reaching out of habit for the knife in her boot before she remembered that she was not wearing boots, nor had she assumed the cloak that concealed her second dagger. If Henry Leveson had been a mortal enemy, she'd be dead.

He caught hold of her arm, his grip merciless. 'Identify yourself.'

'Unhand me, you oaf. You are the one who has no business here.'

'Mistress Jaffrey?' Leveson kept his voice low, but she detected a note of frustration beneath his words. He released her and stepped back, adding more to himself than to her, 'Why am I not surprised?'

'Is your intelligence so poor that you did not expect to find me at Priory House?'

He did not respond to her taunt, asking a question of his own instead. 'Is your husband with you?'

'He is.'

'Then, enjoyable as it is to meet with you in the dark of night, I suggest that he join us before I try to explain my presence.'

'I can guess why you've come,' Rosamond muttered as she opened the shutter on her lantern and led him into the house.

Henry Leveson was a player with the Earl of Leicester's Men. He was also, as she had the best of reasons to know, an intelligence gatherer in Sir Francis Walsingham's employ. He had not come to Priory House by chance.

'You have been here before, else Ludlow would not have let you enter the grounds. And you were already known to Gryffyn.'

'I have and I am,' Leveson admitted.

Rosamond went up the stairs. The guest lodgings at Priory House consisted of three rooms. She lit a few candles and then gestured toward the pierced cupboard that contained a few choice items of food and drink, indicating that Leveson should help himself if he was hungry or thirsty. She left him there and continued on into the bedchamber.

Rob was already awake and dressing. He eyed her attire, eyebrows lifting.

'I am decently covered.'

He ignored the testiness in her voice. 'What has happened now?'

'Henry Leveson.' She found a pair of low-heeled shoes and slipped them on, but did not bother assuming any other garments. The way she was dressed would not disturb their unexpected guest. Leveson had seen her in more than one disguise, including that of a boy.

'God rot the fellow. What is he doing here?'

'Shall we ask him?'

They returned together to the outer chamber.

Leveson had filled a goblet with Rhenish wine and helped himself to bread and cheese. While Rob poured wine into two more goblets, Rosamond lit additional candles. In the flickering illumination, the spy's face looked haggard.

Rosamond had never been certain how old Leveson was. She had always suspected he looked younger than he was. Now she was certain of it. He seemed to have aged a decade in only a few months' time.

Tired gray eyes studied her in return. No doubt he sought some sign of weakness. That suspicion made Rosamond stiffen her spine, set aside her wine, and cross her arms over her chest. If Walsingham had sent an agent to Priory House, it did not bode well for any of them. She needed to know why Leveson was in Cornwall.

'Well?' she demanded. 'You had dealings with my stepfather. Of what nature were they?'

Leveson chewed and swallowed before he replied. 'Need you ask? Sir Walter sent word to Sir Francis every time he met with a certain land pirate by the name of Alexander Trewinard, an alehouse keeper in Boscastle.' He paused to sip more wine. 'In the past, Trewinard has picked up rumors that have proven useful. This last time, or so Sir Walter believed, Trewinard was holding back vital information.'

'And you are only now arriving in Cornwall?'

Chewing industriously, Leveson swallowed before saying, 'It did not seem to be a matter of great urgency until word reached us of the manner of Sir Walter's death.'

'What was in Sir Walter's last report to Sir Francis?' Rob asked.

'You have no need to know that.'

Rosamond was unsurprised by his answer, but she refused to accept it. 'That will not do. Not this time.'

Rob sat back, giving every appearance of being content to let his wife carry on the inquisition.

Leveson sighed. He sipped more wine, studying Rosamond with a bland expression. Abruptly, he caved in. 'Alexander Trewinard is likely privy to a plot that endangers Crown and country.'

'*Another* one?' Rosamond could not quite keep the sarcasm out of her voice. 'I vow, Sir Francis is wont to find treason under every rock!'

'Sir Walter reported that Trewinard seemed afraid to speak freely. As he has been providing your stepfather with information for some years now, that suggests the matter is serious.' Leveson's grave manner was more convincing than his words.

'Does Sir Francis have some inkling of what it is that Trewinard fears?'

'Invasion.'

'There is *always* talk of invasion. If it is not the French, it is the Spanish. You know as well as I do how little basis in fact these rumors have.'

Only a few months earlier, Rosamond had played a crucial role in thwarting one such plan. The intent of the conspirators had been real enough, but the forces they had expected to gather on the Continent to support them had been more fantasy than fact.

Leveson gave a violent shake of his head. 'I grant you there have been false alarms, but it is only by constant vigilance that we protect ourselves. Trewinard has dealings with pirates and smugglers. Such men have an ear to the ground.'

'Or to the water,' Rosamond jested.

'This is no joking matter.'

'England has not been invaded since William the Conqueror. Why should I believe it will happen now?'

'The papists—'

'Oh, not that again! Most of those who still practice the Old Religion are simple folk. They have no interest in overthrowing the queen.'

'Yet that is what the Pope in Rome tells them they must do.'

'If they meant to obey, they'd already have risen, no doubt brandishing pitchforks.'

She found it an easy matter to dismiss the threat of a papist rebellion, even though her association with recusants was limited. There would always be a few malcontents who would plot treason, but monetary and political gain motivated such men far more than religion did.

'Are you such an innocent?' Leveson mocked her. 'I'd not have thought it.'

'Offer me proof of a conspiracy,' she shot back. 'Then I will believe you.'

'That,' he assured her, 'is what I have come here to find. Proof of treason, and proof that your stepfather was murdered. I warrant someone associated with Alexander Trewinard was behind his death.'

Although she had been expecting just such an admission, it gave Rosamond a jolt to hear the words spoken aloud. She glanced at Rob. He, too, looked shaken by the conviction in Leveson's voice.

'So, my mother was right.'

'What does she know?' Leveson leaned forward, suddenly avid.

'Only what she saw when she examined his body.' Rosamond summarized Eleanor's observations and her conclusion.

'A rock?' Incredulous, he shook his head. 'I did not expect to hear that he had died from a bullet wound or that he was stabbed, even if such a death could have been passed off as an attack by robbers, but poison would have been a surer means of silencing him.'

Rosamond shuddered. It mattered little *how* Sir Walter had died. He was gone and there was no bringing him back. The best she could do for her stepfather was make sure that his killer was brought to justice. Leveson could help them achieve that end, even though his mission was somewhat different. His goal was to discover *why* someone had thought it necessary to murder Sir Walter, and use that information to keep England safe.

'I have already talked to Gryffyn, there in the stables,' Leveson said. 'As soon as may be, I will question Carnsey. Then I will have him take me to Boscastle so I can interrogate Alexander Trewinard.'

'Why should the alehouse keeper talk to you?' Rosamond asked. 'Come to think of it, will he even admit to understanding English? Some Cornishmen cling to the old ways and refuse to speak our language.'

'If it becomes necessary, Carnsey can translate.'

'But how will you know if he tells you true?' Rosamond asked. 'Sir Walter's murderer could be anyone – Carnsey, Gryffyn, even Trewinard.'

'Even your mother?' Leveson asked.

Rosamond shot to her feet. She would not dignify that sugges-tion with an answer. Looking down her nose at him, she spoke in a haughty voice that would have done Eleanor proud. 'Rob and I have already made plans of our own to travel to Boscastle. We leave first thing in the morning. If you wish to come with us, I advise you to avail yourself of a few hours of sleep.' She gestured toward the third room of the guest lodgings. 'You will find an unused camp bed in there.'

Rob placed his empty goblet next to Rosamond's untouched one and addressed Leveson. 'You can question Carnsey as we ride.' Then he offered an arm to his wife.

She smiled at him as she took it, but she paused at the bedchamber door to look back. 'Carnsey is not the only one who can understand the Cornish language.'

'I had not forgotten your facility with foreign tongues.' Leveson drained his goblet and set it aside. 'What do you want in return for serving as my translator?'

'Your cooperation. We share everything we learn, from whatever source. After all, the odds are good that the traitor you hope to thwart and the murderer I wish to capture are one and the same.'

TWELVE

29 June 1584

Lost in none-too-pleasant thoughts, Rob said little during the first part of the sixteen-mile ride to Boscastle. Carnsey was in the lead, since he was the only one who knew the road well enough to serve as their guide. Rosamond rode just behind him, then Rob, with Leveson next in line and Rosamond's men – Charles, Luke, and John – bringing up the rear. It was never wise to travel any distance without an escort, even in daylight.

Struck by that widely-accepted truth, Rob turned his head to stare at Leveson. 'Did you come all the way from London to Cornwall alone?'

The other man's lazy smile masked his thoughts. 'Concerned for my welfare?'

'Curious. Only curious. You may be a very clever fellow, but a solitary man on a horse makes a tempting target for runagates and footpads.'

'Only if he is moving slowly enough for them to catch him. I was authorized to make use of the horses Sir Francis keeps throughout the land for rapid passage from place to place. There are post horses at a dozen stops along the two hundred and some odd miles of road between London and Plymouth.'

Rob considered this. By changing mounts at regular intervals, Leveson would have been able to cover that part of his journey at a rapid pace. As he understood it, a groom accompanied the rider at each stage to return the horse after he started the next stretch. That no groom had arrived at Priory House with Walsingham's man prompted another question.

'Are there also post horses available in Cornwall?'

'Alas, no. I purchased this fine fellow in Plymouth.'

'Do you mean to say you rode all the way from Plymouth last night with no moon and no escort?'

Cornish roads, including the one they were following, were narrow and poorly maintained. It was impossible to achieve much speed in the best of conditions. Had Leveson been fool enough to risk life and limb? Rob sent the other man a sharp look when he failed to answer the question and came to a different conclusion.

'You have been in the area longer than you led us to believe.'

Leveson shrugged. 'I had questions to ask. Unfortunately, as your good wife has already pointed out, many of the local people pretend they do not understand English. It is an effective means to avoid answering questions.'

'How did you persuade Ludlow to let you in without alerting Lady Pendennis?'

'The gatekeeper? In truth, I did not arrive that way. Sir Walter showed me another entrance to the grounds during my first visit. He said he preferred to keep my presence secret from his wife.'

Although Rosamond was riding a little ahead of Rob, she was close enough to overhear. When she abruptly reined in, the entire party came to a halt.

'Gryffyn knew who you were,' she said in an accusatory tone of voice. 'Why did my stepfather trust him?'

'I do not know that he did. Ride on, mistress, I beg you. It will take us all morning to reach Boscastle as it is.'

With a little huffing sound, Rosamond set her mount in motion again. Although the days were long at this season of the year, they did not have time to waste if they hoped to make the trip from Priory House to Boscastle and back again before dark.

They continued on their way, riding through terrain that was virtually treeless – hill and wasteland, covered with scrub and furze. Gradually, wildflowers began to appear. Rob was no expert when it came to recognizing plants and herbs, but young Benet, on hearing that they were to travel this way, had informed him that bird's foot trefoil, eyebright, and devil's-bit scabious grew in the valley fields on either side of the deeply rutted road. Rob found himself wishing he could tell one plant from another. It would keep his thoughts from returning to the reason for their journey.

Instead, he pondered the significance of what Leveson had told them. He supposed he could understand Sir Walter's desire to distance himself from one of Walsingham's agents, but what if it was more than that? Was there someone at Priory House, Eleanor or another, who needed to be kept in the dark? Someone Sir Walter had not trusted? Someone who might have betrayed him to an enemy?

Because Rosamond was mounted on a sidesaddle, her body was angled so that it was a simple matter for her to turn her head to look at the men riding behind her. Her thoughts had apparently been following the same thread as Rob's, for when she addressed Leveson, it was to accuse him of knowing a great deal more than he had said. 'You already suspect someone of my stepfather's murder.'

'I know little more than you do,' Leveson protested. 'Sir Walter had dealings with pirates and smugglers, some of whom have a reputation for violence.'

'Bloodthirsty men,' Rosamond agreed, 'and capable of murder.'

'And yet,' Leveson added, 'I cannot dismiss another possibility, that of domestic malice. A widow inherits at least a third of her late husband's estate, reason enough for some women to do away with an inconvenient spouse.'

'You think my mother killed him?' Outraged, Rosamond nearly tumbled from her saddle.

'Anything is possible, and with her history . . .' Leveson's voice trailed off, letting his hint about some past deceit linger in the mild morning air.

Rob braced himself for an explosion. His wife was at the boiling point. It was all very well for her to criticize her mother, but let someone else disparage Lady Pendennis and Rosamond was like a lioness defending her cubs. He saw the effort it took to sheathe her claws, realizing, as he had, that angry words would not persuade Leveson to tell them all he knew. She rode on, giving them her back as she struggled to regain control of her temper.

'You are a slippery fellow,' Rob said in a quiet voice, 'as are all spies. You reveal no more than you have to, despite your claim that you mean to share information to the benefit of all. That is but a ploy to persuade us to tell you what we have learned.'

To his surprise, Leveson did not dispute the charge. 'A good man is dead, and his work for Walsingham is the most likely cause. Since I cannot question Cornishmen without help, I am resigned to dealing honestly with you and your wife. What do you know of Cornish pirates?'

Rob spared a glance for Rosamond before he answered. Although she did not turn, her posture suggested that she was listening.

'I know pirates are a danger to shipping,' Rob said.

'And smuggling? Do you know aught of that practice?'

'It is common anywhere men can bring goods ashore without being caught.' Some years back, his parents had barely survived a close encounter with smugglers in Rye.

'Trewinard is a land pirate, a receiver of stolen goods. He does business with both pirates and smugglers. In return for information Trewinard passed on concerning other matters, Sir Walter, as the local Justice of the Peace, pretended to know nothing of such illegal activities.'

'So we were given to understand.'

Leveson said no more and as they rode on in silence, Rob vowed to keep his ears open in Boscastle. Men with something to hide were unlikely to talk openly to strangers, but they would

not be so cautious in speaking to each other. Then he remembered
that they were likely to be speaking in Cornish. Rosamond might
be able to understand that language, but he could not.

After some considerable time, the riders reached a section of
road lined by massive oaks.

'These oak trees signify that we are close to Boscastle,' Carnsey
announced. 'This is the only place near the exposed, north-facing
coast of Cornwall where they grow so thick.'

A few minutes later, with the sun directly overhead, they rode
down a steep, curving road and entered the village. Rob's first
good look at the harbor surprised him. 'I had thought we would
be able to see the ocean from here.'

Carnsey made a wide gesture. 'It is there, beyond the harbor.
You can see it if you climb the headland.'

'This seems an uncertain haven.' A narrow, twisted body of
water formed the harbor and it was further obstructed by a quay
under construction.

'It is the best to be had along some forty miles of coastline.'
Carnsey's lopsided grin was once more in evidence when he
turned to look at Rob over his shoulder.

'For that reason alone,' Leveson put in, 'I understand it is
much favored by smugglers and the like.'

Rob regarded the scene with a critical eye. 'A winding inlet
of this sort is no doubt fraught with perils. A sailing ship must
have to be hobbled in.'

'Hobbled?' Leveson asked. 'I know the term with horses,
but—'

'Hobbler boats tow larger vessels,' Rob explained, 'aided by
gangs of men on shore who use ropes to keep the ship in the
middle of the channel.'

'And to make the harbor even more hazardous,' Carnsey said,
'there is an island just at the entrance. Larger vessels must ferry
cargo to shore.' When they had ridden closer to it, he pointed at the
quay. 'That has been in ruinous condition ever since it was damaged
by a tempest during the reign of King Henry, but this year the sheriff
ordered it rebuilt.'

'George Grenville,' Leveson supplied, 'although no doubt his
more flamboyant cousin, Sir Richard, will take credit for it.'

Alert for any intelligence Leveson might accidentally reveal,

Rob pondered his words. As Sheriff of Cornwall, Grenville had the unenviable task of mustering troops and securing the ports against the possibility of invasion. Once it had been the French who threatened their shores, but ever since the death of Catholic Queen Mary and the ascension of her Protestant half-sister, Elizabeth, the enemy most likely to make war on England was Spain. Rumors of an armada readying itself for an all-out attack by sea had been rampant for several years. Whether they were true or not was anyone's guess.

Was that what Trewinard had been afraid to speak of to Sir Walter? It was possible, Rob supposed, but the alehouse keeper's secret could also be something much more mundane.

The babble of excited voices reached him just as he sighted the alehouse, its identity made clear by a wand hung out a window. Suspended from it was a simple wooden sign depicting a hand – the universally understood signal that brewing had taken place.

A handful of people had gathered in the street in front of the alehouse door. They fell silent at the appearance of a band of strangers. Suspicious eyes bored into each member of the mounted party until one in the crowd recognized Carnsey and called out his name.

Sir Walter's secretary barked a question in Cornish at the nearest villager. Rob had already dismounted and was helping Rosamond off her horse by the time the fellow answered. His words, spoken in that same incomprehensible tongue, meant nothing to Rob, but Rosamond went very still. He watched her face drain of color and her eyes go wide. Thinking she needed his support, Rob kept hold of her waist.

He should have known better. When she spoke, it was disappointment he heard in her voice, not shock or horror. 'We have arrived too late to question Alexander Trewinard.'

'He's dead?' That conclusion was not much of a leap, given the number of villagers collected in front of the alehouse.

'Not just dead,' Rosamond said. 'Murdered.'

THIRTEEN

S tepping away from Rob, Rosamond addressed the same villager Carnsey had been questioning. It was unlikely he knew who she was, but the richness of her clothing and the quality of the horses marked her as a person of wealth and importance. Even so, had she demanded answers in English, she would have been ignored. That she spoke in Cornish made all the difference. She listened intently as he gave his answers.

'The constable now guarding the alehouse door has sent for the coroner,' she told the others a few minutes later. 'And, as the law requires, he has notified all free men over the age of twelve who live nearby to stand ready to serve as jurors at a coroner's inquest.'

'The coroner has not yet arrived?' Rob asked. 'Most of that breed are eager to earn their fee.'

'This one is an elderly gentleman who lives in Padstow, eighteen or more miles away by road, and no coroner is under any obligation to rush to the scene of a death. The inquest cannot be held until he views the body, whether that be three hours or three days after its discovery.' She eyed the alehouse, a sturdy stone tower with substantial wooden buildings attached. 'If we can persuade the constable to let us in, I should like to examine both the victim and the place where he was murdered.'

'There is little chance that the killer left behind a clue to his identity,' Leveson said.

'It cannot hurt to see for ourselves.'

On a previous occasion when Rosamond had viewed the corpse of a recently murdered man, she had been able to determine the manner of his death – poison – from certain signs and symptoms. She hoped to observe something that would be of equal value in solving this crime.

The man in the crowd spoke again.

Rosamond grimaced, but rewarded him with a halfpenny piece for his honesty.

'What did he say?' Rob asked.

'That likely the wife did it, since she stands to inherit a profitable business.'

Boscastle's constable was a simple villager, chosen by his fellows to serve for the term of one year. He did not want to admit them to the alehouse.

Sir Walter Pendennis, as a justice of the peace, would have been allowed to enter, but even he would not have had the authority to investigate. Only after the coroner's jury made an indictment of homicide, if it was known who was guilty and the coroner ordered an arrest, would he have been able to act in an official capacity. Arraignments, Rosamond recalled, took place before two justices of the peace, who either dismissed the charges or ordered the accused felon bound over for trial.

'Does this man know you?' Rosamond asked Carnsey. 'Will he accept your word that I, or rather my *husband*, has temporarily assumed Sir Walter's duties?'

This was a bald-faced lie. Rob was too young to be appointed to such a post, even in an interim capacity. But he *was* a man. As such, other men would accept his authority far sooner than they would that of any woman.

'There is no need for Master Jaffrey to trouble himself,' Carnsey said. 'As Sir Walter's secretary, I am already authorized to carry out the queen's business on his behalf.' He repeated this statement, a better lie by far than Rosamond's, in the constable's native tongue.

Leaving Charles, John, and Luke with the horses, Carnsey, Leveson, Rob, and Rosamond entered the alehouse. The interior had an appearance typical of such places, with the exception of the corpse laid out atop a table to one side of the single room. A black and white cur lay beneath the makeshift bier that held his dead master's body.

It felt damp inside, for at this time of year there was no welcoming fire blazing in the chimney corner. The faint smell of tobacco lingered in the air, mixed with the stink of spilled drinks and the tang of the sea. The furnishings were all heavy and rough-hewn – two trestle tables and assorted benches, stools, and chairs. A narrow flight of stairs at the back led up to the next level. Barrels and casks ready for tapping were ranged along another wall, hard by a collection of earthenware pots and cups and wooden cans. Rosamond did not see a single pewter vessel, confirming her sense that this was the poorer sort of tippling house.

Her survey complete, she turned her attention, briefly, to the widow. As the wife of the proprietor, she likely brewed all the ale and beer they served. She was a big, buxom woman in brown wool banded with black. Her corset-like bodice was tightly laced over her shift, revealing an expanse of white flesh that no doubt delighted the alehouse's rowdier patrons.

Just now, she stood with shoulders slumped. She glanced at Rosamond and then away, revealing wide-spaced green eyes red with weeping. Her hands twisted in the wrinkled folds of her apron, kneading the fabric into sodden lumps.

Carnsey questioned the constable in Cornish. After a few minutes, he announced in English that the body had been moved.

'Where was he when he was found?' Rob asked.

'Here.' Carnsey indicated the floor behind the table where Trewinard lay.

The cur lifted its head and growled. Rosamond studied the mongrel dog, taking in his size, his short hair, his half-pricked ears, and the short tail that almost looked as if it had been cut. It had not. Many curs were whelped that way. What puzzled her was that Trewinard had kept such a dog. For the most part, curs were owned by farmers who used them to drive cattle. The dogs nipped at the animals' heels to force them to go in the correct direction.

Having been warned that curs bit most keenly, Rosamond was wary, but this was an old fellow with gray in his muzzle. Most of those once-sharp teeth appeared to be missing. Slowly, she knelt and extended one hand.

'We are here to help,' she whispered. 'There is no need to guard your master from us.'

After a moment, the animal deigned to sniff her fingers. She continued to speak softly to him, some words in English and others in Cornish, until he signaled his full acceptance by licking her hand and wagging his stub of a tail.

'Good boy.'

She shifted her attention to the spot where Alexander Trewinard had been found. Lying there, he'd have been half hidden by a bench. Leaning closer to the dog, she examined the area beneath the table. It was too dark to see blood, but she could smell it. The metallic tang was sharp enough to overpower spilled beer and ale and the mud and other matter left behind by patrons' boots. She suspected that it had been some time since the rushes were last changed.

Rising, Rosamond looked down at the body. There could be no doubt about the cause of death. Trewinard had been struck repeatedly about the head.

Swallowing convulsively, Rosamond had to force herself to ignore the gouts of blood and the ruins of the dead man's face. It helped that she had never met the alehouse keeper in life. She could tell herself that he was nothing more than a means to an end. A close study of his person and his wounds might help her solve her stepfather's murder.

'How old was he?' She was pleased to hear no tremor in her voice.

'A few years younger than Sir Walter,' Carnsey said. 'Fifty or so.'

Somewhat older than his wife.

Rosamond continued the examination. His hair was sparse and of a faded, indeterminate shade. What she could see of his skin, where it was still undamaged on his neck and hands, was deeply tanned, making her wonder if Trewinard had taken an active role in the capturing of ships to relieve them of their cargoes.

'Fists alone did not do that much damage,' Rob observed.

'No,' Leveson agreed. 'The killer used a blunt weapon of some sort – a cudgel, I warrant – with considerable force behind it.'

The widow mumbled something. Rosamond caught only two words. 'Lowss' meant hit. 'Nuddick' was the word for head . . . but not in Cornish. She spoke in a local dialect of English. Rosamond filed away that detail to think about later.

'One well-placed blow would have rendered him insensible,' Leveson said. 'One or two more would have been enough to finish him off.'

'That would not require great strength.' Carnsey sent a significant look in the direction of the widow. 'Only determination and ruthlessness.'

He turned to the constable and asked, in Cornish, if there had been any sign of a bloodied cudgel or some similar weapon at the scene.

There had not.

After consulting with Rob and Leveson, Carnsey barked out a string of orders. The constable was to conduct a thorough search for the murder weapon. If he found naught before darkness fell, he was to resume the search the next day. As he went, he was to ask all and sundry if they had seen anyone enter the alehouse in the hours before the hue and cry was raised.

These commands struck Rosamond as sensible. Assuming Trewinard had not been killed by his wife, he had likely admitted his murderer to the alehouse. In a village this small, there was always someone about. With luck, the killer had been seen, mayhap even recognized. Whether anyone would admit to knowing the identity of the culprit was another matter.

After coaxing the dog out from under the table, Rosamond turned her attention to Goodwife Trewinard and left further examination of the body to the men. She addressed the widow in English. 'You have my deepest sympathy for your loss.'

Perhaps emboldened by Rosamond's behavior toward the cur, the other woman eyed her speculatively. Instead of replying in the same tongue, she spoke in Cornish, demanding to know when she could prepare her husband's body for burial.

Rosamond felt certain Widow Trewinard understood the Queen's English perfectly well, but she did not press the point. She replied in Cornish, reminding her that it was the coroner's charge to examine the remains for wounds, bruises, or signs of strangulation. She could not move him again before the inquest.

'Have you any idea who might have killed your husband?' she asked.

The other woman shook her head and sniffled pitifully, a display of distress Rosamond found less convincing than her earlier signs of grief. Although the widow had responded to Rosamond's questions, her gaze had remained on the three men examining her husband's body. When Rob bent forward over the corpse, her eyes lingered on his well-shaped backside. She went so far as to wet her lips, as if she envisioned Rosamond's husband as a tasty morsel she'd like to devour.

Widow Trewinard gave a start when Rosamond spoke sharply to her, and at last shifted her attention.

'Are you the one who found him? Answer in proper English, if you please.' Rosamond had already switched to that tongue.

Her demand produced a baleful look and stubborn silence.

'You are strong enough to have killed him yourself,' Rosamond pointed out. 'If you refuse to cooperate, it will be a simple matter for the coroner to decide that you are guilty of the crime.'

Fear flashed in those fine green eyes, convincing Rosamond that she understood the threat, but she continued to resist admitting that she spoke English. Holding on to her temper by a thread, Rosamond took the other woman by the arm and steered her to the second table. The dog slunk after them.

'Let us begin again. I am Sir Walter Pendennis's stepdaughter. I believe your husband was murdered by the same man who killed Sir Walter, but I need your help to prove it.'

More silence greeted this overture, but Trewinard's widow allowed herself to be coaxed into sitting opposite Rosamond.

'Shall we start with your name?' Rosamond asked.

'Morwen.'

'An excellent start. Were you the one who found him?'

Morwen nodded.

'When?'

In a soft, pleasant voice, Morwen at last began to speak. 'I got up at dawn to begin work in the brewhouse. The dog came with me, more's the pity. He likes to lie in the sun of a morning. My husband was up afore me and should have been about his business, unlatching the door to let in custom and serve drinks.'

She not only spoke English, she spoke it well. Morwen Trewinard, Rosamond suspected, was much more than she seemed. 'You were busy, then, for some hours?'

'Until a customer came round to ask why the alehouse was still locked up tight. It was nigh unto noontide by then.'

Rosamond knew that bodies grew stiff shortly after death and that, after a time, the stiffness receded. She had no idea how long that process took, or even if it always occurred. Had Trewinard been murdered just before they arrived in Boscastle, or had he already been dead for many hours?

'You say your husband rose early. Before dawn?' At this time of year, all but slugabeds arose by four of the clock. She had been up before that herself, so that she would be ready to set out for Boscastle as soon as they had sufficient light to show them the way.

Morwen frowned. 'Mayhap he never came to bed at all. I slept sound. His comings and goings never wake me unless he is in an amorous mood.'

Before Rosamond could pursue this possibility, Carnsey drew Morwen's attention by moving purposefully toward the stairs. She rose from the bench to fling herself into his path.

'Where 'ee goin' to?'

'This entire building must be searched for the murder weapon,' Carnsey said, 'including your living quarters. I fear you have no choice in the matter.' He began to climb.

Leveson and Rob, who had been conversing together in quiet voices, broke off their exchange to join in the search. They followed Carnsey up the stairs. Rosamond and Morwen were right on their heels.

In the lodgings Morwen had shared with her late husband, Carnsey stopped short. Two small children stared back at him. The girl, a thumb securely lodged in her mouth, held tight to her younger brother's arm with the other hand. Neither made a sound.

'Best take them below,' Levenson said to their mother.

Only when Carnsey repeated the suggestion in Cornish, turning it into a command, did Morwen, reluctantly, obey.

Rosamond stayed where she was, although she felt certain there was no bloodied cudgel on the premises. What the searchers did discover did not surprise her, either – when they entered Trewinard's inner chamber, they found a room filled, floor to ceiling, with bales and boxes of contraband.

FOURTEEN

Rosamond returned to the ground floor to find Morwen Trewinard waiting at the foot of the stairs, her fists clenched at her sides and her face a mask of anger. Her children sat on the rush-covered floor nearby, quiet as little mice.

The dog had returned to his late master's side and appeared to be standing guard.

'What are their names?' Rosamond nodded toward the girl and boy.

Morwen seemed surprised by the question. She looked around, as if noticing her offspring for the first time. 'Wenna,' she said, 'and Santo.'

They had been named after their mother and father, Santo being the Cornish diminutive for Alexander.

'And Rover,' Morwen added, pointing to the black and white cur.

Rosamond smiled in spite of herself. Another name for pirates was sea rovers. 'Shall we continue our earlier conversation?' She returned to the table and seated herself on a stool.

Morwen glared at her, but she instructed her daughter to take the boy and the dog outside. While still upstairs, Rosamond had glanced out a window and taken note of a fenced-in area between the stone tower and the brewhouse. A small garden took up part of the space, but the rest was open. She imagined that the children could entertain themselves for a considerable time with the ball and the hoop they took with them.

When they had gone, Morwen joined Rosamond, once more seating herself on the bench opposite. 'What do you want to know?'

'Were you present when Sir Walter Pendennis last visited your husband?'

'Someone had to wait on customers while they talked.'

The aggrieved note in her voice was impossible to miss. How many of Trewinard's duties, Rosamond wondered, had he habitually left to his wife?

'Did you overhear their conversation?' The alehouse was not large. Unless those customers had been noisy, every word should have been audible.

Morwen's face worked. 'Not enough to be of help to you, mistress.'

'Let me be the judge of that.'

'I was busy. Who do you think brings the jug to refill cups with ale?' Morwen stared at her work-roughened hands, clasped before her on the table, but Rosamond did not think she saw them. She was looking inward, searching her memory of another day.

'I warrant their voices carried, even if they spoke in whispers. Mayhap one of your customers heard what they said to each other.'

'They were intent on their drink, and on making lewd suggestions to me.'

'Local men?'

'I had never seen them before and have not seen either since.'

'Do you remember what they looked like?'

She shook her head. 'I had no reason to pay attention to them.'

'Could they have heard what your husband said to Sir Walter?'

'If I heard naught, neither did they.'

Rosamond tried another tack. 'Did anything strike you as odd about that day?'

Morwen started to shake her head once more, then stopped, frowning. 'Once, when I turned toward my husband, I saw that he was staring hard at the window.'

'Did someone look in?'

'No, but there were men on the ale bench.'

'Local men?' Rosamond asked again, remembering that ale and beer sold out of doors cost less and that those who had to pinch their pennies often chose to brave the elements for the savings.

'Two or three were. The others were the escort Sir Walter was accustomed to bring with him, Master Carnsey and the groom, Gryffyn.'

'You knew them by name?'

'They came here often enough.' Annoyance flashed in her eyes. 'Alexander was always secretive about his business with Sir Walter, even though all of Boscastle knew he passed on bits and pieces of news to keep the local justice sweet.'

Rosamond smiled. 'In your place, I would have made certain I was close enough to overhear what they were saying.'

Morwen admitted nothing.

'I will make it worth your while.' Rosamond fingered the small leather purse she had brought with her, causing the coins within to clink together.

'Money will help me little if I am charged with a crime.'

'No one cares about the contents of that room upstairs,' Rosamond said. 'Unless they find the murder weapon, you have nothing to fear.'

'They will not find it among *my* possessions.'

Not even if she had been the one to use a cudgel to kill her husband, Rosamond thought. Morwen impressed her as being far too clever to have left the murder weapon lying about. Removing a gold angel from her purse, she placed it on the table.

Morwen lost no time collecting the coin. 'I did hear Sir Walter remind my husband that Alexander had sent for him for a reason. But then Alexander did nothing more than talk about the death of Sir John Killigrew.'

Rosamond did not know the name. 'Who was he?'

'Killigrew? A justice of the peace like Sir Walter, and captain of one of the queen's castles on the south coast, and the head of the queen's commission on piracy for Cornwall. He died in early March. Old Lady Killigrew, Sir John's mother, was a Trewinard before her marriage. Alexander was kin to her.'

This seemed irrelevant, but Rosamond had no way of knowing what would prove to be important. 'Go on. What else do you remember?'

'Alexander waved me away when I would have refilled his black jack.'

Rosamond saw no significance in that, either. A black jack was a wooden can treated with pitch on the inside and fitted with leather thong handles. It held an impressive quantity of beer or ale. Most men, unless they were habitual drunkards, would be content with one serving.

'I heard him mention the pirates captured last summer off the coast of Dorset.'

'Had Sir John Killigrew aught to do with that?' Rosamond asked.

Morwen gave a throaty laugh. 'The Killigrews are notorious pirates themselves, even the women of the family. Sir John's wife, now his widow, narrowly escaped being tried for piracy when she orchestrated the taking of a Spanish ship at anchor in the harbor below Arwennack House at the mouth of the Fal. Some claim she ordered the murder of its crew, but the only charge made against her in court was that of receiving contraband,

and that charge was dropped. The Killigrews have powerful kin at Court.'

'You said your husband was watching the window. It is located hard by the door. Could he have been expecting someone?'

'If he was, it was not someone he wanted to see. It was almost as if he was *afraid* of what he might see.'

'Did you hear anything more?'

'Only a name – Diggory Pyper.'

Rosamond had to school her features to hide her surprise. The Pypers were a prominent family of merchants based in Launceston. When she was a child, Sampson Pyper had already been wealthy enough to style himself a gentleman. Thus, she had met his youngest son on several occasions. Diggory was a friendly, outgoing lad only two or three years her senior.

'Young Pyper is lately made captain of his own ship,' Morwen said, 'and I have heard he means to take over where Captain Piers left off.'

'Who is Captain Piers?' It was not a name Rosamond had heard before.

'He *was* the most notorious of all the Cornish pirates, until he was executed some two years back.' Morwen looked up, startled, as a commotion began just outside the door.

It had been quiet for some time, the crowd of neighbors having dispersed when the constable asked for volunteers to search for the murder weapon. If there had been other goodwives among the villagers, ready to help the widow prepare her husband's body for burial, they had not lingered. From what Rosamond had seen of the alehouse keeper's wife, this did not surprise her. Morwen was not the kind of female other women took to.

If she had been born and bred in Boscastle, she would have kin to stand by her. That none had thus far appeared seemed to indicate that she was on her own. Rosamond wondered if she was about to be proven wrong in that assessment, but it was not another woman who entered the alehouse.

At the sight of the newcomer, Morwen sprang to her feet and dropped into a curtsey. Rosamond rose more slowly, regarding the fellow with a jaundiced eye. He was one of the tallest men Rosamond had ever seen and the very model of a country gentleman. Modestly but expensively dressed, he sported a beard that had been carefully trimmed but was styled in a fashion that had been out of favor in London for several years.

He regarded her with equal curiosity. 'Good day to you, mistress. I am John Hender of Bottreaux Castle.'

'Bottreaux Castle is a ruin, and has been so for decades.'

His laugh was rich and warm. 'But it is my ruin, purchased from the Earl of Huntingdon along with its land. And you are?'

'Mistress Jaffrey,' Rosamond replied. 'Sir Walter Pendennis was my stepfather.'

'Ah. I am sorry for your loss.' His gaze cut to the body on the table. 'And for yours, too, Goodwife Trewinard. The constable tells me that Master Dodson – the coroner – has been sent for, but that Sir Walter's man is giving orders in the interim. Carnsey, is it?'

'If you are the local justice . . .?' Rosamond began.

Again, he laughed. 'I own a good deal of land hereabout, but that is the extent of my authority. If Carnsey wants to trouble himself with the matter, I wish him well.'

'You know him, then?'

Rosamond wondered why her stepfather's secretary had neglected to mention Master Hender. It was only to be expected that the local gentry would take an interest in Trewinard's murder. She would have appreciated a warning, and some hint as to Hender's true importance in this part of Cornwall.

'Some months ago, your stepfather and his man partook of my hospitality when they were in Boscastle. Sir Walter was good enough to admire the mansion house I have been building since I settled here with my family.'

Since that statement marked him as a relative newcomer to the area, Rosamond felt herself relax. He was unlikely to challenge Carnsey's authority, although his appearance on the scene seemed likely to present her with another dilemma. His next words confirmed that suspicion.

'It is too late in the day for you to return to Priory House before darkness falls, Mistress Jaffrey. You must sup and stay the night with us. My wife and daughters will be delighted to meet you. Isolated here in the wilds of Cornwall, we hear little news of the wider world.'

Rosamond doubted that was true, not if Boscastle was as busy a harbor as she'd been led to believe. Still, she smiled at the

gentleman to keep him sweet while she tried to think of some
way to refuse his offer. In the best of circumstances, she did not
enjoy spending time with a bevy of gentlewomen. Such females
had little interest in anything beyond fashion, needlework, their
children, and the latest rumors about misbehavior on the part of
other members of the gentry.

But Hender was correct in saying she must stay overnight in
Boscastle. Padstow was farther away than Launceston. It was
unlikely the coroner would arrive any earlier than the morrow.
To accept Hender's invitation, however, would take her away
from the alehouse when she had not yet exhausted her search
for connections between Trewinard and Sir Walter.

'Your pardon, Master Hender.' Morwen spoke softly and in
perfect English.

Something in her tone of voice commanded the gentleman's
attention. He went to her side, taking her hands in his and looking
deeply into her emerald-green eyes. 'What troubles you, my good
woman? How can I help?'

'I am afraid to be alone here after what happened to my
husband,' Morwen said in a small voice. 'My children . . .' She
broke off with a sob.

She was angling, Rosamond realized, for an invitation to
move into the mansion house. Once there, it would take a
Herculean effort to dislodge her. As much to save Master Hender
a future filled with trouble as to benefit her own ends, Rosamond
spoke up.

'You poor creature! You must not worry. It is my duty as a
Christian woman to look out for you. I will remain here, Master
Hender. Although I do appreciate your invitation, I will wait for
a happier time to meet your family.' She paused, smiled, and
added, 'Or mayhap you can pay a visit to Priory House. I feel
certain my mother would welcome the company.'

Still elaborating on this suggestion, she escorted him to the door.
Within minutes, he was on his way home, pleased to have received
an invitation to enjoy the hospitality of so good a gentlewoman as
Lady Pendennis. He could see the advantage in cultivating the
widow of a knight, especially one who had served the Crown as
courtier, diplomat, and justice of the peace.

Rosamond repressed a twinge of guilt. Her mother was fully

capable of refusing to admit Master Hender and his wife to Priory House, despite the country custom of offering hospitality to travelers. Still, she was satisfied with the outcome of her ploy. By staying close to Morwen, she hoped to learn more about the late Alexander Trewinard.

Carnsey had come downstairs while Hender was leaving. He was deep in conversation with the widow, but they broke apart when Rosamond approached. Without a word, Morwen flounced off.

'Where is she going?' Rosamond asked.

'To prepare food. Has it escaped your notice that we have not eaten since we left Priory House?'

At the reminder, Rosamond's stomach growled. Despite her proximity to a corpse, she was indeed surpassing hungry.

FIFTEEN

Following Rosamond's announcement that they would remain overnight at the alehouse and the departure of Master Hender, Goodwife Trewinard provided food and drink. Rob and the others had found no trace of the murder weapon, nor had a bloodstained cudgel been located elsewhere in Boscastle. As for the contraband, a strange mixture of goods that included everything from soap to Turkey carpets, Leveson seemed uncertain what to do about it and Carnsey expressed no opinion.

Those two seemed to have settled into an uneasy alliance, first one and then the other taking the lead in dealing with the extraordinary situation in which they found themselves. Neither one appeared to realize that it was Rosamond who made all the important decisions.

At dusk, everyone retired for the night. Rob and Rosamond were to sleep in the small inner room at the top of the stone tower, while Leveson and Carnsey occupied the outer chamber. Charles, Luke, and John bedded down in the stable with the horses.

Rob sat on one end of the bed, tailor-fashion, watching his

wife as she freed her plaited and coiled hair from its bag-shaped coif. She unbraided it and combed through the disordered locks with her fingers, then gave her scalp a vigorous rubbing. A look of pure bliss came over her features.

'You have no idea how fortunate men are to be able to wear their hair short, especially when the day is overwarm.'

Taking the hint, Rob rose and attempted to open the room's one small window. After a struggle, it yielded, but only damp salt air rushed in. The chamber remained close, humid, and uncomfortable. When he turned back to his wife, he saw that she had begun to loosen the long laces that closed her kirtle, in preparation for disrobing. Since they had not intended to be away from Priory House overnight, she had not brought so much as a night robe with her.

That thought made him smile, even as he spoke. 'You may wish to wait a bit before you undress.'

She sent him a questioning look. 'Are we to have a visitor?'

'I would be surprised if we did not. Earlier, we could not speak freely of matters Leveson shared with us, not with Carnsey present, and later the widow and her children hovered nearby.'

'What does Leveson know that we do not?'

'A good deal, I should think. I predict he will come to us, not so much because he wishes to share his information as because he wants to know if you discovered anything of importance from Trewinard's wife.'

They had a considerable wait, but the bed provided comfortable seating, once they determined where the lumps were, and smelled pleasantly of new mown hay from the lady's bedstraw mixed with the filling. Rosamond used the time to repeat everything Morwen Trewinard had said to her.

'What she overheard suggests that her husband did not confide in Sir Walter,' Rosamond concluded, 'but someone else, watching from a greater distance, may have thought otherwise.'

'I agree, and it seems obvious that the two murders are connected. What eludes me is why either man needed to die.'

The soft swish of the door opening heralded Leveson's entrance. He held one finger to his lips. Rosamond rolled her eyes.

'The walls are thin,' Leveson said. As if to prove it, the sound of ragged snoring reached them from the adjoining chamber.

An amused smile blossomed on Rosamond's face.

'If we keep our voices low,' Leveson said, 'Carnsey will likely *stay* asleep. Tell me quickly – what did you find out?'

'This is not a one-sided conversation,' Rosamond warned him. 'I will share what I learned only if you tell us what was in Sir Walter's last communication with Sir Francis Walsingham. All of it.'

'I doubt I know all of it, but I will tell you what Mr Secretary Walsingham was willing to repeat to me.'

After a moment's hesitation, Rosamond relayed the information she'd gleaned from Morwen Trewinard. 'They talked of pirates,' she said again when she'd finished her tale, 'as you did on our journey here.'

Leveson had seated himself on a stool, his back against the outside wall. This was far enough from Rob and Rosamond that the candle by the bed did little to illuminate his face. 'I also talked of smugglers, and of your stepfather's failure to stop Trewinard's illicit activities, and—'

Rob interrupted him. 'What was in Sir Walter's last report?'

Holding up one hand, Leveson listened. The snoring in the next room seemed even louder than before. Satisfied, he continued, 'Trewinard had heard whispers that the crews captured last year in Dorset had been pardoned . . . on the condition that they enter the queen's service.'

'Granting pardons to lesser offenders is not uncommon,' Rob mused. 'It is recruiting them that seems odd. I, for one, would not put my trust in a reformed sea rover.'

No matter the queen's intent, Rob doubted her lord lieutenants would have much success taming men who'd chosen to pillage rather than plow. When they'd gone to sea as pirates, they'd not been after fish. If they captured a ship while sailing for the Crown, they'd not like being obliged to share what they looted with the queen. That Her Majesty would demand her share went without saying. It was common knowledge that Elizabeth Tudor had as sharp a mind for business as any man.

'I do not understand why such recruitment caused Trewinard

concern,' Rosamond said. 'If he had friends among the pirates, he should have been glad that their lives were spared.'

'The reason for his apparent fear remains unclear,' Leveson admitted.

'Morwen said nothing about pardons. Nor did she mention rumors of an invasion, yet that seemed to be your main concern when you first arrived at Priory House.'

Because Rosamond sat next to Rob on the bed, their bodies were lightly touching. He sensed no anger in her now, only a profound curiosity. He was the one who felt annoyed that Walsingham, and through him, Leveson, insisted upon holding his cards so close to his chest.

Rob glanced at his wife, envious of her aura of calm. Tonight, at least, Rosamond was better able than he was to accept the futility of demanding answers. Secrets that could not be coaxed or extorted out of Leveson would have to be discovered by other means.

'How will the government use these pirates?' Rob asked.

'I do not know,' Leveson said. 'All I can tell you is that this was the information Sir Walter passed on to Sir Francis.'

No doubt Walsingham was the one who had secured pardons for the pirates in the first place. Rob was well aware that the queen's principal secretary was accustomed to use both extortion and bribery to recruit agents. He'd even persuaded a few imprisoned Papists to gather intelligence for him – for the good of the realm.

'I have been thinking about this latest murder,' Leveson said. 'We must not forget that Trewinard received stolen goods. It is possible he cheated one of the smugglers, or failed to deliver contraband to someone who had paid for it.'

'Possible, but not likely,' Rob said. 'From what little Carnsey let slip while we searched, Trewinard was, after his own fashion, an honest man.'

'Then, unless Trewinard's wife killed him, we are left with the conspiracy Sir Francis fears.'

At Rob's side, Rosamond made a sound of annoyance. '*What conspiracy?* The only plot Trewinard revealed has all the earmarks of one of Walsingham's own making – sparing the lives of captured pirates in order to bolster the queen's navy.'

'Sir Walter's letter suggested that Trewinard had knowledge of something else, something of greater import, something that struck fear into the alehouse keeper's heart.'

'I doubt my stepfather expressed himself in such melodramatic terms.'

'Yet you have just told us that Trewinard's wife said much the same thing to you, that her husband seemed fearful.'

'She said he watched the window. That is all.'

Had he been expecting someone else to arrive? Rob wondered. Someone he did not want Sir Walter to meet? Or had it been someone he hoped would never know that Sir Walter had visited Boscastle to speak with him?

'It is a great pity that Sir Walter did not do more to pursue this matter,' Leveson said. 'He sent what information he had to Walsingham and was awaiting further instructions.'

'For all he knew, Trewinard's intelligence might have been of no interest to the queen's spymaster.' Rosamond sounded defensive, although Rob did not think Leveson had meant his comment as a criticism of her stepfather.

'Do we *know* that he did nothing more?' Rob asked. 'Mayhap he did, and that is why he was murdered.'

'And the fact of Trewinard's murder may signify that the alehouse keeper did indeed know something of importance to the Crown.' Rosamond twitched as her agitation grew stronger. 'It seems obvious to me that he was killed to keep that secret, whatever it is, from coming to light.'

'Or because he had heard of Sir Walter's murder and could guess the killer's identity,' Rob suggested, earning a glare from his wife.

Leveson stirred in the shadows, making Rob wish he could see the other man's face. Despite his profession, the player-spy was not much better than any other man at hiding his emotions.

'Sir Francis was prepared to dispatch me to Cornwall even before Sir Walter's death,' Leveson said. 'My orders were to locate the pirate Trewinard named.'

'Diggory Pyper?' Rosamond asked. 'Did Sir Walter's message to Walsingham say aught else about him?'

'He reported that he stopped in Launceston after leaving Boscastle, hoping to find Pyper there. He did not.'

'You might have mentioned that detail earlier,' Rosamond said. 'The sensible thing to do next is to follow in Sir Walter's footsteps and speak with Pyper's kin.'

'I have already been to Launceston. Pyper is the captain of his own vessel, the *Sweepstake*, and is currently at sea.'

Feeling the vibrations of Rosamond's growing irritation, Rob placed a hand on her arm.

She shook it off and snapped at Leveson. 'He may have returned by now, or there may have been further news of him. And it is likely Sampson Pyper, Diggory's father, will be more forthcoming with me than he was with you.'

Leveson responded with ill grace, all but leaping off his stool. 'Do as you like. It is late and I am for bed.'

Once he had left the room, Rob dedicated himself to coaxing Rosamond into a better frame of mind. Once he'd helped her out of her clothing, he enjoyed a goodly measure of success, enough to allow them to sleep soundly for some hours.

It was well after midnight when he was awakened by faint sounds from beneath their open window. Moving quietly, in the hope that he could avoid disturbing his wife's slumber, Rob crept from the bed and made his way to the small, square opening. At first, he could see nothing in the darkness, but the sounds he heard allowed him to guess what was happening.

Rosamond came up beside him. As he had, she strained to see and hear. 'The contraband is stored in the room below this one, is it not?'

'It is, and it would appear that it is being taken out of the building by way of a window.'

'Should we try to stop them?'

'I see no need. We examined everything in that room. None of it has any bearing on Trewinard's murder. The smuggling that goes on in this part of Cornwall is none of our concern. Besides, I feel sorry for the widow. She must make do without a husband from now on. She has need of the income from his . . . business.'

'Morwen Trewinard will manage quite well without a man.' Rosamond sounded amused, and she accompanied him back to bed without insisting that he raise the alarm.

SIXTEEN

30 June 1584

Master Dodson, the coroner, arrived in Boscastle before the morning was far advanced. It did not take him long to gather jurors to view the body and instruct them to hand down a verdict of murder by person or persons unknown. This gentleman, a lawyer by profession, regarded Rosamond with extreme distaste when she asked if he knew how long it took a body to lose its stiffness after death.

'It is of no importance *when* Trewinard died, Mistress Jaffrey. What happened here is obvious.'

'Not to me.'

He spoke to her as if she were a child, and a slow-witted one, at that. 'This is a place of ill-repute, catering to brigands and smugglers. No doubt there was a quarrel over a reckoning. Two men fought. One died. As there were no witnesses, there is no hope of apprehending the villain unless he confesses. I think that most unlikely.'

After making this remarkable statement, and before Rosamond could formulate an adequate reply, Dodson departed. She started to go after him, then thought better of it. What good would it do to badger the fellow? Clearly, he knew nothing that would help her discover who had killed the alehouse keeper. Since Morwen was anxious to begin preparing her husband for burial, Rosamond decided that her time would be better spent examining the body one last time.

It had not yet gone rigid when she'd first seen it the previous day. Now, it most assuredly had. That Trewinard had been cold to the touch probably meant he had been dead for several hours by the time she arrived on the scene, but she could not say how long had passed. She wondered if it was possible that he had been done to death the night before he was found.

Rosamond glanced uneasily at her companions. They looked

as anxious as the coroner had been to be gone, and it was true
that they had a long ride ahead of them, but she was determined
to keep an open mind. That meant she must suspect everyone.

She could be certain of Rob's innocence. He had been with
her for the entire time in question. Could Carnsey have ridden
to Boscastle in the dark of night, killed Trewinard, and returned
to Priory House in time to leave with them in the morning? She
could not think why he would do such a thing, and such a journey
would have been treacherous, but he knew the way well, and he
had known both Trewinard and Sir Walter in life.

Leveson was not free from suspicion, either. He had admitted
he was in the area before he arrived at Priory House. What if he
had traveled from Launceston to Boscastle and murdered
Trewinard? He might well have done so on Walsingham's orders.
Or he might be hiding some dark secret of his own.

Fanciful as these possibilities seemed on the surface, Rosamond
did not dare disregard any explanation. She could not dismiss
Morwen as a suspect in her husband's murder, either, although
the widow was not high on her list. The two deaths seemed likely
to be connected and it would have been difficult, if not impossible, for her to kill Sir Walter.

'Rosamond?'

Rob's voice recalled her to their plan for the day. The morning
was already gone, as was midday. They must set out for
Launceston without further delay.

Rosamond accepted several packets of food Morwen had
prepared for their journey, bade her farewell, and stepped out of
the alehouse into a steady drizzle. Resigned to hours of misery,
since the road would soon be a quagmire, she mounted her horse
and pulled the hood of her cloak over her head. It kept the rain
off her face but made her overwarm. She foresaw a long, uncomfortable journey ahead. They would be fortunate to reach
Launceston before dark, and what awaited them there would not
be pleasant, either.

At that realization, she came to a decision. The confrontation
with Sampson Pyper could be postponed until the morrow. Once
in Launceston, they would bespeak rooms in a comfortable inn,
one that also offered filling meals and fires to dry their clothing.
Before she faced Master Pyper with questions sure to provoke

his anger, she would have a good night's rest on a soft featherbed.

SEVENTEEN

1 July 1584

A merchant's property reflected his standing in the community. The yard of the double-sized plot belonging to Sampson Pyper, who had been mayor of Launceston three times, was bounded by a stone wall. Within were a detached kitchen, a well, the usual rubbish pile and latrine tower, and the house itself, a timber-framed dwelling above a cellar built of stone. The roof was of Cornish slate bedded in mortar. It was decorated with ridge tiles and finials and boasted two chimneys.

Rob escorted Rosamond inside by way of a narrow ground-floor passage that ran the length of the house. Ignoring the way into the shop at the front of the building, they continued on into Pyper's hall, the principal room of the living quarters. It was well furnished with carved cupboards and chests, painted wall hangings, and a dining table flanked by several benches and one chair. A fireplace lined with decorative Flemish tiles took up the middle part of the north wall with windows to each side of the hearth. Two more were positioned high up in the south wall and all of them were covered by iron grilles that put Rob in mind of the bars on a prison cell.

Sampson Pyper, a distinguished-looking man of about Sir Walter's years, emerged from an inner room to greet them. 'You are Lady Pendennis's girl.' He regarded Rosamond with keen interest, but the glance he spared Rob was one of thinly disguised disdain.

'I did not think you would remember me,' Rosamond said.

'You made something of an impression when you trounced my son at bowls. I was sorry to hear of Sir Walter's death.' He shook his shaggy white head. 'A terrible accident.'

'I am told that my stepfather came to see you not too long before he died.'

Pyper's eyes narrowed. 'Aye.'

'He wanted to speak with Diggory.'

'My son was at sea and could not help Sir Walter with his inquiries.' He did not sound at all regretful.

A faint sound from the top of the stairs at the lower end of the hall caught Rob's attention – someone else in the household taking an interest in their business. He was not surprised. Although they had not given notice of their coming, the arrival of a large party on horseback could not have gone unnoticed. That only two of their number had entered the house likely provoked even more curiosity.

Returning his attention to his wife, he saw that Rosamond was smiling at their host. 'Has Diggory returned to Launceston since Sir Walter's visit? There is an urgent matter I would discuss with him.'

'Have fond memories of my lad, do you, lass? I thought once you two might make a match of it, but your mother had other ideas.'

Rob's teeth clenched until his jaw ached with the effort to hold back hasty words. The thought of Rosamond married to another man, let alone a pirate, had his hands curling into fists, but what made him take a step forward before he realized that he had done so was Rosamond's failure to mention that she had already been acquainted with the man they were seeking.

'I made my own choice and am happy with it.' Rosamond reached out to catch Rob's arm. 'This is my husband, Robert Jaffrey.'

Pyper's nod was barely civil. 'Is there aught else I can do for you, Mistress Jaffrey? I was working in my counting house when you arrived. Mornings at midweek are a busy time for me.'

His failure to offer them refreshment made it clear they were not welcome to linger, and if Sampson had a wife, she did not appear. They were on their way out when Rob caught a glimpse of a girl peering at them from the top of the stairs. When she realized she'd been seen, she ducked out of sight.

'I told you this was a waste of time,' Leveson said after they had emerged into the street and Rosamond had reported her failure to discover Diggory's location.

She ignored his complaint and they rode in silence until they had left the shire town behind them. For another short span, on the road to Priory House, the only sound to be heard was the plop of horses' hooves on a road still muddy from the previous day's rain.

'How old is Diggory?' Rob asked, giving in to the temptation to ask about this hitherto unknown rival for Rosamond's affections.

'Five and twenty,' Rosamond answered.

'Knew him well, did you?'

'I knew the entire family when I lived in Cornwall. There is an older son, Arthur. I expect he has a wife and a house full of children by now.'

'And the girl on the stairs?'

Rosamond smiled. 'Was there one? How old?'

'Fourteen, at a guess.'

'That would be Grace, then. She was scarce out of leading strings the last time I saw her. I suppose, after the manner of most little sisters, she is devoted to her older brother.'

'What do you know of brothers and sisters? Until Benet, you had neither.'

'I watched your sisters with you,' Rosamond shot back. 'Kate and Susan adore you, although I cannot fathom why.'

Rob preened a bit at that.

Rosamond sighed. 'What a pity we could not talk with young Grace in private. She might have been more forthcoming about Diggory's whereabouts than her father was.'

Rob did not like the affection he heard in Rosamond's voice when she said Pyper's name. 'He is a pirate, Ros. Likely he is the one Trewinard was afraid of, in which case, he is the murderer we have been seeking.'

Rosamond shook her head. 'Diggory's name was the one Trewinard gave my stepfather. To me, that suggests just the opposite – that Diggory has the same concerns that troubled Trewinard and that Trewinard thought he was brave enough to share them with Sir Walter.'

'The fellow's damned elusive for someone who wants to be helpful.'

'After two murders, he is right to be cautious.'

'He absented himself before Sir Walter was killed.'

'He took his ship to sea, as I suspect you yourself meant to do with the *Rosamond*.'

With an angry flick of the reins, she urged her mount into a trot before Rob could remind her yet again that he was the *Rosamond*'s owner, not her captain. He had to increase his speed to keep up with her but the chase did not last long. The road was unsuitable for any speed faster than an amble.

'Diggory Pyper is a *pirate*, Ros.'

'Perhaps so, but not all pirates are bloodthirsty brigands.'

Rob wanted to shout at her to take off her blinders where Pyper was concerned, but he knew his wife well enough to realize that such a tactic would only cause her to defend her childhood friend more stoutly.

He should know! He was the childhood friend she *had* married.

EIGHTEEN

They were back at Priory House by midday. Once again, Rosamond's mother chose not to dine with them, but she was up and about. She had resumed her normal routine as soon as they'd departed for Boscastle. Once Rosamond had eaten, she climbed the stairs to her mother's solar. She heard Eleanor's voice well before she reached the room's open door, berating some poor soul at full volume.

'Fix your caul,' Eleanor shouted. 'Your hair has come loose again.'

'Yes, madam.'

Rosamond identified the second speaker as her mother's young companion, Audrey. She entered the room in time to see the girl, her head bowed and her eyes averted, feel for a stray reddish-brown strand and poke at it in a futile attempt to stuff it back into a bag-shaped hairnet.

'So,' Eleanor exclaimed, catching sight of Rosamond, 'you have decided to honor me with your presence!'

Since Eleanor rarely bothered to conceal her distaste for her only daughter, Rosamond had become expert at concealing hurt feelings. Knowing that any reply she made would be taken the wrong way, she said nothing as she advanced into the room.

It was a pleasant chamber, filled with the things her mother most valued. There were Turkey carpets on the floor as well as on the tables. An embroidery frame had a canvas stretched over it, waiting for Eleanor's nimble fingers to take up her needle. She kept a selection of silks nearby, and since the room was directly above Sir Walter's study, it had windows on three sides to provide an abundance of sunlight to stitch by.

The view at this level was as impressive as it was from the chamber below. Far less pleasant was the expression on Eleanor's face. She looked as if she had bitten into something sour.

'You may go now,' Eleanor said, dismissing Audrey. 'You, too, Melka.'

The older woman had been standing so still that Rosamond had not noticed her. Melka shuffled to the door and went out, closing it behind her.

'Alexander Trewinard is dead,' Rosamond announced. 'He was murdered.'

Eleanor's eyes widened but she said nothing.

'It seems likely his death is tied to certain information Sir Walter hoped to gather for Sir Francis Walsingham. Walsingham has sent one of his intelligence gatherers, a man named Leveson, to investigate—'

'Henry Leveson?' Eleanor interrupted.

'You know him?'

'I know the name. Walter spoke of him. He did not trust the fellow.'

And Sir Walter had not, according to Leveson, trusted Eleanor. He'd given Leveson instructions to visit Priory House in secret. Rosamond was uncertain who to believe.

'Nevertheless, Mother, he is here. He has been charged with discovering the truth behind Sir Walter's death.'

Eleanor pondered this slight exaggeration on Rosamond's part as she resumed stitching the hem of a handkerchief. 'It is good that Sir Francis has taken an interest in Walter's murder. Someone must pay for taking my husband away from me. We were meant to grow old together, your stepfather and I. He should have had years left.' Her sigh was long, drawn out, and not entirely convincing.

'It was too soon to lose him.' Despite her doubts about her mother's sincerity, Rosamond felt a moment's empathy with the older woman. She could imagine how she would feel if it had been Rob who had been murdered. 'I am not at all surprised that you want vengeance.'

Eleanor's mouth curved into an unpleasant smile made even less appealing by the scarring on her cheek. 'I warrant you understand revenge. After all, that is why you married beneath you, is it not?'

'What? No!'

Her motives might not have been entirely pure, but she had not wed Rob out of spite. She'd been trying to protect herself from her mother's machinations. Her intent had been to gain control of the fortune left to her by her father. That outcome had been possible only if she chose an acquiescent husband. But Rob had always meant more to her than a means to an end. They had been the best of friends throughout their childhood. He was, she realized with a sense of certainty that momentarily distracted her from her mother's vitriol, the one she wanted to father her children.

'I understand how easy it is to yield to such an impulse. Indeed, I do. Why else would I have taken young Audrey in?'

Rosamond blinked and tried to focus. This was one of those times when her mother's rapid conversational shifts threatened to make her dizzy. Seating herself on the stool beside Eleanor's chair, she begged for clarification. 'Pray tell me, Mother, what has your companion to do with me or with Sir Walter?'

'Have I never told you the story of my life with Lady Quarles?' Eleanor asked.

The name did ring a distant bell. Rosamond frowned, trying to summon up the memory. 'She was your kinswoman, was she not? She took you in as her companion. It was when she visited London that you met my father.'

'Even so. Then the dreadful old besom threw me out of her house without so much as a cloak to keep me warm.'

'Only after she discovered you had been sneaking out to lie with a married man. Had you still been living with your parents, your father would have beaten you soundly and locked you in your chamber.'

'You should be grateful I escaped that fate, else you would never have been born.'

In bits and pieces, Rosamond recalled more of the story. Lady Quarles had treated Eleanor, her poor relation, like a slave. It followed, since Eleanor appeared to abuse young Audrey in a similar manner, and Audrey hailed from Westmorland, that the girl was kin to Lady Quarles.

'Who is Audrey Gravitt, Mother? Why is she here?'

Eleanor stopped stitching and met Rosamond's eyes, her expression gleeful. 'Audrey's father was Lady Quarles's nephew and heir. After he squandered every penny of his inheritance, I stepped in to rescue the girl.'

'You mean you sent for her so you could take revenge on Lady Quarles through her. That seems rather senseless, since the old woman is long dead.'

'I took her in out of Christian charity.' Eleanor's smirk belied the claim.

'What happened to Audrey's father?'

'He died. When I heard of his death, I at once asked Walter to send Jacob to Westmorland to fetch the poor orphaned girl to me.'

Poor girl, indeed, Rosamond thought. But they had wandered from the purpose of her visit. 'I have questions about the day Sir Walter died.'

'I have already told you all I know.' Eleanor's voice was a well-honed blade. 'Besides, now that Walsingham's agent has arrived, I do not need your help any longer. You and your husband can return to London. Go and pack.' She made a shooing motion with both hands. 'You can leave on the morrow and return to the life you chose over the glorious plans I made for you. If you wish to make amends for disappointing me, do so by preventing the Court of Wards from selling my son's wardship to anyone but me.'

'I thought you did not trust Henry Leveson.' Remaining still required effort. Of their own volition, Rosamond's hands, until then resting quietly on her lap, clenched into a tight ball.

'It was Walter who did not trust the fellow. I am willing to accept that Sir Francis Walsingham vouches for his good character.' She paused to take a few more careful stitches. 'Although it pains me to admit it, I need you in London, Rosamond, to look out for your brother's future.'

'There is no need for me to be present when the Court of Wards meets to make its decision. Jacob Littleton is there to represent you and he has retained a man of law to help him settle the matter. I promise you, Mother, on my honor, no stranger will take control of Benet's inheritance.'

Whether Eleanor was given custody of her son or Rosamond and Rob took charge of him remained an open question, but Rosamond kept the latter possibility to herself. She forced her features into what she hoped her mother would perceive as a reassuring smile.

Eleanor turned sulky. 'I want you there.'

'You want custody of Benet. My fortune is merely the means by which you may keep him. You would do well to remember, Mother, that I am, in truth, under no obligation to help you.'

'You will, though. You just gave me your word. And you know full well how difficult it is for a child to be separated from its mother.'

Rosamond could not believe what she was hearing. 'I gave my word, yes. And I will keep it. But I was not separated from you. You left me behind.'

With a careless wave of one hand, Eleanor dismissed this as a trivial distinction.

As Rosamond rose from the stool, out of patience with her mother, Eleanor caught her forearm in a claw-like grasp. 'Go home, Rosamond. No one wants you here.'

Rosamond broke free of the tight, painful grip and left the solar with as much dignity as she could muster. She found Melka lurking just outside the door.

'London?' the Polish woman asked.

'Only after Sir Walter's murderer has been found. Will you return with us?'

Melka shook her head. 'I stay here.'

Rosamond was not surprised, although she felt more than a twinge of regret at the thought of parting with the tiring maid she had come to trust and depend upon. She would miss Melka's taciturn companionship, her blunt speech, and her unwavering determination to keep her mistress safe, but she knew full well that Eleanor had the prior claim on Melka's devotion.

'My mother is the most exasperating woman on the face of creation,' Rosamond muttered. 'I wish you joy of her.'

Melka answered back, in Polish, chastising Rosamond.

Rosamond held up a hand to stop the flow of criticism. 'How am I to pity her for her suffering when she takes so much delight in making the lives of others miserable? And nothing in heaven or on earth will ever make me regret my decision to marry Rob.'

Turning her back on Melka, Rosamond made her way down the stairs. Opposite the entrance to Sir Walter's study was the door that opened into the parlor. She entered and walked briskly through the series of connecting rooms – great hall, screens passage, and service wing – to reach the stairs that led to the guest lodgings.

The sound of laughter distracted her as she passed the exit that gave onto the herb garden. Curious, she stepped outside into bright afternoon sunshine.

Audrey was sitting on the stone wall surrounding a bed planted with marjoram. Beside her was a small striped kitten, batting at her extended hand with playful abandon.

'Oh,' said Audrey when she caught sight of Rosamond. 'I did not mean to—'

'What? Enjoy yourself?'

The picture they made, girl and kitten, was precisely the antidote Rosamond required after her interview with her mother. A snort escaped her first, then a chuckle, and finally full-bodied laughter so overpowering that there were tears running down her cheeks by the time she regained control of herself again.

It felt good to give way to emotion. Cathartic. Wiping her eyes with the back of one hand, she sat down next to Audrey, taking note of her apprehensive expression but ignoring it to reach for the kitten and tickle it behind one ear.

'I have a cat at home,' she said. 'Watling. He is quite spoiled, and ten times the size of this little fellow.'

'I dote upon the creatures.' Audrey's wariness grew less when she saw how gently Rosamond dealt with the small feline. 'I borrowed this one from the litter in the stable.'

The kitten yawned, opening its mouth wide enough to show many fine, sharp teeth.

Rosamond smiled. 'I am reminded of the first time I encountered Watling. It was on the street for which he is named. For some reason, he chose to enter the road just as I rode past. He stopped right in front of my horse, looked up at me with a hard stare, and sat down. I had to rein in so hard that my mount reared, else I would have trampled him.'

A look of horror came into Audrey's face as Rosamond described the scene.

'Having narrowly avoided disaster, I dismounted and squatted down beside him and extended one hand. Watling eyed it with such a hungry look that I nearly retreated, but there was something about his attitude that I could not help but admire. In the end, I removed my glove and let him sniff my fingertips. He surprised me by following that action with a lick, and the feel of his tongue on my bare skin was so rough that my whole body jerked. The next thing I knew, I was sitting on my backside in the middle of Watling Street, with passersby on horseback and on foot giving me a wide berth. The glances they sent my way made it plain that they thought me fit for Bedlam.'

'I think it was wonderful of you to rescue Watling.' Tears welled up in Audrey's eyes and in the next moment she flung herself off the wall and onto her knees, assuming the pose of a supplicant. 'Can you find it in your heart to rescue me, too? I beg of you, Mistress Jaffrey, take me with you when you leave for London!'

'Audrey, stand up at once!' Embarrassed by the girl's display of emotion, Rosamond spoke more sharply than she intended.

Sobbing, the girl scrambled to her feet. 'You think me ungrateful to abandon the woman who took me in,' she said, sniffling between every word, 'and I do owe her my gratitude, but that does not mean I want to spend the rest of my life in her service.'

'You are my mother's companion, Audrey, not a servant bound to this household for a set term. You can leave at any time.'

'I have no place to go,' Audrey wailed, 'and I lack the wherewithal to travel even so far as Launceston.'

'If it is money you want—'

'I wish to *earn* my keep. Turn me out in London if you must, but let me accompany you that far. It is a long journey to make without a tiring maid, and what gentlewoman would willingly travel so far in naught but the company of men?'

'I travel with my husband, Audrey.' Rosamond's lips curved into a reminiscent smile. 'I assure you that he is most adept at helping me in and out of my clothing, even as his very presence protects my reputation.'

Audrey's shoulders slumped in disappointment. She stared at the ground in front of Rosamond's feet. 'I thought you could save me, but I see now that I was mistaken.'

Her movements stiff, she reached past Rosamond to scoop up the kitten. Clutching it to her bosom, she fled into the house.

NINETEEN

That evening after supper – a meal at which Eleanor once again failed to appear – Rob and Rosamond ventured into the new wing of the house where the steward lived with his family and kept a small office devoted to the business of the estate. The lands that Benet would inherit at the age of twenty-one were well run but this upper servant, although adept at overseeing day-to-day operations of the estate, was not as skilled as he should have been when it came to keeping careful records. Sir Walter had managed most of the accounts himself.

Together they examined the ledgers. It did not take long to discover that there was little ready money in the Priory House coffers.

'Your mother spends freely,' Rob observed. 'You spoke with her today. Is she fit to have charge of Benet?'

'She is as impossible as ever!' Abandoning the table where they had been working, Rosamond roamed the confined space. The snarl beneath her words reinforced her likeness to a caged cat.

Rob sympathized. His mother-in-law was a trial to his wife. So was his mother, but unlike Jennet Jaffrey, Lady Pendennis

had a long history of taking advantage of the good nature of
others. 'Tell me, love.'

She stood with her back to him, staring out the room's sole
window into the gathering dusk. He doubted she saw anything
of the scene before her. Her thoughts had clearly gone back to
earlier in the day and the encounter in her mother's study.

'Why is it that she and I cannot be in the same room for
more than a quarter of an hour before she finds something to
criticize?'

Perhaps because you are too much alike, Rob thought, but he
was wise enough to keep that suggestion to himself. As hard as
Rosamond tried to avoid rising rise to the bait, she would always
speak up to defend herself from her mother's verbal attacks.
Voices would rise. Sparks would fly. Venom would spew.
Husbands and servants alike knew better than to remain within
range of words that could stab like poniards.

'What did she say to you this afternoon?'

Words tumbled out, along with all of Rosamond's hurt and
confusion. She had endured an emotional day. Even though she
would never admit it, Rob suspected that she still craved her
mother's love and approval. Rob doubted she would ever win
either.

When she at last fell silent, Rob deemed it safe to join her
at the window. He slipped one arm around her waist and shifted
her so that she was nestled against his side. 'Why do you
suppose she is willing to let Leveson take charge of the
investigation?'

'She never wanted me here.' Rosamond's voice was bleak.
'She has seized upon his presence as an excuse to send us away.'

'But she means to keep Melka.'

'To spite me!'

'And Audrey? You might have repaid your mother in kind if
you'd yielded to the girl's pleas. Her story tugs at the heart.'

'If it is true.' Turning in his arms, she looked up at him with
haunted eyes. 'I cannot help but wonder if Mother *wants* me to
accept Audrey into my service. What if this is just a ploy to place
another spy in my household?'

'That seems unlikely, given Audrey's desperation. Shall we
take her with us when we go?'

'I will have to know her better before I decide. At present she has only one point in her favor – she likes cats.'

Rob chuckled and brushed a light kiss into his wife's hair. 'A good start. And the boy?'

'I do not know that answer yet, either. Mother's heats are alarming, and she clearly despises me, but I do not think she would ever harm her son.'

'She does not appear to mistreat him,' Rob agreed, 'but from all I can discover, she does not spend much time with him, either. Before Sir Walter's death, she left him to his father. Since then, he has spent most of his time with his tutor. There is also an uncle he is fond of – Tristram Pendennis. Benet accompanied Sir Walter on visits to his older brother on several occasions.'

'I remember him, I think, although he did not often come to Priory House when I lived here.' Rosamond moved out of Rob's arms and seated herself on a settle. 'Is Benet deeply attached to his mother? Or to Priory House? He has just lost his father. How can I rip him away from the only home he has ever known?'

'I cannot say.' He sat beside his wife, but made no attempt to touch her. This was her decision to make, but he was glad to be offered the opportunity to share his thoughts on the subject.

'I wish I could be certain how Mother truly feels about him,' Rosamond said.

'Her feelings for the boy aside, is she fit to take charge of his inheritance? I question not only her temperament, but also her ability to manage a large and prosperous estate. Her spendthrift ways could do great damage if they continue unchecked.'

'I have been thinking that I should write to Jacob and instruct him to purchase Benet's wardship in my name rather than my mother's. Then it will be up to me to decide if he remains here.'

'That would uphold your promise that Benet's wardship will not go to a stranger,' Rob agreed, 'and allow you to impose certain safeguards in case Lady Pendennis's erratic behavior worsens with time.'

'Safeguards? What safeguards?'

'Tristram Pendennis. Sir Walter's brother lives near enough to keep an eye on his nephew. Why not give him the authority to intervene?'

'It is an idea worth considering,' Rosamond said.

Rob was about to propose a visit to Sir Walter's brother when Henry Leveson interrupted them. He was not alone. He had brought the gatekeeper with him.

'Ludlow here has been at Priory House for many years,' Leveson said. 'He was born and bred in Cornwall. As such, he knows something about piracy in these parts.'

The gatekeeper stood twisting his cap between his hands. He kept his head down, avoiding looking at either Rob or Rosamond. 'I know passing little, Mistress Rosamond. Sir Walter was a justice, but he did not have dealings with such men. Pirates be tried by Admiralty Court.'

'But you have heard tales of Cornish pirates,' Leveson insisted. 'There is always . . . talk.'

Ludlow heaved an unhappy sigh. 'If 'tis Captain John Piers you would hear of, I can oblige. He was the most notorious pirate ever born in this part of Cornwall, for all that he operated for the most part out of Studland Bay in Dorset.'

'We need information on the current whereabouts of local pirates,' Rosamond said, gesturing for Ludlow to seat himself on a stool. Leveson remained standing, his back braced against a wall.

'No use looking to Piers for help, then. He was caught, tried, and executed some two years back.'

'But Morwen Trewinard mentioned his name,' Rosamond said. 'She said Diggory Pyper wants to be the new Captain Piers.'

'Some say Piers died a wealthy man, but all I know is that he delivered stolen goods to his mother in Padstow and she took them to Bodmin to sell.'

'A land pirate.' Leveson's eyes lit up at this revelation. 'Tell us more about her.'

'Old Annie Piers was caught trying to sell a set of silver buttons. Charged with receiving, she was, and that was why Sir Walter took an interest.'

'If this Annie Piers is in prison,' Leveson said, 'the hope of freedom may loosen her tongue. And if she escaped punishment, then she can be threatened with gaol.'

Ludlow scratched his chin and thought a while before he spoke. 'The best I can recall is that Old Annie was charged with selling stolen goods at about the same time her son was captured in Studland Bay along with fifteen of his men. He was sentenced to be hanged, but he escaped from Dorchester gaol by bribing the keeper, and then he was recaptured and hanged.'

Rob winced. The custom when executing pirates was to leave the body at the tide mark, hanged in chains, as a warning to others. Beside him, Rosamond shuddered, no doubt envisioning the same scene. He reached out to take her hand and found it was cold as ice.

'We are not interested in her son,' Leveson said. 'What happened to the mother? Is she still living in Padstow?'

The gatekeeper shook his shaggy head, but then his brow furrowed, as if he was remembering something more. His voice dropped to a whisper. 'Annie Piers was charged with being a witch.'

'Go on,' Rob said.

'There is not much to tell. The same men already dealing with cases of receiving stolen goods formed a commission to investigate the charges.'

'And they were?'

'Sir Richard Grenville, Thomas Roscarrock, and George Grenville of Penheale.'

George Grenville was the current sheriff, Rob recalled, and Sir Richard was his cousin. 'Not Sir Walter?'

'He assisted, being a local man. But then, they all are.'

'Why was she charged with witchcraft?' Rosamond wanted to know. 'Was there a history of ill fortune falling upon those who angered her? Dead cattle? Cows that stopped giving milk?'

'There was no suspicion of anything like that. It was only that some in Padstow believed her son could not have been so successful in his piracy for so long without the aid of sorcery.'

'Was she tried?'

'She was, and twelve good men and true ruled that she was not a witch.' For a moment, a faint smile played about Ludlow's mouth. 'They did all agree on one thing more – that she was a disreputable, loose-living woman who engaged in unsupervised night-walking.'

'How old is she?' Rosamond asked in surprise. 'Night-walking is a charge more commonly made against prostitutes.'

'Far older than I am,' Ludlow replied. 'I have heard that her son began to ply his trade as long ago as the reign of King Edward.'

'Her night-walking, then, most likely refers to receiving stolen goods after dark. How did they punish her for trying to sell contraband?'

'Likely she was held in gaol for a few months and mayhap made to do penance,' Ludlow said. 'After that, most women are released into the custody of their husbands.'

'What is *likely*,' Leveson interjected, 'is that this woman knows a good deal more about how pirates operate in this part of Cornwall than we do. If she can be persuaded to talk, she may be able to help us locate Diggory Pyper.'

'She will have good reason to be suspicious of anyone who comes asking about him,' Rosamond said.

Leveson sent a bland look in her direction. 'She might be persuaded to confide in another woman.'

'Why should she trust me?'

To Rob's annoyance, Leveson grinned. His words were even more provoking. 'You have been successful in the past when it came to winning the confidence of strangers. There is no need to approach her as yourself.'

'I doubt I can disguise myself well enough to fool her into thinking I am not a foreigner.'

'You underestimate yourself. And you know you enjoy playing a role.'

Rob had to admit the truth of Leveson's statement. Back in Bermondsey, Rosamond had several costumes, disguises she had successfully donned in the past when she wished to hide her true identity.

'Or you might try bribery,' Leveson added. 'If she is accustomed to selling stolen goods, why should she balk at taking your coin?'

'Mayhap because she will already have heard of Alexander Trewinard's murder?' Rosamond suggested.

A single glance at his wife's face told Rob that she was intrigued by the prospect despite her objections, and Leveson was correct in saying that she had advantages he lacked, not the least of which was her ability to speak the Cornish language.

'If I go to Padstow, Rob must accompany me,' Rosamond said, 'and so must my men.'

'Excellent,' Leveson said. 'At the same time, I will return to Boscastle. I believe Morwen Trewinard knows more than she told you about this matter.'

Seeing that Rosamond was about to object, Rob cut in. 'We will join you in Boscastle after we talk to Old Annie.'

Leveson frowned even as he nodded in agreement. 'I will take Carnsey with me to translate.'

'Nay!' Ludlow's objection had them all turning to stare at the gatekeeper. His face wore a mulish expression. 'Carnsey must go with Mistress Rosamond to guide her safely across the moor. It is a treacherous place for those who do not know it well.'

'And how am I to understand a word Widow Trewinard says without him?' Leveson sounded petulant.

'That will not be a problem,' Rosamond said. 'Morwen Trewinard speaks perfect English. You have but to persuade her to do so. But why do you think she has more to tell us? My questioning of her was most thorough, I assure you.'

Leveson's superior smile had Rob's hackles rising.

'Because Ludlow here tells me she was Morwen Piers before she wed Alexander Trewinard,' Leveson said. 'The infamous pirate captain was her cousin.'

TWENTY

B efore she retired for the night, Rosamond had one last duty to perform. She did not look forward to speaking with her mother again, but since she meant to remain in Cornwall for an indefinite period of time, she did not want Eleanor to labor under the misapprehension that she was leaving for good on the morrow. The temptation to notify her in writing and avoid another face-to-face confrontation was strong. She resisted. She vowed, too, to hold on to her temper, no matter how much provocation she was offered.

Her plans were thwarted at her mother's bedchamber door.

Melka emerged, shutting it firmly behind her and announced that her mistress had taken a sleeping potion and must not be disturbed.

Hiding her relief, Rosamond settled for leaving a message with the tiring maid. 'Tell her that we will return in a day or two. Master Leveson, too. We are in pursuit of information that will lead us to Sir Walter's murderer.' She hesitated, then added, 'Mother seems to think Walsingham's man has her best interests at heart. He does not. His mission is to unearth treason and capture those who conspire against the realm.'

To Rosamond's surprise, this statement provoked a response from the usually stoic Melka. She gasped aloud, recoiling and backing away.

Rosamond had chosen her words deliberately, picking 'treason' over 'piracy'. Her hope had been that by mentioning the more serious crime, she could convince her mother not to rely on Leveson to bring Sir Walter's killer to justice. She wanted Eleanor to accept that she needed her daughter's help.

Melka's reaction unsettled her, and her attempt to retreat into Eleanor's bedchamber set off alarm bells. Before the older woman could escape, Rosamond caught her by both arms and gave her a shake. 'What did I say?' she demanded. 'What are you afraid of?'

Although Melka understood English perfectly well, she rarely spoke the language. Rosamond switched without conscious thought to Polish. 'What are you hiding?' she asked. 'What has Mother done?'

Melka insisted she knew nothing, but then, as if the words were ripped from her against her will, she spoke of a violent quarrel.

'Between Mother and Sir Walter?'

Tears running down her pale cheeks, Melka nodded.

'When? When did they quarrel?'

'Augsburg,' Melka said.

Rosamond blinked at her in astonishment. Then she laughed. 'Augsburg? That was *years* ago.' She sobered quickly at the look on Melka's face. Leveson had hinted that there was something sinister in Eleanor's past. 'Tell me.'

It *had* been years before. Fifteen years, to be precise, when Walter had still been acting as the queen's special envoy abroad. Melka insisted that she did not know the cause of their anger at each other, but it had run deep. After a heated exchange, Eleanor had left the house, too furious to watch where she was going. Moments later, she had been struck down and run over by a heavy horse-drawn wagon.

Rosamond saw the horror of that event reflected in the maidservant's eyes. Melka remembered it as clearly as if it had happened yesterday. Rosamond knew her mother's injuries had been terrible. Some of her broken bones had healed well. Others had not. The scars, both visible and hidden, remained.

'It must have been devastating,' she murmured, 'for both of them.'

Melka made a strangled sound, following it with a torrent of words. Rosamond did not want to believe what she heard, but she had no reason to doubt Melka when she said that Walter had left Eleanor in Augsburg with only the servants to care for her and gone home to England alone.

'He expected her to die?'

Melka gave a violent shake of her head: he had *hoped* his wife would die. Eleanor had astonished everyone by surviving.

In her heart, Rosamond knew Melka's version of events was true. She remembered the coldness between her mother and stepfather when Eleanor, dragging Rosamond with her, had first arrived at Priory House and installed herself as its mistress. At the time, she'd been too self-absorbed to wonder what had caused it.

Rosamond supposed her mother might have angered her husband by being unfaithful to him, but that did not account for Leveson's hints. She reached back in her memory, trying to think what great events had taken place at around the time of Eleanor's accident. She did not have far to search before she encountered an unsettling possibility. Fifteen years ago, there had been treason afoot in England. News of an uprising in the north, although it was quickly put down, had alarmed even young girls living in Kent. As she recalled it, the rebellion had broken out in Northumberland . . . and in Westmorland, the county of Eleanor's birth.

No. Impossible. Eleanor had many faults, but she was no traitor.

If his wife had betrayed her country, Sir Walter would never have forgiven her.

But neither would he have allowed her to be imprisoned. He would not have been able to divorce her and she'd not had the courtesy to die of her injuries. What choice would he have had but to tolerate her?

No, she thought again. Surely they had been reconciled. The proof of it was young Benet.

'Were they on better terms once she'd given him a son?' Rosamond asked. She wanted Melka to tell her that they had learned to love each other again, and that Sir Walter had trusted his wife, even though his instructions to Leveson suggested otherwise.

Instead of answering, Melka fled into the bedchamber. Before Rosamond could follow her, the bar on the other side of the door fell into place with a resounding thunk.

Left to stare at the solid wooden barrier, Rosamond sighed. She did not like what she had heard, and she was even less pleased by the speculations spawned by Melka's revelations. If a husband, one who had pledged to love and honor his wife for all their days, could find cause to wish for her death, then it was all too possible that she, even years later, might have had a hand in his.

TWENTY-ONE

2 July 1584

'We need to talk about our future,' Rosamond said.

They had set out for Bodmin only a quarter of an hour earlier, riding side by side. Carnsey led their small party, with Charles, Luke, and John making up the rear guard.

Rob stifled a groan. At least fifteen miles of bad road lay ahead of them before they could rest, a journey difficult enough without the addition of an uncomfortable topic of conversation. He supposed a discussion of their plans for the years ahead need not be unpleasant, but there was something tentative in his wife's voice that struck him as worrisome. Rosamond did not ordinarily lack self-confidence.

'Did something happen when you spoke with your mother last

night?' He'd been asleep by the time she returned from her visit to Lady Pendennis's bedchamber.

'I did not speak to her, and this is not about Mother. It is about us. Do you remember when you were first sent away to school? Everyone assumed that you would pursue a profession, entering either the law or the church.'

'Why bring this up again? It was my mother's idea that I study law, never mine. And you know I would never succeed as a preacher. Can you imagine me in somber black?'

At present, Rob's trunks and hosen were buff-colored, his doublet a rich forest green with a collar of finest lawn. His high-crowned hat matched the doublet. Only his cloak, tied behind the saddle since the day was warm, was a sad color.

'Besides, a degree in divinity would mean staying on at Cambridge for at least another year.' He shuddered at the thought. He had nothing against learning, but he was done with the rules and restrictions of academic life.

'You might have had the living in Eastwold. You would have been an improvement over the current vicar.'

'Now you grow fanciful. Why would I want to live in the village of my ancestors even if I did have a calling? The wider world has much more appeal.'

A little silence fell as they rode along. Rob tried to gather his thoughts before he spoke again. Where was this leading? Ros knew his plans. He had told her about the *Rosamond* during their journey to Cornwall. True, she had not been pleased at first to hear that he had purchased a ship, but she had not objected to the idea of being married to a merchant and he had thought she was warming to the prospect of accompanying him on a voyage or two.

A glance at Rosamond's face told him that she, too, was considering what to say next. Her reticence surprised him, but he was grateful for it. A considerable length of time passed before she said, 'Your mother, as you say, was of the opinion that you should study the law. It is not uncommon to follow university studies with time at one of the Inns of Court.'

'True. Even Captain Carleill went from Cambridge to Lincoln's Inn, although he did not stay there long.'

The mere mention of Carleill's name caused a furrow to appear between Rosamond's brows. Because of the captain's connection to Walsingham, Rob presumed, since Carleill's expedition to the New World was no longer viable. But when his wife spoke, it was to ask what he had against a career in law.

'I am neither scholar nor orator. To be any good at what he does, a lawyer must divide his time between musty law books and pleading cases in the courts. That life is not for me.'

'You prefer to pursue criminals, then? You *enjoy* taking on assignments for Mr Secretary Walsingham?'

'You know better than that!'

She was prevented from replying when Carnsey urged his mount to greater speed, despite the fact that the terrain they were now crossing was rougher than it had been, the road no more than a cart track. Distracted, she turned her ill humor on their guide.

'Faster or slower, I beg you. My very teeth are rattling at this uneven gait.'

'There is no help for it, Mistress Jaffrey, if we are to avoid the mists.'

'Mists?'

'Descend without warning, they do, and even the most experienced guide cannot find his way. Go off the road and you risk being swallowed up whole.'

'By some grotesque creature that haunts the moor?' Her question dripped sarcasm.

'Worse. All you need do is step all unwary into a bog. Many a traveler has disappeared, never to be seen again.'

'It cannot be as dangerous as all that,' Rosamond scoffed. 'Bodmin is renowned as the best market town in Cornwall and the twice yearly assizes are always held in Launceston. People frequently travel this way between those two places.'

'This is *Goen Bren*,' Carnsey said in an ominous tone of voice.

'It is Fowey Moor,' Rosamond countered, 'known for its ancient standing stones and barren landscape. Such places are conducive to fantasies.'

Sensing that Rosamond meant to urge her mount to go even faster, simply to annoy their guide, Rob reached across the distance between them and put a restraining hand over hers. 'The road is too uneven. Nothing will be gained if your horse stumbles and falls.'

Looking around them, he saw a few grazing animals, but for the most part they were passing through an empty, windswept wasteland, one Carnsey knew and they did not. When Sir Walter's secretary kept on at a steady, bone-jarring pace, they followed his lead. Any attempt at further conversation was abandoned.

It was late afternoon before the parish church at the east side of Bodmin came into view. Nearby was the Dolphin, the inn Carnsey recommended. After an indifferent meal in the common room, Rob escorted his wife to their bedchamber. Since she had no tiring maid with her, he offered to help her undress.

Obligingly, she turned so that he could undo the laces. She did not wear finery when traveling on horseback, but a gentlewoman's clothing, no matter how simply constructed, was not easy to remove without help.

'If you cannot see yourself in the church or the law,' she said, her voice muffled, 'and if you could not be a merchant, what would you do?'

'You are like a dog with a bone,' Rob complained. 'What need have I to change the plans I have already made? I have ties to the Muscovy Company. The Merchant Adventurers are—'

'There is no *need* for you to earn a living at all. I am exceeding wealthy. Why not pursue something that interests you?' She turned her head to look at him over her shoulder. 'I have heard that there are antiquarians who do nothing but study the standing stones, attempting to discover how and why they were put in place by our distant ancestors.'

'I was not raised to be an idle gentleman. If you wanted such a fellow for a husband, you should have married one of the men your mother thought suitable.'

Exasperation made her voice sharp. 'What I *want* is a husband who stays at home.' She made a sound of disgust. 'I warrant that if Carleill's expedition had become a reality, you would already be on your way to the New World.'

He let go of her loosened points and backed away. 'I was tempted by the prospect. I cannot deny it. What is wrong with that? Is it not an exciting idea that, in time, men will take their wives and children with them to the land across the Atlantic Ocean? There will be colonies, Ros, English plantations in the Americas, much like the ones we have already planted in Ireland.'

'Better to go to Ireland, then. It is closer to home.'

His laugh contained little amusement. 'I think not, unless you have developed a fondness for pirates.' He wondered if she had, but pushed the thought away. 'Ireland is a popular place for such men to sail the ships they seize. Free from fear of arrest, they unload their cargoes there.'

'And then what? Smuggle the plunder back into England?'

'Even so.'

Rosamond dropped bodice, kirtle, and petticoats and ripped off the coif that had covered her hair. A dark mass of curls tumbled free. In nothing but her shift, she turned to jab her index finger into his chest. The anger he saw in her eyes had him backing up a step.

'Do you swear you do not intend to leave me in search of adventure?'

He caught her hand and held it against his heart. 'Being married to you is adventure enough!'

He expected her to laugh. Instead she shoved him away from her, whirled around, and stalked to the window.

Rolling his eyes heavenward, Rob waited a beat before he came up behind her to place both hands on her shoulders. He did not attempt to turn her around. Instead he dropped a light kiss on the back of her neck before resting his chin against the silken mass of her hair.

'Why are you so troubled, Ros? It is not like you to brood and fret over nothing. You know full well that I am not about to abandon you.'

He felt rather than saw her frown.

'Tomorrow we will go on to Padstow and the next day return to Boscastle. When we have discovered who killed Sir Walter, we will go home.'

'What about Benet?'

He was at a loss. 'What about him?'

Her concerns poured out of her then. She was reluctant to trust Benet's keeping to her mother, even if Tristram Pendennis agreed to supervise his care. She questioned Eleanor's fitness to raise the boy, and yet she also had doubts about herself in the role of guardian. She was confident in her ability to safeguard his inheritance, but she worried that he would fare no better with her than with Eleanor when it came to receiving love and guidance.

'I crave adventure as much as you do,' Rosamond admitted, 'mayhap more so. I will not rest until I have uncovered the truth about Sir Walter's death, even if that places those I love in danger. It was the same before, when I agreed to gather intelligence for Sir Francis Walsingham and again when I was tasked with proving my friend Lina innocent of murder.'

'You are loyal, determined, and committed,' Rob said. 'Those are not bad traits to have.'

'I would have been the first aboard one of Captain Carleill's ships if I could have thought of a way to hide my gender throughout all the many weeks at sea.'

'If you had married a proper gentleman, he would have been appalled at such a notion, but your luck was in when you chose me instead. I have told you this before, Ros – we can sail away together on the *Rosamond* and no one will dare complain of it. I will find mariners who know better than to think having a woman on board ship brings bad luck at sea.'

'What of *our* children?'

'They are still in the future. Unless . . .?'

She smacked him, hard, on the upper arm. 'No!'

But she wanted children, he thought. He'd been blind not to realize that until now. He sent her a knowing look that should have infuriated her, but rather than stamp her foot and rail at him, she seemed to lose all desire to quarrel. She made not a single objection when he removed her one remaining garment and lifted her onto the bed. For the next little while, they did not talk at all.

TWENTY-TWO

3 July 1584

Rosamond was in charity with her husband once more when, at first light, they pressed on to Padstow, some ten miles to the northwest. A mile from Bodmin, they crossed a three-arched bridge over a river – the Camel, Carnsey called it. The entire journey after that seemed comprised of streams, brooks, rivers, and estuaries, some with fords and some with bridges. Rosamond gave up any attempt to remember their names.

Her thoughts strayed to the previous night. She believed Rob when he said he meant to stay with her. Of the accuracy of his observations about her desire for children, as opposed to her yearning for adventure, she felt less certain. She chose not to think too deeply about Rob's assumption. Not yet. There would be time enough later to consider whether or not he was right.

Padstow, when they reached it, surprised her. On the road, they had encountered only a handful of other travelers, but here was a bustling, busy port for all that the town lay a good two miles from the mouth of an estuary.

'Small ships come here from as far away as Brittany to trade for fish,' Carnsey said.

Rosamond laughed. 'I can smell the truth of that!' And unless her ears deceived her, not only Bretons, but Irishmen, too, mingled freely with the good Cornish citizens of Padstow.

The King's Head, where they were to stay the night, was small and badly weathered. She stared up at the sign. Although the crudely drawn head wore a crown, she was unable to identify which monarch it was supposed to represent.

'Athelstan,' Carnsey supplied when she asked. 'The old name of this town is Adelstow – the place of Athelstan.'

It was convenient that Sir Walter had favored well-educated servants, Rosamond thought. Since she'd met him, Ulick Carnsey had supplied many such snippets of local lore. They were of no particular use that she could see, but when they did not annoy her, as they had on the moor, she found them entertaining.

While Rob bespoke a room and arranged for a meal, Carnsey made inquiries in the stables. They had decided not to ask the assistance of the only person they knew in Padstow, Master Dobson the coroner and man of law. Sir Walter's secretary already had results by the time Rosamond and Rob emerged from the inn.

'I know where you can find Annie Piers,' Carnsey said, 'but I fear she will be of no help to you. There are no monuments inscribed with their names and life dates for simple folk, but both Annie and her husband now reside in the churchyard next to a parish church dedicated to St Petrock.'

'Dead?' Rosamond had not expected this, despite knowing that the woman was called 'old' Annie.

'Let us find the vicar,' Rob suggested. 'Confirming Annie Piers's death is the sensible thing to do.'

'His name is Archer,' Carnsey said. 'Robert Archer. But I doubt you'll have much joy of him. I am told he was one of those who testified against Old Annie in court.'

'One of those who urged that charges of witchcraft be brought against her?' Rosamond knew the type.

Carnsey nodded.

'We are forewarned, then, but he may still know something of value. Go you and make more inquiries around the village. We are already conspicuous by virtue of being strangers. The larger the party, the more unwanted attention we will draw to ourselves.'

'How shall we proceed?' Rob asked after Carnsey was well away.

'With caution . . . and a good lie. We will say we have come on behalf of Morwen Trewinard and that she has only just heard of the death of her kinswoman.'

'That will not work if Annie and her husband died some time ago.'

'Was there sickness in Padstow?' Rosamond wondered aloud. 'Were they carried off together?'

'Shall we call Carnsey back and ask?'

'No need. Let us go to the vicar as ourselves. We will say we need to confirm the old woman's death in order to clear up certain paperwork Sir Walter left behind.' Ludlow had said that, as one of Cornwall's justices of the peace, Rosamond's stepfather had played a small part in Old Annie's trial, even though it had been a special commission that had taken charge of the case. 'We will say that you have been ordered to write a report,' she added. 'Since you were not there, it follows that you must question those who were.'

Convinced this ploy would work, Rosamond followed the directions Carnsey had given them to find a house near a gray stone church with a square tower. The vicar's housekeeper, a downtrodden female of indeterminate years, admitted them.

Robert Archer gave his servant a disapproving look. His beady little eyes were no less censorious when they fixed on Rosamond and Rob. That he was dressed all in black, without a hint of adornment, marked him as a Puritan as surely as if he'd had the letter P embroidered on his sleeve.

Rosamond braced herself for trouble.

The vicar's greeting lacked both warmth and welcome and was delivered in a harsh, raspy voice. 'You are not my parishioners.'

'No, Sir Robert, we are not.'

Rob used the form of address customary for men of the cloth, despite the fact that few of them had ever been knighted. This seemed to soften the vicar somewhat, and he permitted Rob to explain that he was on official government business.

Archer ignored Rosamond, and as soon as he heard Annie Piers's name, his negligible chin began to quiver. 'A most ungodly old woman!'

'But dead? That is certain?'

'I buried her myself, out of Christian charity.' For a brief moment, Archer's lips parted in a parody of a smile that revealed large yellow teeth. The two largest overlapped at the front.

'And her husband?' Rob asked.

'Died some six months later.'

'Of what cause?'

'Old age. Shame. She was the sinner, but he harbored her.'

Rob's solemn nod seemed to appease the vicar, as did Rosamond's continued silence. She sat with her eyes downcast and her hands primly folded at waist level. Having met men like Archer before, she knew they never looked kindly upon women who dared have opinions of their own. If she did anything to remind him of her presence, she would likely be ordered to go and keep company with the housekeeper.

'Part of my commission,' Rob continued, 'is to learn if Annie Piers resumed her illegal activities after she was released.'

'I've no doubt she did. Eve was born to sin.'

'And her husband abetted her?'

'He claimed he did not when he was questioned by the commissioners, and he was believed solely because, long ago, he renounced his son for lewdness. Even so, he did admit to going aboard Captain Piers's flagship on one occasion. He accompanied the vicar of Meryn in order to help him collect the seven pounds Captain Piers owed him. Or so William Piers said.'

'And was the vicar paid?'

Archer gave a derisive snort. 'Oh, yes, but not in coin. Piers claimed, so his father said, that he had no ready money. He offered the vicar a bolt of calico cloth in return for forgiveness of part of the debt.'

Rosamond hid a smile. There was no forgiveness in Archer's telling of the tale. His sneer suggested that he had little regard for his fellow clergyman and even less for William Piers, and that he stood firm in his belief that Annie Piers's husband had not been as far removed from his son's activities as he'd wished to appear.

'Who were Old Annie's friends?' Rob asked. 'Who knew her well?'

'Others like her.' Venom dripped from the words. 'Land pirates and smugglers.'

And witches? Rosamond took care not to ask that question aloud.

'Do you know their names?'

The vicar's beady little eyes gleamed with malice. 'Only two – Margery Morgan and Edith Davye. Old Annie denied the charge of receiving stolen goods, even though she was caught trying to sell plate, a silver salt cellar, and silver buttons in Bodmin, but she later admitted to going with those two women to collect a large rug when it was brought ashore from her son's ship. At midnight, mind you. They helped her carry it to a nearby barn, where they left it to be collected by a certain local gentlewoman, the person who had purchased it from Captain Piers.'

He was careful not to identify the gentlewoman. Rosamond took note of the hypocrisy. Unlike Old Annie, the gentlewoman was likely married to someone prominent in these parts, someone who might take it amiss to hear her good name bandied about.

'Were these other women charged with receiving stolen goods?' Rob asked.

'They were not. There is far too much tolerance of such things in the town! Put that in your report, young man, and that Annie Piers was proud of her son. Unrepentant, she was, even in gaol.

She boasted of the great store of money he had made from piracy, although to most observers his profit from plundering ships was nothing out of the ordinary. He dealt in small items – a cask of soap, bolts of cloth. Once there was even a parrot!'

'Where can I find Goodwife Morgan and Goodwife Davye?'

The vicar seemed reluctant to say, or else he did not know. Further questioning revealed that they were not members of his congregation.

'Had Annie Piers any remaining kin?' Rob asked.

The vicar's demeanor abruptly altered at this question. 'You have no call to trouble Honor Piers. She is a good Christian woman. When she was questioned, she readily confessed to having been aboard her brother's ship, but only once, and she never dealt in stolen goods.'

Rosamond felt her eyebrows shoot up at Archer's vehement defense.

'Where will I find Old Annie's daughter?'

Rob's voice carried so much authority that the vicar replied without hesitation, describing how to reach the cottage Honor had inherited from her father. It was only a short walk from the vicarage.

Out in the street again and striding at a brisk pace toward their next destination, Rosamond dragged in a deep breath of fresh air. 'I had the greatest difficulty hiding my dislike of that man! I am glad I am not one of his parishioners.'

'Did you hear him, though?' Rob asked, grinning down at her. 'Talking about how Captain Piers dealt only in *small* items? I swear I heard longing in his voice. I warrant he coveted that parrot!'

Behind them, someone choked back a laugh. Rosamond glanced over her shoulder in time to see a man with a bulbous, red-veined nose cover his mouth. Someone who knew Archer, no doubt. Intent upon their mission, she dismissed him from her thoughts.

'If the daughter did not deal in contraband,' she mused aloud, 'she may know nothing about piracy in these parts.'

'But she should know where we can find her mother's confederates. It cannot hurt to ask, and here is her cottage.'

Rosamond had wondered if the vicar's staunch defense of

Honor Piers's virtue might be based on his attraction to her person, but she discarded that fanciful notion when she saw that the woman who opened her door to them bore little resemblance to her kinswoman in Boscastle. Honor Piers was of middling height with faded yellow hair and pale blue eyes. Her age was impossible to determine.

She greeted them with a surly look and her response to Rob's first question was predictable – she claimed to speak no *Sowsnek*, the Cornish word for English.

Rosamond caught the door before Honor could slam it in their faces and used her forward momentum to gain a foothold. The habit of deferring to the gentry had Honor retreating before she could think better of it. Then it was too late. Both Rosamond and Rob were inside the cottage and had closed the door behind them.

Favoring Honor with a bland smile, Rosamond informed her that she understood *Kernewek* perfectly well. There were likely to be a few mistakes when she spoke in that language, but she felt certain she could make her meaning clear.

'*Oiw osta?*' Honor Piers demanded.

'She wants to know who we are,' Rosamond translated.

She chose to offer a different answer than the one Rob had given the vicar. Since it seemed unlikely that this woman would have heard of Sir Walter's death, Rosamond introduced herself and Rob as his representatives. She hoped that this would persuade Annie Piers's daughter to provide them with the information they sought.

Honor's eyes widened as she recognized Sir Walter's name. With obvious reluctance, she agreed to cooperate, but her answer to almost every question Rosamond posed was '*Ny wonn*' – I do not know. She insisted she had naught to do with any pirate – *morlader* – and Rosamond took care not to broach the subject of murder – *moldra*.

When she asked if Honor knew how they could locate her mother's friends, Goodwife Morgan and Goodwife Davye, a glare momentarily brought life into the nondescript blue eyes.

'They were no friends of hers!' Rosamond translated. 'They gave testimony against her.'

'Mayhap they knew even more than they said,' Rob suggested.

In response to his quiet comment, Honor shook her head. Rosamond hid a smile. She had suspected from the first that the woman understood English and here was proof of it. Honor likely spoke English, too, perhaps as well as her cousin Morwen. The only question that remained was whether or not she knew more about her brother's activities than she was willing to admit.

'Are any of Captain Piers's crew yet living?' Rosamond continued to speak in Cornish. 'I will not reveal who named them.'

'*Ny wonn.*'

'What do you know of Diggory Pyper?'

Although Honor did not reply, her eyes once again betrayed her. Even if she had never encountered the man in person, she most assuredly knew his name.

'He is Captain of the *Sweepstake*,' Rosamond said.

Honor insisted she had never heard of him, but now she grew more and more agitated with every question Rosamond asked. Her fingers clenched and unclenched in her apron. Her lips pursed into a thin line whenever she was not speaking. When her gaze slid toward the door, Rosamond wondered if she was about to bolt. Was she so desperate to escape their questions that she would abandon her own home?

She frowned. Was it that Honor wished to escape their questions, or that she feared the consequences of telling them what she knew?

'We can offer you protection,' Rosamond said. 'If you are afraid to stay here, you can bide awhile in some safer place. With a kinswoman, mayhap?'

Honor mumbled a reply.

Frowning, Rosamond translated. 'She says she has no kin left. They are all dead.' The look she sent Rob silently asked him whether he thought she should mention Morwen Trewinard by name.

He shook his head. If Honor did not yet know about Alexander Trewinard's murder, it seemed best that they not be the ones to tell her he was dead.

To Honor, Rosamond said only, 'We can take you to Priory House. None will dare harm you there.'

The offer propelled Honor to her feet with a heartfelt plea of '*Ke war gamm!*' – Leave me alone!

Reluctantly concluding that she would learn no more from Annie Piers's daughter, Rosamond yielded to her wishes and left. She and Rob walked back toward the King's Head in silence until Rob, being careful to keep his gaze fixed straight ahead, abruptly announced that they would not stay the night in Padstow.

'What is it?' Rosamond had seen nothing to alarm her, but she had been lost in thought and less observant than she might have been.

'We are being watched. Do not look back!'

Rosamond arrested the movement and stared up at her husband instead. 'We are strangers. It is natural that we attract attention.'

'Curiosity I can understand, but this has a malevolent feel.'

In the ordinary way of things, Rosamond did not put much faith in premonitions. On the other hand, she was practical enough not to take unnecessary chances. Besides, Honor Piers had lied to them on at least two counts. She understood English. And she did have kin yet living. For some reason, she had not wanted to acknowledge a connection to Morwen Trewinard and the smugglers at Boscastle.

They left Padstow an hour later, delaying that long only because they had to wait for Carnsey to return to the inn.

Since Padstow was located on the western side of an estuary, they were obliged to ride southward, even though their destination lay along the coast to the northeast. Rosamond had briefly considered hiring a boat, but there were too many in their party to make leaving by sea inconspicuous. Worse, they would have had to leave the horses behind. That would attract almost as much unwanted attention as hiring a barge to ferry themselves and their mounts to the other side.

The road was better than most in that part of Cornwall, and straight enough that she was able to see that they were not being followed. That left the question of where they would spend the night. Not every village boasted an inn. Some of the smaller hamlets did not even have a proper alehouse.

'What do you suggest, Carnsey?' Rob asked.

Curiously, Sir Walter's secretary had not asked why they chose to leave the comfort of the King's Head. Rosamond supposed he had been trained not to question Sir Walter's decisions and now extended that courtesy to them.

Carnsey eyed the sky, estimating how much daylight remained. It was not long after Midsummer. They could ride for some distance yet before the sun set. 'We have time to reach St Kew.'

'Is there a respectable inn in that village?' Rob asked.

'Better.' Carnsey favored them with his lopsided grin. 'A house called Bokelly. It is owned by William Carnsey, a distant kinsman of mine.'

Rosamond had never met the gentleman, but the rules of country hospitality would oblige him to offer them beds for the night. She agreed to Carnsey's proposal with a sense of relief.

It took nearly as long to reach St Kew as it had to travel from Bodmin to Padstow. They rode south and then east to reach Wadebridge before turning in a more northerly direction. The road from Wadebridge avoided a wooded valley to climb to higher ground, taking them through several miles of good, arable land before plunging into the woodlands that surrounded William Carnsey's dwelling. It was already dusk before Rosamond caught her first glimpse of Bokelly.

A lane wound between sparse hedgerow trees, leading to the house's forecourt and porch and the entrance to the great hall. When she stood at the top of the porch steps, Rosamond turned to look back toward the hills to the southwest. The last rays of the setting sun glistened on the water of the numerous creeks and rivers that crisscrossed the landscape, giving the whole of it a magical glow. Rosamond smiled with pleasure at the sight . . . and at the fact that she could detect no sign of pursuit.

TWENTY-THREE

4 July 1584

Although he could scarce complain about their host's hospitality, Rob was anxious to leave at first light the next morning. They took time to break their fast with bread and beef and ale, and accepted a packet of food for the journey, but they were mounted and under way before Carnsey's kinsman had time for more than one brief prayer.

Rosamond waited until they were halfway to Trelill before she took her husband to task for their abrupt departure. 'There was no need to leave so early,' she chided him. 'I know the real reason for your haste.'

'To reach Boscastle with all speed.' Rob made the mistake of glancing her way.

The mischievous twinkle in her eyes warned him he would not get away with this excuse. 'A likely story! I saw you trying to stifle your yawns.'

William Carnsey, employing no chaplain, took it upon himself to preach to his family, his servants, and his guests. This passed for an evening's entertainment at Bokelly.

'To be fair, he is widely read,' Rob said.

'That may be, but his preference for boring religious tracts by the likes of Thomas Cartwright did not endear him to me.'

'I doubt he is as much a puritan as you think. Did you not hear him say that he plays at bowls of a Sunday afternoon?'

'I stopped listening when he began to ramble on about his sandridge.'

Rob chuckled. 'A good husbandman cares about such things.'

The sandridge, composed of sea-sand and manure and compost, would be used to fertilize crops. Master Carnsey had begun his the previous week. In a few days' time, he planned to start adding to it by as much as thirty loads of dung a day.

'We were fortunate to escape without a lecture on the best way to shear sheep,' Rosamond said. 'The maidservant assigned to serve as my tiring maid told me that task is to be done a fortnight hence.'

They passed through Trelill and on to St Teath without incident. From that point they could follow the southern shore of the Severn Sea. As they rode over heather-covered hills toward Tintagel, they had a fine view along the rocky coastline in both directions.

'We might stop to eat nuncheon amid the ruins,' Rob suggested. 'I have heard that the ancient castle is a popular spot for such excursions.'

'And I am told there is a dungeon,' Rosamond said.

'That might be interesting to explore, so long as we cannot be locked in.'

'Reportedly, it sits on a high crag surrounded by the sea and can only be reached by means of a drawbridge.'

'The chapel dedicated to St Ulette once stood within the dungeon,' said Carnsey, who was their guide from a few yards in front of them. 'It has lately fallen into disuse. Nowadays the place is overrun with grazing sheep.'

Reminded that Sir Walter's secretary could not help but overhear everything they said to each other, Rob fell silent. He supposed it must have been Carnsey who would have told Rosamond about the dungeon in the first place, just as he'd been the one to make Rob aware of Tintagel's suitability for a meal taken out of doors. The fellow had a quiver full of such obscure facts.

Since Tintagel was only three miles from Boscastle, Rob considered changing his mind and riding straight on to their destination, but it had been several hours since they had broken their fast and he was hungry. So, he imagined, was Rosamond, who always had a hearty appetite.

When they had dismounted and Rosamond had divided the food – bread, eggs seethed until they were hard, and thick wedges of cheese – Rob ordered their escort to remain close to the tethered horses, took his wife by the hand, and went in search of a place where they could eat in private. Soon, perched atop a broken wall softened by the addition of their cloaks, they were looking out across the water as they munched.

'Wales is there somewhere,' Rob said, pointing to their right.

'And Ireland,' Rosamond agreed, squinting at the sun in an attempt to judge direction, 'lies whichever way is northwest.'

'Eastbound ships sailing past this point are bound for Bristol.' He considered saying more, but given the mixed feelings Rosamond had about the ship he had named for her, he could not predict her reaction. Best to wait to broach that subject.

'Shall we explore the ruins?' Rosamond asked when they finished their simple meal.

'If you like. There is no hurry to reach Boscastle and the distance remaining is short, especially if we do as Carnsey suggests and take the trail that winds over the cliffs.'

It was windy on the headland, but the gusts sweeping across the heights were invigorating. The view was spectacular. Rob could imagine few more stimulating places on earth than this isolated spot on the north coast of Cornwall. It was easy to become lost in the sight as he leaned over the castle wall and contemplated the drop to the churning water below.

He jerked upright when Rosamond cried out in alarm, momentarily disoriented. Two men armed with cudgels seemed to have appeared out of nowhere. Rendered slack-jawed and speechless at the sight of them, Rob froze.

The first man rushed at them, cudgel raised, the light of battle in his small, pig-like eyes.

Steel swished against leather as Rosamond drew the knife she kept in her boot, rousing Rob from his stupor. She had another hidden in her cloak, but that garment was still spread across the crumbling wall and was well out of reach.

He reached for the short sword with which he had armed himself for travel, prepared to defend both himself and his wife. He was only just in time to parry a blow from the cudgel. Ducking, he came up on his opponent's off side, but before he could go on the offensive, his attacker turned and came at him again.

Distant shouts and cries told Rob that the others in their party were also under attack. They could expect no help from that quarter. Rosamond's men would be too busy fending off additional villains to come to her rescue.

Rob risked a glance at Rosamond as he danced out of range of the cudgel. Holding her ground as a giant of a man bore down on her, she steadied herself and threw her dagger. She made a small sound of frustration when the blade struck his shoulder instead of some more vulnerable target, but the damage was enough to make him reel back, crying out in pain.

The villain attempting to flatten Rob faltered. What had just happened to his companion left him looking as stunned as if he'd just seen an earthworm turn into a viper. Rob seized the opening. Holding his sword two-handed, he aimed for the heart.

At the last possible moment, his target realized his danger and defended himself. Rob's blade struck the cudgel and stuck there. He gave a mighty heave, trying to wrench his weapon loose, and fell to the ground when both sword and cudgel abruptly came free. His attacker, left unarmed, turned and fled like the coward he was.

Still sprawled in the dirt, Rob looked for the man Rosamond had wounded. He had dropped his cudgel when the hand holding it went numb, but while Rob had been preoccupied with his own battle, he had used the other to jerk Rosamond's dagger out of his shoulder and toss it aside. Once again armed with his cudgel, he stalked her as she sprinted toward the wall where they had eaten their nuncheon.

While Rob struggled to his feet and fought to free his sword from his opponent's abandoned cudgel, Rosamond retrieved her cloak, extracting the second dagger it concealed. She brandished it, taunting her foe.

'Come closer,' she called, and stepped nimbly out of the way when he swung the cudgel at her. 'Closer! I need but one small opening to slit your throat from ear to ear.'

Her attacker swayed, dizzy from loss of blood. He looked down at the profusely bleeding wound in his shoulder, took another step toward Rosamond, and faltered.

Taking advantage of that moment of indecision, Rob gave a shout and charged. Sun glinted off the steel of his sword, momentarily blinding his enemy. Throwing his good arm up to shield his eyes, the brigand took several rapid backward steps before looking around for his friend. Finding himself alone, he lost his nerve entirely, stumbling away as fast as his legs could carry him.

Rob did not chase him. His concern was all for his wife.

Eyes bright, her face wore a broad, triumphant grin. 'We make an excellent team,' she said as she joined her husband, giving his sword an admiring glance before she calmly collected her bloodied knife.

'You caught them by surprise. If they had been expecting us to fight, we would likely be dead by now.'

'My men would have—' She broke off, belatedly realizing that those two villains had not come alone, and started to run toward the place where they had left their men and the horses.

Rob overtook and passed her, dreading what they might find. Stones fallen from the ruins and uneven ground slowed their speed, but it took no more than a few minutes to reach the others.

Carnsey was sitting on the ground, one hand gingerly examining the back of his head. No one else had been injured, although Charles, Luke, and John had all been fully engaged in battle. They had defended themselves with short swords, knives, and fists.

'I was struck from behind.' Carnsey sounded incredulous. 'I never saw them coming.'

No one could agree on how many men had attacked them, but Rob reckoned there had to have been at least five. When routed, they had fled in the direction of St Teath.

'They must have been after the horses,' Carnsey said.

Luke disputed this, swearing he'd heard the sound of rapidly retreating hooves.

'That they already had horses of their own does not rule out the theft of more,' Rosamond said, 'but if all they wanted were our mounts, they could have made off with them without venturing beyond this point.'

'They were not ordinary thieves,' Rob agreed. 'They came here bent on murder. What I cannot fathom is why. As far as I can tell, we have made no progress at all in our investigation. We do not know who killed Sir Walter or Alexander Trewinard and we do not know what secret Trewinard was keeping.'

'But we must be getting close to the truth.' Rosamond's voice was grim. 'Let us hope Leveson has fared even better, and that he is still alive to share what he has learned.'

TWENTY-FOUR

Rosamond and her escort rode in all haste to Boscastle and went straight to the alehouse. Business was brisk. A half dozen Boscastle men and one woman had gathered to drink ale and amuse themselves by singing ballads. In a larger establishment, there might have been dancing.

Henry Leveson sat alone, brooding into an empty earthenware cup. From the morose expression on his face, he had not been able to persuade Morwen Trewinard to confide in him. He sent

Rosamond a sour look as she seated herself beside him on the bench. Rob settled in next to his wife.

'She'd have thrown me out if she dared,' Leveson complained.

'No doubt you have offended her.' Rosamond hid a smile. An empty cup was the sort of minor inconvenience a woman inflicted on a man when she wanted to make him feel her displeasure.

'How could I offend?' Leveson asked. 'She refuses to acknowledge that she understands a word I say.'

He stared with intense longing at the ale jug Morwen held, but she remained where she was. To all but the sharpest of eyes she did not appear to so much as glance their way. To add to the insult, when the rest of Rosamond's men came in after seeing to the horses, she was quick to wait upon them.

'Widow Trewinard inherited a flourishing business,' Rob said.

'A pity we cannot conclude that she killed her husband for it,' Leveson muttered.

'Did he beat her?' Rosamond asked. 'Mistreat her in any way? Were you able to persuade any of the villagers to talk to you?'

'A few. By all accounts, Alexander Trewinard was an indulgent husband and a good father.' He made the effort to shake off his ill humor to ask what luck they'd had in Padstow.

'We made someone nervous,' Rob said. 'We were set upon when we stopped to refresh ourselves at Tintagel. A small band of men armed with cudgels attacked us. Ros wounded one of them before they fled.'

Leveson leaned forward, his expression eager. 'Can you describe them?'

Rosamond sent him an incredulous look. 'There was no time to memorize their faces. They were great ugly brutes in country clothing. They fled as soon as they realized we could defend ourselves.'

She frowned, trying to recall details. The man she'd wounded had worn a coat that had a shaggy look to it – frieze, no doubt. It had been the dull brown color she associated with coarse, loosely-woven wool. The fellow attacking Rob had been able to afford a bit better – no coat, but a doublet of russet cloth. She described these garments to Leveson, but he dismissed their importance. They both knew how easy it was to use clothing as a disguise.

'Scars?' he asked. 'What color hair had they?'

'They did not doff their caps.' She paused, considering. 'But the caps were ordinary. Not the sort I've seen on soldiers or on men who go to sea.'

Soldiers favored Monmouth caps, knitted and fulled and brimless, while most of the sailors she'd seen in Padstow and elsewhere wore thrum caps knitted with a shaggy covering of loose threads. She'd been told this helped repel water.

'Why attack your party?' Leveson asked. 'You traveled with guards. That should have been sufficient to discourage any ordinary thief.'

'I should think that is obvious.' Rob looked surprised by Leveson's lack of insight. 'We made someone nervous by questioning Honor Piers.'

At the mention of her kinswoman, Morwen's head snapped around, a startled expression on her face.

Leveson looked almost as surprised. '*Honor* Piers?'

'Annie Piers's daughter,' Rosamond explained. 'Old Annie is dead. She and her husband both. Honor – a singularly inappropriate Christian name – claims to know nothing of her mother's activities or of Diggory Pyper, but I do not believe she told us the truth.'

'Someone was watching us when we left her cottage,' Rob said. 'I thought we lost them when we left Padstow, but we must have been followed.'

Carnsey joined them, carrying a jug of ale and three more cups. Leveson seized the jug and poured. He and Rob at once quenched their thirst and refilled their cups, but Rosamond took no more than a sip of hers, thinking it a pity that Morwen did not sell barley water as well as beer and ale.

'What is most likely,' Carnsey said, 'is that we were set upon by a gang of masterless men. Vagabonds populate all the roadways of England. Their presence is the reason most people travel in well-armed groups.'

'Then they would have taken the horses and left us alone.' Rosamond knew she sounded impatient, but Carnsey's theory did not become any more palatable with repetition.

'How could anyone know we would take that road?' Carnsey argued. 'If someone intended us harm because we visited Padstow, would they not assume we would return to Priory House afterward?'

'Unless they knew Leveson was here in Boscastle and suspected that our plan was to meet him and share information.' Rosamond frowned, beset by the certainty that she was missing something.

'How would someone in Padstow know that?' Carnsey asked.

The answer that came to Rosamond was stunning in its simplicity. She felt like a fool for having overlooked the obvious. Glancing around, she spotted Boscastle's constable among Morwen's patrons and summoned him with a preemptory gesture.

'How did Master Dodson travel here from Padstow?' she asked him.

His reply was the one she expected – by boat.

The overland journey might be long and tedious, but by water, especially when the wind and weather cooperated, it was not. Fishermen went out every day. News of deaths, or of strangers asking questions, could travel quickly and easily between Boscastle and Padstow.

TWENTY-FIVE

5 July 1584

For some reason, the bed in Morwen Trewinard's alehouse seemed even harder and more lumpy than Rosamond remembered. It was, in truth, no more than a sack stuffed with sheep's wool. If not enough care had been taken in the making of it and the fleeces felted together, not even a good shaking would fluff them again.

Restless, she spent a goodly portion of the night regretting that she had not sought out Master Hender and availed herself of his hospitality. A manor house, especially one newly built, would likely provide accommodations far more amenable than this. When she finally slept, she dreamed of a feather bed stuffed with the down of eider ducks.

She was awake again long before first cockcrow, listening to the irregular rhythm of Rob's soft snores. The sound grated on her nerves. Worse, though, was that she could not shut down her swirling thoughts.

When asked about Honor Piers the previous day, Morwen had admitted nothing, not even that she recognized the name. She had been stubbornly close-mouthed about everything, declaring that she would answer no more questions, no matter who asked them.

Then there had been the matter of the children. Morwen paid so little attention to Wenna and Santo that Rosamond had been moved to approach the little girl. A few words had reassured her that the youngsters were not neglected. They had been given their supper, and as Rob had pointed out, leaving them to their own devices in Morwen's lodgings while she remained below to wait on customers in the alehouse could not be helped.

'Besides,' he'd said, nodding in the direction of the sleeping dog, 'they have Rover to look out for them.'

'And is he to sound the alarm if one of them is sick or injured?' The cur was old and seemed to spend most of his time asleep.

Rob had grinned at her before yawning hugely. 'I am delighted to discover that you possess maternal instincts, sweeting. Shall we adjourn to our bed?'

Annoyed, she'd pretended reluctance. To her dismay, he'd taken her at her word and had been fast asleep by the time she rose from her knees after saying her private evening prayers.

Once the first pale light of day crept through the open window, Rosamond rose and began to struggle into her clothing unaided. This process took more than a quarter of an hour but once she was decent, she crept through the outer chamber. Carnsey was stirring but Leveson still slept like the dead. She hurried on down the stairs and out into the bracing morning air.

It was only when she saw that no fishing boats had gone out that she remembered it was Sunday. The alehouse, she noted, was hard by the village's archery butts. That was doubt-less good for business, since Sunday afternoon after church was the traditional time for archery practice. Every able-bodied male in the realm was expected to become proficient with the longbow. The fathers of boys between the ages of seven and seventeen were even required by law to provide each son with a bow and two arrows. Rosamond supposed that obligation would fall to Benet's guardian, now that Walter was dead. To her? The possibility did not seem quite so daunting as it once had, especially when she imagined herself practicing archery right along with her young half-brother.

Lost in contemplation of the future, she walked toward the half-completed stone pier. The steep sides of the river valley that formed the natural harbor at Boscastle rose up on either side of her. Gulls dipped and wove over her head, their cries loud and raucous in the morning air. She saw other birds, too. One odd looking one was all black with a white belly. Another she tentatively identified as a cormorant.

The tide was fully out, leaving a strip of sand and rocks between the water and a row of small fishing boats drawn up on the bank. A boy of no more than fourteen, skipping stones, was the only person in sight and she fell to watching him. When he tired of the game, he set off in the direction of the beached boats.

Rosamond turned to walk back to the alehouse. The first rumblings of hunger had emerged from her belly and she thought to beg a heel of bread, a wedge of cheese, and a cup of ale from Morwen before church.

She was stopped in her tracks by a high, shrill cry. The boy's scream shattered the peace of the day. By the time Rosamond hiked up her skirts to sprint toward him, he was doubled over and retching with alarming violence.

At first, outcroppings of rock and the bulk of the boats obscured her view. Then she saw it: an arm where no arm should be. A moment later, she reached the body and threw herself to her knees beside it. She saw at once that it was already too late to render aid.

The boy approached, staggering a bit and coming to an unsteady halt a few feet away. His eyes were wide in a face that had lost every vestige of color. 'Is she dead?'

'I am afraid so.'

Rosamond was not much given to premonitions, but as she grasped the limp shoulder to roll the body toward her, she felt with eerie certainty that she knew the victim. When the face came into view, her stomach lurched. It was a ghastly sight. She had been in the water long enough for fish to nibble at her, but there was enough left to recognize the dead woman as Honor Piers.

The crunch of footsteps warned her that others were approaching, drawn by the boy's outcry. She looked up as two Boscastle men stopped beside her.

'Drowned,' said one, looking down at the body.

The other repeated the same verdict in Cornish.

Rosamond willed her breathing to steady and her heart to stop racing. She was exceeding grateful she had not yet broken her fast.

'Leave her to I, mistress,' the English-speaker said. 'Her's not the first drowny here.'

From somewhere nearby, his companion had already produced a door.

Rosamond had to stare at it for a few heartbeats before she realized that they meant to use it to transport Honor's body. She objected at once. 'She must not be moved. She must remain where she was found until the coroner has seen her.'

The two men ignored her. She could not say she blamed them.

'Where are you taking her?' she asked when they hoisted their grisly burden onto the door.

'To the church,' the second man said in Cornish.

The first man balked. 'Be the Sabbath.'

Rosamond decided her wits must have gone wandering with the shock of recognizing the dead woman. Gathering them up with a firm hand, she spoke in an authoritative tone of voice. 'Best take her to the alehouse, good fellows. She is kin to Morwen Trewinard.'

The two men exchanged a look Rosamond could not interpret, but they were not inclined to argue. They changed direction just in time for the local constable to intercept them. He stared at the dead woman's face, a puzzled expression on his own, and asked who she was.

'Honor Piers,' Rosamond said.

He swore in Cornish and then announced in the same language that he would send for the coroner.

The sad little procession made its way to the alehouse, where Rosamond broke the news to Morwen. She showed no emotion at hearing her cousin was dead, but it was clear she was not happy about having another body lying on one of her tables.

Rosamond left her berating the constable and went up to the top floor of the tower to wake Rob. This proved difficult, although as a general rule he rose as early as she did. He, in turn, roused Leveson and Carnsey, the latter having, apparently, gone back to sleep after Rosamond passed through the chamber. Some considerable time later, all four of them gathered around the corpse.

Rob took one look at the body and swore. His voice was husky. Whether that was from sleep or with emotion, Rosamond could not tell.

Leveson yawned and blinked sleepy eyes at the remains. 'Honor Piers?'

Rosamond nodded.

'Poor woman,' said Carnsey.

'But what is she doing here?' Leveson asked.

'I have no idea, but I think I must take it upon myself to examine her body for marks of foul play. Honor Piers should be in her cottage in Padstow, not here, freshly deposited at Boscastle by the tide.' Squaring her shoulders, Rosamond approached the table.

'How can anyone discern the difference between bruises caused by the sea and the rocks and injuries inflicted by man?' Carnsey fiddled with his collar. Since he had dressed while still half asleep, it was askew.

Rosamond ignored him and concentrated on the dead woman's hands and wrists before moving on to examine her ankles. She saw no indication that Honor had been bound when she went into the water, but that meant little. If she could not swim, simply tossing her into the sea would have signed her death warrant.

Calling upon Morwen to assist her, Rosamond stripped off Honor's sodden clothing. While the men retreated to the other table and broke their fast, she studied every bump, bruise, and cut on the body.

'There is a gash at the back of her head that looks suspicious,' she reported when she had finished her examination, 'but what caused it is impossible to say.'

'Should you not leave determining the cause of death to Master Dodson?' Carnsey asked.

Rosamond made a derisive sound. 'I know already what he will say. He will give the body a cursory glance and instruct his jury to rule her death an accident.'

'What else can he say?' Leveson asked. 'You have found no proof that she was beaten, bludgeoned, or stabbed to death.'

Rosamond did not trouble to argue with them, but she was of the opinion that it might indeed have been a blow from a cudgel that had sent Honor Piers into the sea. A cudgel had likely been used to kill Alexander Trewinard. The men at Tintagel had been armed with cudgels, too. And now a new thought came to her. Was it possible that the same weapon had been used to kill Sir Walter?

TWENTY-SIX

Rob seated his wife at the table where Leveson and Carnsey were waiting for them. He watched her closely, concerned about her well-being. She was too pale, and the events of the day had drained her reserves of strength and resilience. He wanted to wrap her in velvet and protect her from the rest of the world, but he knew he'd be that world's greatest fool if he thought she would put up with such treatment.

Rosamond propped her elbows on the table and came straight to the point. 'Now that the coroner has come to his wrongheaded conclusion, we need to discuss this latest murder and how it relates to the other two.'

Before Morwen had retired to her lodgings for the night, she had been persuaded to supply them with a jug of ale. Rob filled the two remaining wooden cups for himself and Rosamond while the other men waited in gloomy silence for her to continue.

'I have been thinking about why Honor Piers would leave Padstow,' she said. 'Indeed, I have thought of little else all day. Even in church, I found myself testing one explanation after another and discarding them one after another, too. My conclusion is that the visit Rob and I paid to Honor frightened her. She set out for Boscastle by boat, hoping to arrive before we did.'

'Why?' Leveson asked.

'Perhaps to consult with her cousin, Morwen.' Rosamond heaved a deep sigh. 'I fear we will never know for certain.'

'It is a great pity that she was unwilling to let us protect her.' Rob took another swallow of his ale. Whatever else Morwen was, she was expert at brewing.

'Honor told us very little,' Rosamond said, 'but she did talk to us. What if someone thought she told us more than she did, just as someone believed that Alexander Trewinard confided more than he did in Sir Walter? Honor might have been running away from that someone, alarmed by our questions because she knew, or suspected, the reason Trewinard was killed.'

After mulling over this possibility, Rob decided he agreed with it. He glanced at their companions. Carnsey had his head down, hiding his thoughts, but Leveson's skepticism was obvious in both the twist of his lips and his tone of voice.

'Are you suggesting that she was involved in treason?' he asked.

'Why not? A woman can be as deadly as a man. Were you not the one who suggested that Morwen might have killed her husband?'

'Then how did she end up drowned?'

'Doubtless betrayed and murdered,' Rosamond said, 'just as Trewinard was.'

'You have no proof that anyone helped her into the sea.' Carnsey's head remained bent over his cup. 'Many a poor soul drowns by accident in these waters. If she attempted to manage a small boat on her own, it is no surprise that she came to harm.'

'Is it not more likely that she hired a fisherman to bring her here?' Rob asked.

'Then why did no one sound the alarm when she went overboard?' Rosamond asked. 'The weather has been mild, the water calm. Rescue should have been possible, unless she asked the wrong person to bring her here. To discover who provided her with transportation, we must inquire in Padstow.'

Carnsey pondered this, his cup gripped in both hands and his gaze fixed on the rough wooden surface of the table. Then he sighed. 'Someone must inquire, but you'd do well to let me undertake that task. Padstow men will talk more readily to another Cornishman than they will to you.'

Although she clearly begrudged the necessity, Rosamond conceded his point.

'Your questions will seem suspicious now that the woman is dead,' Leveson said. 'It will be a waste of time for you to go there. Besides, she need not have been bound for Boscastle at all. What if her destination was Bristol, or Lundy Island?'

Rosamond sent him a questioning look. 'Lundy Island?'

'It is a notorious haven for pirates,' Carnsey explained. Turning to Leveson, he smiled his crooked smile. 'Never fear, friend. No one will suspect a man generous enough to escort that poor woman's body home for burial.'

While Leveson continued to argue against the journey to Padstow, Rob's thoughts drifted into other, even less pleasant byways. When Carnsey excused himself to visit the privy, he hastily shared them with Rosamond and Leveson.

'The only people who knew that we planned to go to Padstow to talk to Old Annie Piers and travel to Boscastle afterward were those who were at Priory House before we left – members of Sir Walter's household.'

'You think that one of them is a traitor?' Leveson cocked an eyebrow at him. 'It is possible.'

'Can we rule anyone out?' Rosamond asked. 'Carnsey was with us.'

'That does not mean he can be trusted.' Leveson drummed his fingers on the table, as if to aid his thinking. 'Mayhap, to make certain of him, I should accompany him to Padstow.'

'And who will keep an eye on you?' Rob asked.

'You can trust me. I act for Sir Francis Walsingham.'

'But is Walsingham your only employer? Loyalty can be bought.'

Leveson glowered at him. 'Suspect me all you like, but if your theory is correct and both Carnsey and I are innocent, then you had best be careful when you return to Priory House.'

'On that we can agree,' said Rob. 'No one except the members of Rosamond's family are exempt from suspicion.'

Leveson gave a short bark of laughter. 'You are a fool if you do not believe them capable of betrayal.'

'You mean my mother, I assume,' Rosamond interjected, 'since the only other kin I have left at Priory House is young Benet.'

'And the girl – Audrey. I have heard more than one rumor about Lady Pendennis and her connections.'

'And the facts? What are they?'

'My dear Mistress Jaffrey, I had no need to know.'

Rosamond gripped the edge of the table, making Rob wonder if that was to keep herself from going for Leveson's throat. 'I grow weary of your insinuations,' she said through clenched teeth.

'Then it is a great pity that you did not think to ask Jacob Littleton about Lady Pendennis's past before you left London.'

With that, Leveson rose and headed for the stairs, going up to bed without saying another word.

'What an exasperating fellow he can be,' Rosamond said.

'That is especially true,' Rob agreed, 'if there is any possibility that he is right.'

TWENTY-SEVEN

6 July 1584

Rosamond and Rob set out for Priory House at dawn on Monday, leaving Carnsey and Leveson to depart Boscastle for Padstow as soon as they had secured a cart in which to transport Honor Piers's body. Rosamond spent the long morning's ride organizing her thoughts. Rob had been right, and Leveson's warning was one she must heed. She must be wary of everyone who had been privy to their plan to travel from Padstow to Boscastle.

Having worked with Henry Leveson before, she was inclined to trust Walsingham's agent, but she despised his sly hints about her mother's past. She did not suspect Leveson of betraying his country. Further, she knew he would have been hard pressed to murder Alexander Trewinard when he was riding toward Boscastle in her company at the time the alehouse keeper died. But the fact that he was a player by profession meant that he was especially skilled at deception. His duties as one of Sir Francis

Walsingham's agents made him even more secretive. If he thought it necessary, or was ordered to do so by Walsingham – for the good of Crown and country – he would not hesitate to betray his dearest friend, let alone Rosamond, Rob, or Sir Walter.

Her first task must be to verify Leveson's whereabouts at the time of Sir Walter's murder. She would talk to Ludlow first, she decided. The gatekeeper must have met Walsingham's man at least once, on the occasion of Leveson's first visit to Priory House.

By the time she reined in at the gate, bracing herself for an enthusiastic greeting by the two mastiffs, she was prepared with questions. Before she could ask any of them, Ludlow burst into speech. His news drove every other thought out of her head.

Jacob Littleton had arrived at Priory House during their absence.

Ludlow spoke to Rob, too, but Rosamond did not hear what he had to tell her husband. She was already urging her mount into a trot, anxious to reach the house.

She found Jacob in Sir Walter's study. At her entrance, he looked up from the desk with a smile, slowly removing the spectacles he wore when reading.

'I saw you ride in.' He indicated the windows. 'Were you successful in your quest?'

'If anything, I am more confused now than I was before we left. But how is it that you are here, Jacob? Should you not still be in London, awaiting the pleasure of the Court of Wards?'

'That matter is settled.'

When he avoided meeting her eyes, Rosamond's heart missed a beat. 'Oh, no! Never tell me that some stranger persuaded them to grant Benet's guardianship to him!'

'Not to a stranger, no, but not to your mother, either. Upon careful consideration, I took the great liberty of proposing an alternative. *You* have been granted Benet's wardship and the right to arrange his marriage. You will think I presumed too much, but I deemed it unwise to leave control of either in Lady Pendennis's hands.'

Sinking into the Glastonbury chair, Rosamond tried to absorb what this would mean for her and Rob. 'It is for the best,' she said aloud. 'You did well, Jacob.'

'Ah,' he said. 'I see. I presume, then, that time has not improved Lady Pendennis's temperament?'

'She is . . . erratic. You must have seen that for yourself.'

'As it happens, I have not. She has not deigned to receive me.'

'Then she does not yet know I am Benet's guardian?'

A wry smile confirmed it. 'All things considered, I thought it best to wait to tell her until you returned.'

That placed the burden on her shoulders. Rosamond could not repress a small shudder. 'We will wait a while longer, then, before putting our heads on the chopping block. There are other matters that need to be settled first.'

'Melka told me where you went and why, and informed me that you believe Sir Walter's death was not an accident, but—'

'Melka did? I did not realize that you spoke Polish.'

'A little. And Melka has, as I am certain you are aware, more English than she likes to admit to. We communicate quite well.'

Was he blushing? Rosamond shook her head to clear it. Jacob . . . and Melka?

He did not give her time to speculate further. Clearing his throat, he asked what she had learned in Padstow and Boscastle.

'Only that someone is willing to kill to keep a secret and that no one seems to know what that secret is.'

Jacob's lips curved into the smallest of smiles. 'If they knew,' he pointed out with gentle humor, 'it would not be a secret.'

In no mood for jests, Rosamond sprang to her feet, her hands curled into fists at her sides. 'If I am to die for it, I should like to satisfy my curiosity first.'

'My dear girl, were you hurt?' He started to rise.

She waved him back into the chair, ashamed of her outburst. Jacob had not intended to upset her. 'The men sent to ambush us failed in their task. Carnsey has a bump on the head, but nothing worse befell us.'

Subsiding, every trace of levity banished, Jacob folded his hands over his slightly concave abdomen and regarded her with the utmost seriousness. 'You had best tell me everything.'

Resigned to recounting most of what had happened since she and Rob arrived in Cornwall, she settled herself on the flat-topped

traveling chest, curled her legs beneath her, leaned back against
the casement, and began. When she had finished, Jacob looked
even more solemn.

'I worked with your stepfather for many years. I knew
Alexander Trewinard when Sir Walter first began to use him as
a source of information. And I have met young Diggory Pyper,
too. I am not certain I can be of much use to you, having lived
in London these last few years, but I will do all I can to help
you put the pieces together.'

'Were you a spy, too?' She had always wondered.

'I . . . assisted.'

She sat up straight, grinning at him, and suddenly felt more
lighthearted than she had in days. Walter might be gone, but a
part of him remained in the memories of his faithful manservant.
To Jacob she could and would give that rare and valuable
commodity, her trust.

'We will discover who killed Sir Walter,' she said. 'I am sure
of it.'

'You and your husband were attacked,' Jacob reminded her.
'Is revenge for your stepfather's murder worth the risk that these
villains may come after you again?'

'*Justice* is, but, yes, I do want revenge. Revenge and justice
are very nearly the same when it comes to making someone pay
for Sir Walter's death.'

'Your stepfather was always most particular when it came to
meting out punishment. He made certain he had proof of guilt,
especially in those cases where the accused would be hanged or
burnt to death for committing a crime.'

'I remember hearing one or two of his lectures on the subject,'
Rosamond admitted.

When a man could be executed for stealing property worth no
more than a shilling, it behooved a justice of the peace to show
mercy. Many juries agreed, bringing in a verdict of not guilty,
even when the proof was overwhelming. Repeated felonies were
less often forgiven, but it had been Sir Walter's belief that most
criminals deserved a second chance.

Not murderers, she thought. *And not traitors.*

She slid off the chest, once again too agitated to sit still. 'I
know so little!'

Jacob winced at the sharp-voiced complaint, but he remained calm. 'There must be a few suspects you can eliminate.'

'You. Myself. Rob. Benet. No one else. Not even Mother.' She crossed the room to stand in front of him. 'Henry Leveson has been hinting that she has some dark secret in her past, something that affects her actions even now.'

'You cannot think Lady Pendennis conspired to bring about her own husband's death!'

'Why not? Mayhap asking for my help in solving his murder was only an attempt to divert suspicion. What is it that I do not know about her? You must tell me, Jacob.'

The old man sighed deeply. 'It was a long time ago and best forgotten.'

'But it has not *been* forgotten, else Henry Leveson would not know of it. Tell me, Jacob.'

He sighed again and waved her into the Glastonbury chair, then inched his own chair closer to her and took her hands in his. 'You were still a small child – seven or eight? It was at the time of the rising of the Northern earls.'

Rosamond closed her eyes. This was what she had feared after she had talked with Melka. Somehow, her mother's ties to Westmorland had led her to betray her country.

'Catholic malcontents rose up in Yorkshire and Northumberland,' Jacob said. 'They wanted to overthrow the queen.'

'Not in Westmorland?'

'The *Earl* of Westmorland was one of the leading rebels,' Jacob corrected her, 'along with his countess, and one of the women in the countess's household was your mother's cousin. Through letters to this cousin, Lady Pendennis gave aid and comfort to the rebels in the days before the uprising. She was privy to your stepfather's correspondence, you see, since he had no reason to think he needed to hide it from her. She sent intelligence to those who would commit treason and thus was guilty of treason herself.'

With every word, the ache in Rosamond's heart grew more painful. She'd had little reason to think her mother a paragon of virtue, but this was a terrible betrayal, not only of England, but of Sir Walter's love and trust in his wife. She had to swallow a few times before she could speak.

'At the least, she should have been tried and imprisoned in the Tower for what she did. How did she escape punishment? Was she pardoned?'

'She claimed she had been acting in Sir Walter's best interests. She was ambitious for him. She wanted him to be named ambassador to France. His goals were different. He'd planned all along to rusticate in Cornwall once he completed his duties as the queen's special envoy abroad.'

'So he protected her? After what she'd done?'

'I do not know what he intended. He may not have known himself. In the end, it was not necessary for him to do anything.'

A quarrel, Rosamond remembered. Melka had told her that Sir Walter and his wife had fought just before Eleanor ran out of the house and into the path of that heavy-laden wagon.

'The accident,' she whispered. 'Mother was horribly injured. It was thought she would not live.'

Jacob nodded. 'It was Sir Walter's duty to care for her when she survived. He did so grudgingly at first. In time, after she joined him here in Cornwall, he forgave her and they were reconciled.'

'How did he ever dare to trust her again?'

'She was his wife, and Sir Walter wanted a son and heir.' Jacob released her hands to toy with his spectacles. 'I must admit that I have never been certain he could count on her loyalty, and my worst suspicions were revived when I was ordered to travel to Westmorland to fetch Lady Pendennis's kinswoman, the orphaned daughter of a known recusant, and deliver her here to Cornwall.'

'Audrey?'

'Even she.'

'Was her father executed?'

'Nothing so bad as that, but he was in prison when he died. For years, he had paid the fines for not attending church, but when he ran out of money, he was arrested and what little he still owned was seized by the Crown. The girl was left with two choices – enter service or starve. Your mother's offer of a post as her companion was most generous.'

'And most suspicious.' Rosamond could not keep the bitterness out of her voice.

If Audrey's father was a recusant, then she had been raised in a Catholic household, taught to obey Rome above the queen. Audrey must have attended church since her arrival in Cornwall – to refuse to do so would not have been tolerated while Sir Walter was alive – but in all probability she was still a secret Catholic. Rosamond did not believe all papists were innately evil, but she knew from firsthand experience that some of them *did* plot against queen and country.

Had she wasted her time riding hither and yon in search of Sir Walter's killer? If her mother and young Audrey had been plotting together, then the answers Rosamond sought were to be found right here at home.

TWENTY-EIGHT

7 July 1584

As he dressed for the day and broke his fast, Rob wondered if he was searching for a murderer or a spy or both? His theory that someone at Priory House had betrayed them had been bolstered by what Jacob Littleton told Rosamond the previous day. That Lady Pendennis had refused to speak with her daughter gave him even more reason to suspect she knew more than she was saying, but as yet they had no proof against her.

Rob did not enjoy looking with suspicion at every man and woman in the household. Most people, or so he had always believed, were inclined to be good-hearted, even generous. No one could have asked to be raised in a more loving environment than the one he and Rosamond had shared as children.

Still, someone had been responsible for the deaths of three people and the attempted murder of six more at Tintagel. That same someone was, allegedly, neck-deep in treason. What little they had been able to discover about the crimes seemed to lead straight back to Priory House, for the villain they sought for murdering Sir Walter was most likely one of those with whom he had interacted on a daily basis.

Rob was glad Rosamond would be questioning Lady Pendennis, but she had delegated him to deal with Ludlow, Gryffyn the groom, Sutton the tutor, Sir Walter's steward, and the others who had served Sir Walter. It was his task to determine, if they did not know already from the first time they'd questioned the servants, where each of them had been when Sir Walter went out riding. In addition, he hoped to learn if any of them were wont to write letters or send messages, and if so, to whom. He planned to ask if they had entertained any visitors, mysterious or otherwise, and to discover if any of them had papist leanings.

At least one did – Audrey Gravitt. Along with Jacob's report on the Court of Wards' decision and Lady Pendennis's history, Rosamond had also shared what their faithful family retainer had told her about Lady Pendennis's companion. Rob and Rosamond had talked long into the night, going around and around with theories and suppositions.

Neither Rob nor she believed that everyone who followed the Old Religion was bent on regicide, but ever since the Pope's proclamation urged all true believers to rebel against their heretic queen, there had been those disposed to carry religious fervor too far. He prayed none of them lived at Priory House.

He began his inquisition with Master Sutton, invading the schoolroom in the new wing of the house. He was unsurprised to find not one, but two young boys seated at a long table, heads bent over their books. It was not unusual to educate a servant's children along with the master's offspring. That was why not only Rob, but also his two sisters, had shared Rosamond's lessons.

Mathy Ludlow was the first to notice Rob. He elbowed Benet in the ribs and jerked his head in the newcomer's direction. Master Sutton, hands clasped behind his back, stood by the window staring out into the rain. He seemed oblivious to the intrusion until Rob spoke.

'A word with you, Sutton?'

The tutor turned slowly, his pallid countenance almost ghost-like above the solid black of an academic gown. Rob studied that face, noticing for the first time that the man was trough-eyed, with one slightly lower than the other. They were a murky blue in color, like a pond where the mud at the bottom had recently been disturbed. The body concealed by his loose garment was unremarkable, neither corpulent nor lean, but spindly legs and the lack of breadth in the shoulders hinted at thinness.

Such a man might not be adept at using a cudgel, but he was surely capable of throwing a rock at a rider with enough accuracy to kill him. Anyone could fling a stone, even a woman. To hit what one aimed at only required practice, most likely with that most innocent-appearing weapon, the shepherd's sling. Rob's gaze shifted to the boys. Gentlemen's sons and the sons of peasants alike learned to use one at an early age so that they could play at 'David and Goliath' with their friends.

'You interrupt our lessons, Master Jaffrey.' Sutton's reprimand, although mildly voiced, had the weight of generations of Oxford scholars behind it.

'It is a matter of some urgency.'

'I should hope so, for my young charges must not be disturbed for petty reasons.' A superior smirk on his face, he added a phrase in Latin.

Rob silently translated: 'There is only one good – knowledge; and only one evil – ignorance.'

It was a quotation from Socrates and he was expected to reply in kind, preferably taking his text from one of the great Greek or Roman thinkers. Rob had never cared for the pretentious academic habit of capping quotes. He might have responded with Plato's saying that truth was its own reward, or cited Aristotle's belief that all men by nature desire to know, or offered further words of wisdom from Socrates with: 'Nothing is to be preferred before justice', instead he suggested that it might be best if they spoke in the passage.

By now both boys were watching with wide-eyed curiosity. Rob had no doubt they would listen at the door, scrambling back to their places before their tutor returned to catch them at it. When Sutton presented his back to stalk out of the room ahead of him, Rob winked at Benet.

Annoyed by the interruption, as well as by what he must perceive as Rob's lack of scholarship, Sutton let his impatience show. 'What is the meaning of this high-handed behavior?'

'Questions have arisen concerning the death of Sir Walter Pendennis.'

'The man fell from his horse and hit his head on a rock. What is there to question?'

'Whether or not he was *helped* to fall.' Unless Sutton had been living in a cave, he must have heard something of Lady Pendennis's belief that her husband had been murdered.

'As to that, I cannot say. I keep myself to myself.'

'You have a considerable correspondence with other scholars.' Although Rob had not yet ascertained if this was true, it was a reasonable assumption.

'What does my letter-writing have to do with the matter?'

Although Sutton's bewilderment struck Rob as genuine, he pursued the subject. 'To whom do you write and upon what subjects?'

Sutton supplied several names, none of them familiar. 'We correspond on matters scientific and mathematical, and on occasion discuss sermons we have heard.'

This sounded as dull and old-fashioned as the man himself, but Rob preferred not to take any chances. 'Did you ever exchange rumors, or speculate on the fate of the monarchy?'

'You insult me, Master Jaffrey. To do the latter would be high treason and I am no traitor!' He reached for the latch. 'I have wasted enough time on this foolishness. I must return to my charges.'

Rob's hand shot out to brace against the door and hold it closed. 'I crave a word with the boys first . . . without your presence.'

'By what authority do you order me about?'

'By the authority of young Benet's guardian.'

'Lady Pendennis cannot have sanctioned such an outrageous imposition and she is the one who employs me.'

'Are you certain she is the one who holds the boy's wardship?'

Rob let him stew over that statement without elaborating, in part because he was reluctant to say more until Rosamond had informed her mother of the decision of the Court of Wards. Sutton did not look happy. Benet's guardian would have the authority to remove him from his post.

'You may have a quarter of an hour. No more. I am not paid to neglect my charges.'

Rob could not resist. Just before Sutton withdrew into the adjacent chamber, he quipped, in Latin, 'An education obtained with money is worse than no education at all.'

As he had expected, the two boys were waiting just inside the door. Belatedly, Rob wondered if Benet knew that his father had been murdered. He felt certain every servant in the household was aware of Lady Pendennis's claim, but they might have conspired to protect the young master from that knowledge.

He knelt at the boy's side. 'How much did you overhear?'

'That you seek my father's murderer.' Benet's expression was solemn but not distressed. 'I have been thinking about that ever since you and my sister left here for Padstow. I know who I would question.'

'Do you, now?'

His eager nod had Rob hiding a smile. 'But first I would know who has been named my guardian.'

'So you overheard that, too, did you?' Rob grasped the boy's shoulder as he stood. 'The Court of Wards gave your wardship to your sister.'

'Does that mean I must leave Priory House?'

'That has yet to be decided. Do you want to stay here?'

Benet looked at Mathy and quickly away. In that moment, Rob decided that if one boy came to live with them in Bermondsey, both boys would.

'Nothing will be settled,' he said aloud, 'until your father's murderer is brought to justice.'

'Then you must question that man Leveson,' Benet said. 'I have seen him before, sneaking in through the old gate.'

'The old gate?'

'This was a real priory once,' Mathy chimed in. 'The ruins are all gone now, but long ago they faced southeast and the old stables were near a gate on the south wall. Sir Walter had the opening walled up – wide enough for carts, it was – but there is still a wicket.'

Rob recalled that Leveson had said he'd come to Priory House in secret, on Sir Walter's orders, but he had not thought to ask the fellow where he had gained entry. He should have done. He saw that now.

'Was Leveson here on the day Sir Walter died?'

Benet shook his head, but Mathy burst into speech. 'He *could* have been. My father would not have seen him, not even if he came past the gatehouse.'

'Why not?'

'Father was away that morning.'

'And how do you know that, lad? Were you not here in the schoolroom?'

'I heard my mother complain of it.' Mathy grinned, oblivious to the fact that he had just cast suspicion on his father. 'She was wroth with him for leaving it to her to open and close the gate.'

'Was there much coming and going on that day?'

'Not until later, after Sir Walter's horse came back without a rider. By then my father had returned. It was the principle of the thing. That is what Mother said. Minding the gate is not her responsibility. She has enough to do taking care of my brothers and sisters and the dogs.'

Rob broke off questioning the boys for fear he would alert Mathy to the new direction of his suspicions. After asking them to send word to him if they remembered anything else about the day Sir Walter died, he left to question Mathy's mother.

TWENTY-NINE

Rosamond did not look forward to announcing the Court of Wards' decision to her mother and the steady downpour hammering against the windows only increased her reluctance. For one cowardly moment, she considered instructing Jacob to undertake the onerous task, but she could not in good conscience ask anyone else to venture into the lioness's den. She drew in a deep, strengthening breath and stepped through the door to Eleanor's bedchamber.

At first, no one noticed her. Her mother was still abed and Melka had her back to the door while she fussed over something stored in a dome-topped wardrobe chest.

Rosamond welcomed the respite, no matter how brief, and took advantage of it to study her mother's lair. It did not appear that much had changed during the years she'd been away. When she inhaled, she could smell the mint and burnt fleabane strewn among the rushes on the floor. Ash-colored hangings trimmed with lace adorned her mother's high, ornately carved and painted bed. A livery cupboard contained Eleanor's ewer, basin, and chamber pot, as well as a goodly collection of perfumes and salves. Chests and coffers held her clothing. An imported chair of Spanish make was in its accustomed place close to the hearth. Nearby was a stool covered in green Turkey-work with double rows of fringe.

That was where Rosamond had been accustomed to sit, at her mother's feet while Eleanor attempted to instruct her in the finer points of embroidery. She grimaced at the memory. She'd never been any good with a needle, being too impatient to make small, careful stitches.

Her gaze shifted to a pedestal table covered with a Persian carpet. A pitcher and a small coffer were in their proper places on top of it. The pitcher would contain barley water and the coffer was doubtless still used to store comfits. On occasion, Eleanor had offered her one as a reward for good behavior, but those treats had been few and far between.

Rosamond turned slightly in order to see the rest of the room. Where once a tapestry map of Cornwall had hung on the wall there was now a portrait, a very fine one, of Eleanor and Benet. Stepping closer, Rosamond studied the two painted faces. The similarities between mother and son had been emphasized by the artist. Within two pale, perfect ovals, he had painted identical turned-up noses and hazel eyes.

Eleanor had taken care to present her good side, hiding the scars that slashed across the other cheek. These had faded with time and were no longer livid, but they would be visible as faint white puckers as long as she lived. Women disfigured by smallpox wore visors to hide the damage. Curiously, Eleanor rarely did so. That was admirable, Rosamond supposed. Or mayhap her mother's other injuries, being so much more serious, had allowed her to discount mere disfigurement . . . except when being painted for posterity.

She started at the sound of Eleanor's voice.

'My powder, Melka! I need a dose of my powder before

I deal with that wretched girl! I told her to go back to London. Disobedient creature! She continues to defy me.'

As Melka turned away from the wardrobe chest, she caught sight of Rosamond. A look of consternation momentarily disrupted the placidity that was her usual expression.

Squaring her shoulders, Rosamond resolved to hold her tongue, no matter what cruel things her mother might say. She would ignore the inevitable criticism. Once she and Rob left Cornwall, they would go on with their lives whether she had been reconciled with Eleanor or not.

Even as these thoughts flashed through her mind, Rosamond's eyes followed Melka's movements. The tiring maid opened the small coffer atop the pedestal table, revealing that it no longer contained sweets. Instead there were at least a dozen apothecary's papers inside. Melka extracted one and emptied the contents, a fine white powder, into a cup of barley water. When she carried it to Eleanor's bedside, a pale, thin hand darted out, seizing hold of it with such haste that some of the liquid slopped over the edge and spattered onto the silk coverlet.

Rosamond circled the bed, beset by an intense feeling of uneasiness. The hangings had been pushed apart, giving her a clear view of her mother as Eleanor gulped down the posset. Melka leaned in to adjust a plump bolster covered with tufted velvet so that it would better support Eleanor's neck and back. When she stepped away, Eleanor's gaze fell upon her daughter. Her eyes narrowed. Her mouth tightened into a thin line.

'Good morrow to you, Mother.'

'How dare you enter my bedchamber without an invitation!'

'It is necessary that I speak with you. There are certain matters we must discuss.'

'I told you to go back to London.'

'You no longer have the right to order me about.'

'You never listened when I did.'

'And thus, you should have known better than to think I would obey you now. Why did you want me to go, Mother? What are you afraid I will discover if I stay?'

Eleanor did not answer, but because Rosamond was watching her mother so closely, she witnessed a remarkable change. From one moment to the next, Eleanor went from snarling beast to contented cat. At the same time, her pupils enlarged until they were twice their normal size.

Rosamond turned on Melka. 'What was that powder you gave her?'

The tiring maid kept her mouth tightly closed, a mulish expression on her face.

'Such a fuss,' Eleanor murmured. 'It is medicine. Effective medicine. Better than poppy juice.' Her long, thin fingers plucked at the lace trim on the coverlet Melka had drawn up to her waist. Spots of hectic color rose on her cheeks and her pupils had now grown so enormous that only a minuscule rim of color showed around the black center.

'Where did it come from? A physician? A cunning woman? In the wrong dosage, such nostrums can be deadly.' Taking too much of any potion could have dire, even fatal consequences.

'There is naught to fear. I distill the herbs myself.' Eleanor's smile was euphoric. She looked for all the world like a woman deep in her cups. Slowly, her eyelids drifted down and her words slurred. 'All is well.'

Rosamond stared at the vacant expression on her mother's face, alarmed but at a loss as to what to do. She would not deny anyone relief from constant pain, but her mother's magic powder – doubtless some sort of opiate – appeared to have a dampening effect on her mind.

She turned again to Melka. 'How long has she been taking this powder?'

'Since she first came to Cornwall.'

Melka's clipped words left Rosamond in no doubt that she had discovered the cause of her mother's erratic behavior. Habitual use of an opiate, week after week, year after year, impaired one's mental powers. A deep sadness laced with pity came over her. She sat on the side of her mother's bed, anxiously studying Eleanor's face. How long, she wondered, would she stay in a stupor?

Without warning, Eleanor opened her eyes and sat bolt upright. Her pupils were smaller than they had been and her gaze at once fixed on Rosamond. 'What are you doing here?'

Rosamond sighed. 'I came to talk to you.'

'Have you discovered who killed Walter?'

'Not yet, but there are other matters we must discuss.'

At least, she thought, Eleanor's addiction made it unlikely that she was the one behind the scheme to kill her husband and betray her country.

Ignoring her daughter, Eleanor called out for Audrey. When Melka appeared instead, Eleanor frowned, but her confusion lasted only a moment. Imperious as a queen, she demanded to be dressed.

When Melka divested her of her night rail, tugging it off over her head, Rosamond looked away. Scars disfigured much of her mother's body. She had seen them before and had no desire to be reminded of how numerous they were.

It had been a wonder that Eleanor could walk at all on her misshapen lower limbs, but now Rosamond understood how she managed without the help of crutches or a wheeled chair. Putting weight on those damaged bones would have been agonizing had she not dulled the pain by taking her powder.

When a shift had replaced the night rail, Rosamond hesitated no longer. She suspected that her mother's wits were sharpest just after she had dosed herself. There would never be a better time to ask questions.

'Were you here all day on the day Sir Walter died?'

'Where else could I be? I cannot venture far from home.' With Melka's help, Eleanor swung her legs over the side of the bed and eased to her feet.

'Did you see him leave?'

'He went out early. He liked to ride of a morning. I prefer to lie abed.'

She preferred to take her powder in peace, Rosamond thought, when her husband was elsewhere. She glanced toward the second entrance to her mother's bedchamber, a door at the side of the bed. It led to the room where Sir Walter had slept. A thick wooden bar had been lowered across it, preventing anyone from entering.

'Was anyone else in the household absent that morning?'

'Ask the housekeeper or the steward. It is their responsibility to make sure all and sundry are present to perform their duties.'

While Melka added the next layers of clothing, tying points and smoothing skirts, Rosamond wondered if her mother played an active role in running the household. Doubtless she was quick to step in if something displeased her!

'How did you learn of the death of Audrey's father?' she asked.

This time only silence answered her.

'Do you still correspond with your kin in Westmorland?'

'As little as possible.' Sounding irritated, Eleanor waved Melka away with an impatient gesture. The Polish woman was nothing if not efficient and had nearly finished dressing her for the day.

'Is my grandmother still living?' Rosamond wondered why she had never thought to ask about Eleanor's mother before. They had never met, but she had heard Eleanor complain about her often enough. She had cut her daughter out of her life when she remarried. She had lived in comfort while Eleanor struggled to survive.

'She died three years ago.' Eleanor's voice was frigid.

'To know that, you must have been in touch with someone in the north.'

'Her husband wrote to tell me the news. I did not answer his letter. She had two brothers. They are also dead.'

'Cousins?'

'None I wish to acknowledge. One of them led me into great difficulties once. I will not be tempted into such foolishness again.'

Rosamond was about to leap on that statement, certain it was a reference to the rebellions fifteen years earlier, but she was prevented from asking more questions by Audrey's arrival.

The girl bobbed a perfunctory curtsy and directed both it and her words to Rosamond rather than to Eleanor. 'Master Jaffrey sent me to fetch you, Mistress Jaffrey. He asks that you meet him in the gatehouse.'

'Not now. Tell him—'

'He said 'twas important.'

'What the devil does he want with Ludlow?' Now fully armored in her widow's weeds, Eleanor advanced on her daughter. Her pupils had returned to their normal size and it appeared that the powder had effectively dulled her pain. Her limp was barely noticeable and there was only the slightest hint of a lurch in her gait.

'I will not know that, Mother, until I speak with him.'

'Then you had best be off,' Eleanor said.

Exasperated, full aware that she had not yet told her mother who now held Benet's wardship, Rosamond went.

THIRTY

Tamsyn Ludlow was considerably younger than her husband and a comely woman despite a sprinkling of freckles across a prominent nose. She could not have been much older than young Audrey when she birthed her eldest son. She had a way of walking that suggested she courted male attention, but the sour expression on her face and her patently false claim not to understand English, spoiled any positive effect her manner or her looks might have had on Rob Jaffrey.

Rather than remind her that he knew Sir Walter had required all his servants to speak the queen's English, he'd shrugged and sent for a translator. Rosamond would soon make this foolish woman see the sense in cooperating.

His wife arrived within a quarter of an hour of being sent for, slinging off her rain-dampened cloak as she entered the gatehouse. The Ludlow children scattered. Rob had been amusing them while he waited, teaching a girl of no more than six to make shapes with her fingers and a length of string. There were three others, two boys younger than their sister and a baby asleep in a cradle.

He rose and dusted himself off. 'Step aside with me, Ros.'

In a whisper, he explained why he had sent for her. When he told her what Mathy had let slip, her eyebrows shot up in surprise.

'I have attempted to question her,' he added, 'but she only shakes her head and acts as if she cannot understand me.'

Rosamond sent Tamsyn a jaundiced look. 'That ploy becomes tiresome.'

Her tone of voice was sharp with frustration, making Rob suspect that the meeting with Lady Pendennis had not gone well.

Rosamond addressed Ludlow's wife in English. 'If you wish to remain at Priory House, you will answer the questions my husband puts to you. It is not your place to question why he wants to know.'

Tamsyn's eyes burned with resentment, but she had no choice

but to agree. She sent the older children into another room, ordering her daughter to watch over the others. Then she stood, feet braced wide apart and arms crossed over her bosom, and waited.

Rob also remained standing. He began with simple questions – where she had been born, how she had met her husband, and the ages of her children – before he asked, 'Where is your husband?'

Ludlow had not been standing guard at the gatehouse when Rob pounded on the door. The two mastiffs were also absent.

'He does not tell me his business.' She spoke, as she had all along, in the slow, careful manner of someone unused to aping her betters, but now resentment underscored the admission.

'Do you know where your husband was on the day Sir Walter died?'

''E told me naught, didn'a?' The rush of color into her face spoke as loud as her words, telling him that she was still angry about Ludlow's failure to explain his absence.

Rosamond, who had been poking about the gatekeeper's lodgings, returned to Rob's side to address Tamsyn. 'No doubt you were busy with your children and your many wifely duties.'

Rob hid a smile. Given the evidence around them, the woman had slovenly habits. Wooden trenchers and cups had yet to be scrubbed clean. The rushes, as he had reason to know, since he had been sitting in them to play with the children, were overdue for changing. Only the addition of foul-smelling dried wormwood kept them from being infested. As for Tamsyn's linen, the inch or so of a chemise that showed above the neckline of her bodice looked more gray than white.

'It must have been most annoying,' Rob said, 'to be pulled away from your accustomed routine to admit a visitor to Priory House.'

Tamsyn eyed him warily, as if she suspected she was being mocked, but after a moment she admitted she'd taken her time going out when a visitor arrived and that he'd been angry with her for making him wait.

'Who was he?' Rob asked.

She looked at him askance. She had not asked his name and implied it was not her place to do so.

A fine point, Rob thought. It was her husband's job, and hers by delegation, and she had been lazy in the performance of her duty.

'Had your husband taken the dogs with him?' Rosamond asked.

'Aye.'

Rosamond made a tsking sound. 'And what if that man had been bent on mischief, I ask you? There you were, all alone with your babies.'

The matter of the dogs struck Rob as strange, but he was more than willing to let Rosamond take over the questioning, Her show of sympathy for Tamsyn seemed to mellow the other woman. She was even amenable to sitting alongside Rosamond on a bench. Rather than let their rapport be broken, Rob took the stool beside the cradle when the baby began to fuss and rocked the infant until it quieted.

'Did the stranger ask for Sir Walter?' Rosamond asked.

Tamsyn shook her head. Applying herself to the task of speaking as they did at the royal court, she offered what details she could recall. 'He wanted to come in, so I opened the gate. He did not stay long. I'd scarce gone back to my mending before he wanted to be let out.'

'Who did he talk to?' Rosamond asked.

'I do not know.'

Rob frowned as he kept the cradle in motion. If this mysterious visitor had learned from one of the servants that Sir Walter was out riding alone, might he have gone in search of him? Was some stranger the murderer, after all?

'Did he have servants with him?' he asked aloud. 'A groom or a companion?'

Once again, Tamsyn shook her head.

'And you had never seen this man before?' Rosamond asked.

Another shake of the head was accompanied by a baleful look from beneath lowered lashes as Tamsyn grew impatient with being questioned.

'Do you know what Henry Leveson looks like?' Rosamond asked.

'No.'

Rob almost wished they had not left Walsingham's agent behind in Boscastle to accompany Honor Piers's body back to Padstow and ask questions there with Carnsey's help, but there would be time enough to let Tamsyn take a look at him when he returned. If she did not identify Leveson as the stranger, it was still possible that the mysterious visitor had been some other spy sent by the queen's principal secretary. Before Rob could ponder this possibility further, Rosamond asked another question.

'Have you ever met Diggory Pyper?'

For just an instant, Tamsyn looked startled. Then she hastily denied it.

'But you know the name?'

'I do not, mistress. I swear it.'

She protested overmuch, but Rob could not fathom why she would lie about Pyper. The fellow's family had been friendly with Walter and Eleanor Pendennis. He'd have been admitted at once if Ludlow had been the one guarding the gate.

Rather than press Tamsyn on that point, Rosamond asked if she had noticed if the stranger had any distinguishing features. Tamsyn insisted that she had been too busy to pay attention to his appearance.

'What about his clothing? Was he a gentleman?'

That question brought a frown to Tamsyn's face. It deepened with her effort to remember. 'He wore a black cloak,' she said at length.

This observation was not helpful, since many men wore such a garment, but Tamsyn claimed she could not recollect anything else about the way the fellow was dressed.

'He spoke a few words to you,' Rosamond said. 'Were they in English?'

Tamsyn furrowed brow smoothed out. 'Aye, mistress. English.'

'Did he speak like a local man or a stranger?'

'A foreigner for certain, mistress.'

Rob was momentarily taken aback. A Spaniard? A Frenchman? An Irish brigand? Then he realized that Tamsyn would call anyone who lived farther away than Boscastle or Bodmin a foreigner, and she'd not be too certain about the denizens of those towns, either.

'He said Sir Walter's name the way you do, mistress,' Tamsyn volunteered. In common with most West Country folk, she pronounced it 'Water.'

Rosamond leapt on that, her voice cold. 'I thought you said he did not ask for Sir Walter.'

'He did not, mistress, but he asked if this was Sir Walter's house. Indeed, he did.'

She was spared further interrogation by the return of Ludlow and the dogs. The two great beasts bounded into the house, snuffling at everyone and nearly knocking Rob off his stool. The smell of wet dog surrounded him.

The room, not large to begin with, became distinctly over-crowded when Ludlow entered and shut the door behind him. 'What is going on here?'

'We are attempting to ascertain everyone's movements on the day Sir Walter died,' Rosamond said in a calm tone of voice. Her face was carefully devoid of emotion. 'Where did you go that morning?'

He replied without hesitation. 'Langore.'

'Why?' Rob asked. Langore was but a few miles distant, but it was a small place of little account. 'And why take the dogs?'

In spite of his obvious irritation at the barrage of questions, the gatekeeper grinned. 'It was because of the dogs I went, to mate Gorgon with a mastiff bitch.'

'And today?'

'To Langore again, to inspect the new litter.'

'Thee bedder not bring another dog oma,' Tamsyn muttered under her breath.

'Be quiet, woman.' He shifted his attention back to Rob. 'What has she been telling you?'

'Only what she knows to be true. A stranger came here that day while you were away. Do you have any idea who he might have been?'

His answer was a sharp 'No', but it was not as pointed as the look he sent winging toward his wife. 'She should have asked his name.'

Tamsyn's retort was incomprehensible to Rob, but he could guess the gist of it. She thought her husband should have been there to ask for himself. In a huff, she rose from the bench, stalked to the cradle to gather up the sleeping infant, and left the room to join her other children.

Shaking his head, a grim smile on his face, Ludlow turned to

Rosamond. 'In the ordinary way of things, I would have attempted to learn his identity as soon as my wife told me about him, but it was just after my return that Sir Walter's horse came home without him. The uproar that followed wiped all thought of the stranger from my mind.'

Ever-mindful of Benet's accusation, even though he did not put much stock in it, Rob asked, 'How many times have you admitted Henry Leveson to Priory House?'

'Only once, some months ago, but I saw him again, at a distance, speaking with Sir Walter. It was not my place to question how he got in that time, or after you came to Priory House.'

'I am told there is a wicket by the old entrance to the manor.' Rob heard Rosamond make a small sound of surprise, but she did not interrupt.

'So there is,' Ludlow agreed. 'I can remember when the priory buildings still stood, and the former stables, too, but that way in is kept locked.'

An agile fellow like Leveson was capable of climbing over the wall, if no one had been there to let him in. It scarce mattered, since Sir Walter had not been killed at home. His murderer had waited until he was some distance from Priory House before he struck. Not Ludlow, Rob decided, although he would take pains to verify the gatekeeper's presence in Langore that morning to be sure.

'Are you thinking that this stranger is the one who killed Sir Walter?' Ludlow's brow furrowed. 'You must not blame my wife. She'd not have been able to keep him out.'

'She did nothing wrong,' Rosamond said, 'but whatever person he talked to inside Priory House may have told him where to find Sir Walter. Can you think of anyone in the household who'd want Sir Walter dead?'

Ludlow avoided meeting her eyes. 'I have no proof.'

'We do not need proof,' Rob said. 'Not yet. Give us a name.'

'Carnsey,' Ludlow said.

'Ulick Carnsey?' Rob had included Sir Walter's secretary on their list of suspects along with everyone else at Priory House, but the fellow had been so helpful in their investigation that he had placed his name near the bottom. 'Why Carnsey?'

Ludlow's voice was devoid of emotion, but a slight flaring of his nostrils betrayed the depth of his anger. 'He is a fellow always out for the main chance. There's a wealthy widow at Priory House now, but even before Sir Walter died, Carnsey was ever eager to curry her favor.'

'Nonsense,' Rosamond said.

Do not be too hasty, Rob thought. Lady Pendennis might be getting on in years and be crippled besides, but she had inherited a third of everything Sir Walter owned. If she had acquired her son's wardship, control of the rest would have been in her hands until Benet reached his majority at the age of twenty-one. If she remarried in the interim, her new husband, by law, would take possession of it all.

'Ulick dooth not want that old woman.' Tamsyn spoke from the doorway. Her face worked in a way that suggested she was on the verge of tears.

Ludlow glared at her. 'He'd not want you, either, you bran-faced she-cat, not even if you were a widow. Not as a wife.'

Tamsyn seized a heavy brass candlestick from a nearby table and threw it at him before storming up the stairs to the bedchamber above. Rob wondered what she'd done with the baby. Ludlow, without a passing thought for his offspring, gave a low growl and set off after his wife.

'Bran-faced?' Rob asked.

'A reference to her freckles.' Rosamond regarded the ceiling. All was silent above. 'I do not believe we will learn any more here today.'

Together they left the gatehouse. 'Carnsey and Tamsyn? Is that likely?'

'Ludlow seems to think so. Reason enough, I suppose, to accuse him of other atrocities.'

'Do you believe it?'

Rosamond considered before she answered. 'Suspect everyone and trust no one – is that not what we agreed?'

'We did. For the present, then, Ludlow's accusation against Carnsey must carry the same weight as Benet's claim that Henry Leveson is the guilty party.'

THIRTY-ONE

The rain had stopped by the time Rosamond returned to the guest lodgings, but the improvement in the weather did nothing to ease her troubled state of mind. Was anything as it seemed? Her mother was dependent upon some unknown narcotic to ease her pain. Carnsey was making the beast with two backs with Ludlow's wife – or at least the gatekeeper thought he was. What other secrets did Priory House hide?

If there were more, she could not spare the time to delve into them. She had promised to bring her stepfather's murderer to justice. That must be her only concern.

She had bits and pieces of the puzzle, but as yet no notion of the whole. If the murders were tied to a treasonous plot, as Henry Leveson maintained, then the pattern was more murky still. She trusted Leveson, but only up to a point, and she silently damned Sir Francis Walsingham for keeping his cards so close to his chest.

Think, she ordered, flinging herself down full length on the bed and staring up at the tester overhead. Her mind strayed to pirates, although piracy had no connection to Sir Walter that she knew of. Pirates took their captured prizes to Ireland. She tried to remember what she knew of England's presence there.

The Irish were a rebellious lot. Englishmen sent to govern in the Irish pale frequently bankrupted themselves in the queen's service. When she had been living in Kent, she had heard talk that Sir Henry Sidney, whose home was nearby at Penshurst, had refused the queen's offer to create a barony for him because, thanks to his service in Ireland, he no longer had the wherewithal to support a title.

Who was governor now? She had no idea, but she did know that there were English plantations in Ireland, settlements founded to enhance England's right to govern there. More were planned. Rosamond frowned. If English rule was widespread in Ireland, the authorities there must be taking the same stand against piracy that prevailed at home, but if pirates used Irish ports, they'd apparently met with little success. Mayhap that was what pardoning so many pirates was meant to accomplish. The pirates sworn to serve Queen Elizabeth were expected to betray others of their kind.

Did any of that matter? Rosamond pounded her fists on the coverlet in frustration. She must not allow herself to be distracted from her most pressing task – to find Sir Walter's killer. Pirates might not be involved at all if the person behind his death was someone at Priory House.

Rob had gone from the gatehouse to the stables to talk with Gryffyn and the other grooms. Instead of hiding in her bedchamber, brooding, Rosamond should have been questioning the women of the household. One of the maidservants might have seen the mysterious visitor Tamsyn Ludlow had admitted. One of them might be able to describe him. One might even have recognized him.

She would speak with Audrey first, Rosamond decided. She needed to question Eleanor's companion about that powder, as well, and now that she thought about it, she was also curious to hear Audrey's account of her life in Westmorland.

With renewed determination, Rosamond left the guest lodgings for the main part of the house. She glanced into the solar, but only her mother and Melka were there. She crept away again before either of them noticed her.

Melka had taken over the small room hard by Eleanor's bedchamber, displacing Audrey. Rosamond considered where the girl might now be lodged. The maidservants shared dormitory-style quarters in the garret of the same wing that housed Benet's schoolroom, but there was also, she recalled, a tiny private chamber there. A series of governesses had occupied that room when she was a girl. As Audrey was a female retainer of slightly greater importance than a maidservant, that seemed the most likely place for her to be housed.

A few minutes later, Rosamond paused just outside the little room. She could hear faint sounds within – the rustle of a skirt and the swish of a page being turned. Easing the door open, she slipped quietly inside.

The ceiling sloped sharply above her head. The only light

came from a small window set into a gable. At this hour of the day, it was on the wrong side of the house to provide much illumination. Audrey had lit a candle to read by.

The girl sat on a bench, turned so that she was facing away from Rosamond. Although she was unaware that anyone had come into her bedchamber, Rosamond had no qualms about spying on her. She was intrigued by what she observed. Audrey squinted at the words on the page before her, using her index finger to guide her from one to the next. It appeared that she had been taught the rudiments of reading but had not perfected the skill.

Stepping closer, still without attracting Audrey's attention, Rosamond peered over the girl's shoulder. The text that leapt out at her provoked an involuntary gasp. This was not a book approved by the *English* church!

Audrey's head snapped around. Her eyes went wide when she realized that Rosamond had seen what she was reading. She tried to slam the book shut and whisk it out of sight, but Rosamond was too fast for her. She wrestled it out of Audrey's grip.

One look at the title confirmed her worst fears: *The Exercise of a Christian Life*, written in Italian by the Reverend Father Gaspar Loarte of the Society of Jesus and newly translated into English by I.S.

'This is a forbidden book. A Jesuit book. You could be thrown in gaol simply for possessing it.'

Audrey snatched back the contraband volume. 'You have no right to take what is mine.'

Rosamond drew in a deep, steadying breath. She wanted Audrey's cooperation, not her hostility. 'Explain to me, then, why you keep it, knowing how dangerous it is to own.' She sat on the bench Audrey had just vacated and tried to look non-threatening.

'You . . . you will not tell Lady Pendennis?'

'Why should I? I have seen how badly she treats you and I know why.'

'Then you know more than I do.'

'Shall we exchange information?' Rosamond slid sideways to make more room on the bench.

Audrey stared at her for a long moment, her indecision plain. Then she sat.

'Your father inherited the estate of an elderly relative, a Lady

Quarles. When my mother was young, she was in service to Lady Quarles. She was treated badly. When she displeased the old woman, she was turned out to fend for herself.'

'There is more to the story,' Audrey guessed.

'There is, but you have no need to know it. Why did you accept Mother's invitation?'

Bitterness seeped through every word Audrey spoke. 'How was I to know? It was obvious that I must be beholden to someone, and here was a wealthy kinswoman offering to make me her companion.'

'You had no other kin to take you in?'

'None who were welcoming. Father's fate had made them wary. He . . .'

When she faltered, Rosamond took pity on her. 'I know what happened to him, and I can guess why they were reluctant to offer to keep you. His dedication to his beliefs must have made the local authorities take a hard look at all members of the family.'

Audrey nodded. After taking a moment to compose herself, she spoke in a voice so soft that Rosamond had to strain to catch her words.

'Most of them make a show of attending church on Sunday, but they keep to the tenets of the true faith at home. They have much to lose if there is a raid while mass is being celebrated.'

'As you did.' Rosamond did not lack sympathy for the girl, but she could and did blame Audrey's father for being so blatant in his defiance of the law. Had he given no thought to what would happen to his daughter?

'I stayed for a time with a neighbor, but I knew I would have to find a way to support myself. Entering service was my only choice, other than to try to escape to the Continent and become a nun.' She smiled a little at that. 'I lack vocation. Then, at my last confession, the priest advised me to accept what I had been offered with gratitude and humility. He said I was fortunate that a distant relative had heard of my plight and was willing to find a place for me in her household.' She gave a humorless laugh. 'The generous kinswoman we imagined does not exist. She did not offer me a home out of kindness. I do much doubt she has an unselfish bone in her body. All she wanted was a poor relation who would be so indebted to her that she could order her about with impunity.'

'You have good food in your belly and a roof over your head,' Rosamond reminded her.

'I am little more than a slave!'

Rosamond's heart went out to the girl. She was tempted to rescue her and give her a home at Willow House, but the fact that she had papist leanings was reason to hesitate. Then, too, she had not yet established that Audrey was innocent of any involvement in murder and treason.

'If I had been expected to act only as a tiring maid instead of a companion,' Audrey said, 'I think I could have borne the humiliation with better grace, but your lady mother never hesitates to order me to empty the chamber pot into the privy, or help her clean herself with a rubbing cloth, or perform any number of equally demeaning tasks. It is not to be borne, and yet I must bear it.'

A draft caused the candle to flicker and sent smoke curling upward to tickle Rosamond's nose. Audrey's eyes began to water. Or was she crying? With a strangled cry, the girl slammed her fist onto the tabletop. The candlestick wobbled. The candle went out.

Rosamond did not relight it. The dimly illuminated bedchamber lent itself well to the exchange of confidences. She waited until Audrey's breathing slowed and she sensed that the girl was ready to listen.

'Will you tell me about this book?'

'It was a gift from my father and our priest said it was my sacred duty to read it and follow its precepts.' She sighed. 'In truth, I do not understand half of what it says. I was taught only the rudiments of reading at home.'

'It is a book of advice, then?' Rosamond had to admit to a certain curiosity about its contents.

Audrey nodded. 'It offers guidance to English Catholics cut off from Mother Church by the laws of our homeland. I did not need to read it when my father was alive. I did not have to hide my faith then. It was no secret that our household clung to the old religion. Father recused himself, and me, from attending church services, even though that meant he had to pay a heavy fine for each absence. There were other recusants nearby – a community. We supported each other in our beliefs and when the priest came, we celebrated the sacraments together.'

'Those days are gone, Audrey. You must accept that.'

The girl stared at her hands, clasped tightly in her lap. 'Everything must be done in secret now, or the consequences are terrible. I had hoped . . . the priest said there were Catholic families aplenty in Cornwall. If there are, I have never met any. How could I? Every Sunday I must attend church in the local parish. Lady Pendennis is no Puritan, but she has no use for recusants, either.'

'Possession of this book could condemn you to prison.'

'I keep it hidden.' Audrey hesitated, then blurted out a confession. 'I have thought of destroying it, but it is all I have left of my father.'

She stood, taking the book with her, and moved to the chest that contained her meagre possessions. The bedchamber was so small that she had only to turn to reach her bed. It was a poor thing compared to the luxury in which Eleanor slept, but Audrey did have a well-stuffed mattress and an adequate number of blankets.

A faint click drew Rosamond's attention. Audrey had opened a panel at the side of her chest. On the front, one of the carved rosettes was twisted out of alignment. Before the girl could consign the volume to its hiding place, Rosamond caught her arm.

'Let me take the book. I will keep it safe and make certain no one can use it to persecute you for your beliefs.'

Audrey clung to the book. 'Why should I trust you?'

'Why should you not? You have already shown me your hiding place. I mean you no harm, Audrey. I will try to help you if I can. And you, mayhap, can help me.'

The forbidden volume clutched tight against her bosom, Audrey stared at her. 'What do you want of me? Why did you seek me out?'

'To ask you questions.' She subsided onto the bench once more. 'The first is about the powder my mother takes. Was she already using it before you arrived at Priory House?'

'She was.'

'Was Sir Walter aware of his wife's habit?'

'I do much doubt it.' She hesitated. 'They were not a loving couple, no matter what she would have the world believe now that he is dead.'

'How often does she take the powder?'

'She cannot do without it for so much as a single day. If she is late with a dose, she falls into terrible heats, berating the servants and bewailing her fate.'

How Walter could have remained oblivious puzzled Rosamond, but she supposed he had become inured to Eleanor's complaints. She had always had a temper and had always thought of herself first.

Rosamond grimaced, knowing she shared those traits. She prided herself on *trying* to suppress them.

'Will you tell me everything you remember of the day Sir Walter died?' she asked Audrey.

'I have already done so.' Audrey placed the book in its hiding place and closed the panel that concealed it.

Rosamond pretended not to notice. 'Was what you told us you saw when you helped my mother prepare the body for burial the truth?'

Audrey shuddered at the memory. 'It was. I swear it.'

'A stranger arrived at the gate shortly after Sir Walter rode out but before his horse returned without him. Did you see this man? Do you know who he was?'

The girl gave a start of surprise, but her denial came out in a rush. 'I saw no one.'

Rosamond did not believe her. 'It is possible this mysterious visitor was the one who killed Sir Walter.'

Color rushed into Audrey's face. For a moment, Rosamond thought she was about to leap to the stranger's defense. Instead, she once again denied any knowledge of him.

'Someone at Priory House must have spoken to him,' Rosamond said.

'I was in attendance on Lady Pendennis all that morning.'

'My mother claims she was still abed when Sir Walter rode out. Do you mean to tell me that she rose before Sir Walter left?'

'I have no doubt that she did, Mistress Jaffrey. She does not sleep well unless she takes yet another powder, and she does not often do so. She says that one makes her head ache most abominably.'

Audrey's earnestness would have been more convincing had she been able to meet Rosamond's eyes. Clearly she was lying, but Rosamond did not understand why she had chosen this particular lie. If she was complicit in Sir Walter's murder, the safest and most sensible thing to do would be to admit that she had talked to the stranger and claim that although she had informed him that Sir Walter was not at home, she'd had no inkling of his evil intentions.

Rosamond hid her suspicions. After reminding the girl to be careful to keep that book well hidden, she left the garret.

As she had planned, she talked to the rest of the female members of the household and that evening she and Rob compared what they had learned during the day. They were unable to reach any useful conclusions. Too many people at Priory House were keeping secrets.

THIRTY-TWO

8 July 1584

They were in their bedchamber, breaking their fast with a modest repast of bread, cheese, and ale, when the letter arrived. Rob would have liked a bit of beef to go with the rest, but it was Wednesday and therefore a fish day when no eating of flesh was allowed. Once he closed the door behind the servant who'd brought the mysterious missive, he remained standing, staring at it. It had been folded into an oblong shape and sealed with red sealing wax imprinted with a signet ring. His name was inscribed on the outside, together with the words: 'Priory House, Cornwall.'

'I do not recognize the crest,' Rosamond said.

'Nor do I.' But he had the uneasy feeling that he would not like what it contained.

'You will never know who sent it if you do not open it.'

Rob managed a faint smile. 'Are you so certain of that? Here – what do you see?' He thrust it into her hands. 'Was this penned by the sender or by a clerk?'

Rosamond carried it to a window seat where the light was better. She sat, curling her legs beneath her, to study the writing.

'Italic script, but was it written by a man or a woman? One of my earliest tutors, one who did not hold that position long, claimed that Italic, developed from the Roman hand, was the easiest cursive script to learn and therefore the only style of writing suitable for girls. Females, he claimed, lack the patience to take pains with their education. Boys, whose capacity for learning is naturally greater, are taught the Secretary hand.'

Rob laughed as he joined her. 'In truth, boys are often taught both, as were you, but you must allow that Italic is both easier to write and easier to read.'

'Oh, yes,' she agreed, 'and easier to forge, as well. Have a care, Rob. This may be an attempt to lure you into a trap.' Although she spoke the words lightly, there was a flicker of concern in her eyes.

Rob reclaimed the letter, broke the seal, unfolded the page, and read the message. The signature, if not the handwriting, was familiar – Christopher Carleill.

'Well?' Rosamond demanded.

'Read it for yourself.' He watched her warily while she devoured the contents.

'Lundy Island?' She frowned. 'Someone mentioned that place not long ago. Where is Lundy Island?'

'In the Bristol Channel.'

'Carleill can scarce expect you to swim there!'

'He does not.' Rob sighed. 'Before we left London I left orders for the *Rosamond* to sail to Bristol as soon as she was seaworthy. Word was waiting for me when we returned from our trip to Padstow and Boscastle that she arrived there safely. I planned to surprise you when it was time for us to go home and make the return journey by sea.'

'Carleill appears to have plans of his own for both you and your ship.'

'So he does.' The captain's instructions, politely worded but with the force of a command behind them, were for Rob to come with all speed to Lundy Island and bring Henry Leveson with him.

'I suppose you cannot simply ignore this summons?'

Rob shook his head. 'I promised him that I would be at his disposal. I owe him that much.'

'I know. You feel you owe Carleill your life, but clearly Walsingham is the puppetmaster behind this venture. Are you willing to dance to *his* tune?'

'Carleill's letter says only that he has been delegated to patrol the coast of Ireland in search of pirates. Piracy must concern us all.'

'And how, pray, does he expect you to help him capture pirate ships? The *Rosamond* is a merchant vessel.'

'I feel certain he has a plan.' He also felt sure there was a great deal that Carleill had left out of the letter.

'This is tied to Leveson's talk of conspiracy. It must be.' Leaping to her feet, Rosamond began to pace. 'Why else would he instruct you to bring Walsingham's agent with you?'

Rob stood more slowly. 'Mayhap if I join in this endeavor, I will discover the answer to that question, and with it the identity of the man who killed Sir Walter.'

She stopped short, whirled around, and reached for him, clutching handfuls of his linen shirt in her fists. 'It is too dangerous. You must not go.'

'Not even if the answers we have been seeking are on Lundy Island?' Gently, he freed himself and turned back to the window, staring down into the stable yard below as he considered the matter. 'Even if the murderer belongs to this household, he did not act alone. If you stay here to pursue—'

'Rob, no! You cannot risk your life battling pirates.'

He smiled to himself. Trust Rosamond not to use the argument that he should stay at Priory House because she wanted him here with her. 'I will be aboard my own ship, Ros. If the danger is too great, I can always sail away from it.'

'And if some pirate decides the *Rosamond* would make an excellent prize? You may not be given a chance to flee.'

'Knowing Carleill, he is gathering an entire fleet of ships. There is safety in numbers.'

He spoke with more confidence than he felt, but he hoped what he said was true.

'Nothing need be decided today.' Rosamond's glower was fierce.

'True enough,' Rob agreed. 'We must wait for Leveson to return.'

'Then let us hope,' Rosamond muttered, 'that he is delayed for a considerable time longer in Padstow.'

THIRTY-THREE

10 July 1584

Contrary to Rosamond's wishes, Leveson and Carnsey returned to Priory House the day after Rob received the letter from Captain Carleill. They'd had no luck discovering how Honor Piers had traveled to Boscastle or why she'd left Padstow in the first place.

The following morning, Rob left, taking both men with him. Rosamond forced a smile when her husband looked back to salute her, but it faded as soon as he faced forward again.

She told herself it was not as if she wished to go with them. She had more than enough to keep her busy right where she was. For the rest of that morning, however, her thoughts continually drifted to the little party riding toward Boscastle, where they would hire a boat to take them on to the anchorage where the *Rosamond* waited.

It was near noontide before Rosamond ventured into her mother's solar. She found Eleanor, Melka, and Audrey seated in a circle near the window, bright fabrics spread across their laps and needles busy. A heavy bowl brimming with sweets sat on a nearby table.

Eleanor glanced up, caught sight of her daughter in the doorway, and sneered. 'A pity you did not leave with your husband.'

Her casual contempt roused Rosamond's temper. A powerful urge to retaliate had her blurting out what she'd come to say without a hint of finesse. 'The matter of Benet's guardianship has been settled. The Court of Wards has given him into my keeping.'

Her mother's face drained of color before it flashed red with anger. She threw her embroidery to the floor. 'How dare you take what is mine!'

'Would you prefer a stranger had charge of him?'

'In truth, I would. You will turn my child against me.'

'I will protect your child and his estate. What he thinks of his mother is your doing and yours alone.'

'Ungrateful wretch!' Eleanor seized the dish full of confits and hurled it at her.

Rosamond ducked. Melka and Audrey abandoned their stools to scramble out of Eleanor's range. The sound of other items being thrown followed Rosamond out of the solar and down the stairs.

For the rest of the day, she stayed well away from her mother. She talked to the men of the household, confirming what the each of them had already told Rob, and once again questioned the women servants. She learned nothing new about Sir Walter, nor could she confirm that there was an illicit relationship between Ulick Carnsey and Tamsyn Ludlow. She did discover that the two had something in common. Neither had troubled to cultivate friendship with anyone else at Priory House.

Toward evening, after she supped alone in her lodgings, Rosamond repaired to Sir Walter's study to commit to paper all she had learned about the three murders and the events surrounding them. She included the report she'd received from Leveson upon his return the previous day.

He and Carnsey had found no one in Padstow who would admit to knowing when Honor Piers had left her cottage or who might have given her passage by sea to Boscastle. Rosamond had not been surprised by that outcome. Leveson had been forced to rely upon Carnsey to translate both questions and answers. That fact alone had marked them as persons no local man should trust.

But Leveson had also relayed one additional bit of information. Rosamond smiled to herself as she recorded it. It seemed that her questioning of the coroner after Alexander Trewinard's death had annoyed that good gentleman. Upon his return home, Master Dodson had complained of her unwomanly curiosity to his friends, one of whom was a coffin-maker. This fellow, who could boast of a more than casual acquaintance with dead bodies, had been the one to take charge of Honor Piers's remains and had shared with Walsingham's agent his observation that a dead body stayed warm up to three hours after death. Beyond that, the body became rigid and cold, but by a day and a half later, it was no longer stiff.

Rosamond could not recall if Alexander Trewinard had been warm to the touch when she examined his body, but she knew that it had still been possible to move his limbs. Therefore he had been killed that morning, most likely not long before her arrival. That meant that neither Leveson nor Carnsey could have killed him. They had been with her at the time.

She wished she could also rule out the possibility that Leveson was working with another of Walsingham's agents, or with a traitor to the realm, but she could not. With a sigh, she read over the pages she had filled, then sharpened her pen and once more dipped it into the inkwell. On a fresh sheet of paper, she made three columns, writing the name of one victim at the top of each.

The list of those who might have killed Honor Piers was short, consisting of 'person unknown' and, since she had disliked him so intensely, the vicar, Robert Archer. 'Person unknown' also appeared among the suspects in Trewinard's murder, along with Morwen Trewinard and Diggory Pyper. Although the list under Walter's name also included 'person unknown', this time she added 'in black cloak'. She might have included everyone at Priory House on that list, but she limited herself to those who had behaved most suspiciously – her mother, Ludlow, Leveson, and Audrey. She hesitated, then added Gryffyn and Carnsey, simply because they had been with Sir Walter on his last visit to Boscastle.

She could not decide if she had too many suspects or too few. In frustration she flung the pen across the room.

'Damnation,' she swore, staring in dismay at the spatter of ink it left behind. Black specks stained the edge of the expensive Turkey carpet covering a nearby table and dotted the rushes on the floor.

A sound from the doorway sent a wave of embarrassment washing through her. Bad enough that she had let her temper get the better of her for a second time that day, but to have Jacob witness this latest lapse was the final indignity. It was only when she saw the morose expression on his face that she realized it was not her behavior that concerned him.

Her first thought was that something had happened to Rob on his way to Bristol, but it was too soon to have word of the travelers. The trouble had to be closer to home. With a grimace, she asked, 'What has my mother done now?'

Jacob entered the room, stopping to pick up the pen and shake his head at the damage to the carpet before he returned it to her. 'This is as nothing compared to the ruin of your mother's solar. She broke a window and a stool and she used the broken stool leg to strike Melka on the arm. Young Audrey fared only slightly better. Lady Pendennis boxed her ears.'

Rosamond sighed. 'I fear I am to blame for those things, too. I mishandled telling Mother that I am Benet's guardian.'

Jacob took off his spectacles and cleaned them with his handkerchief, not speaking until they were once again perched on the end of his nose. 'Mayhap that is true, but Lady Pendennis's heats are nothing new. Her servants have oft times been similarly mistreated and for less cause. There was no need for the girl to run away.'

'The girl? You mean Audrey? She's gone?'

'With all her possessions,' Jacob said. 'She left by the wicket. I sent men out to search for her, but they were unsuccessful. It is possible that she had help to escape.'

Rosamond looked at the list she had made. Audrey's name leapt out at her. Had the girl – the papist girl – left because she could no longer tolerate Eleanor's treatment of her . . . or because she feared that her part in a murderous, treasonous conspiracy was about to come to light?

THIRTY-FOUR

12 July 1584

A fishing boat with a crew that knew how to navigate the hazards of the Bristol Channel brought Rob and his companions safely into the anchorage called King Road. It had not been an easy journey. Tidal currents between Boscastle and the mouth of the River Avon often ran at twice the speed of a heavily-laden ship. Shallows, flats, islands, reefs, and outcroppings of rock added to the danger, as did the possibility of a sudden fierce northwesterly gale.

The *Rosamond* awaited them at anchor, her name a beacon in fresh paint. She was a bark of fifty tons with a crew of eighteen men. Other ships, all of them caravels of 100 to 150 tons, bobbed alongside her. Lighters and ships' boats darted in and out among the larger vessels.

Most of the ships anchored off Portishead were waiting for the tide to carry them seven miles upriver to the harbor in the heart of Bristol. Since the Avon twisted and turned and passed through a narrow gorge before reaching its destination, they would also need the services of a river pilot to reach port and unload their cargoes. Then they would, most likely, wallow in shallow water, bearing a strong resemblance to beached whales, for nine hours out of the next twelve, before the next high tide would lift them free of the mud.

Other ships in the anchorage, including the *Rosamond*, awaited a favorable wind to carry them down channel. Now that Rob had arrived, the ship he owned would sail at the first opportunity. He felt a healthy burst of excitement, as well as a deep sense of pride, as he scrambled up the boarding steps sticking out from the side of the hull like a series of shallow shelves.

Once on deck, he turned. Leveson was right behind him, but so was Sir Walter's secretary. Rob had not expected Carnsey to come aboard. More surprising still, the fishing boat that had brought them from Boscastle was already pulling away from the *Rosamond*.

'Do you mean to travel overland to return to Priory House?' Rob asked. 'If so, I am told there is a ferry that will take you downriver to Bristol for tuppence.'

'If it is all the same to you, I would rather accompany you to Lundy Island. Since Sir Walter's death, I have had little to do and Jacob Littleton appears to have assumed responsibility for those few tasks that remained.' Carnsey offered a self-deprecating smile. 'I find myself in need of occupation.'

'This is not a pleasure jaunt,' Rob warned him.

'I am not a fool. It is plain enough that you and Master Leveson have been called away by duty. But it is also clear that this business has some connection to those brigands who attacked us at Tintagel and I would welcome a chance at revenge.'

Carnsey had proven himself a loyal retainer in that skirmish, Rob reminded himself. In truth, there was less reason to mistrust Sir Walter's secretary than to suspect Leveson of deceit. Walsingham's man had been acting in a most peculiar manner ever since they boarded that fishing boat in Boscastle. While Rob had found the journey exhilarating and was looking forward to the next stage, it was obvious that Leveson did not share his enthusiasm.

Taking both his traveling companions with him, Rob began his inspection of the *Rosamond*. Given that she had just been overhauled, he anticipated no problems. One deep breath assured him that caulk and tar had been recently applied. Yet another strong smell confirmed that the inside of the ship had been thoroughly scoured and doused with vinegar.

A sudden swell had all three of them staggering to keep their footing. Rob smiled, remembering that it had taken him several days to get his 'sea legs' on the voyage to Muscovy. Carnsey grunted but stayed upright. Leveson groaned, his face pale and a look of desperation in his eyes.

Rob's smile broadened as he belatedly understood the reason for the other man's odd behavior. The greenish tinge to Leveson's skin confirmed his deduction. Rob clapped Walsingham's agent on the back and spoke in a hearty voice.

'Be of good cheer. It is not possible to die of seasickness.' He held off warning Leveson that the constant rocking of the *Rosamond* at anchor was as nothing compared to the sometimes violent motion of a ship under sail.

The afflicted man broke away from his companions and raced for the rail. When he had cast his most recent meal into the water, Rob helped him to the captain's cabin, vacated to provide lodging for the vessel's owner.

'When we meet with Carleill,' Rob said, 'you can ask to be put ashore.'

Looking more miserable than ever, Leveson shook his head. He reached inside his doublet and drew forth a grimy, much-folded paper. 'My orders come direct from Walsingham. I go where you go, Jaffrey.'

Seizing the page, Rob smoothed it out to read for himself, but it was written in code. That fact did more to convince him of its authenticity than anything Leveson might say. For all Rob knew, it was naught but a laundry list, but he was inclined to think otherwise, especially when Leveson took it back, declared that Walsingham's instructions were too dangerous to keep, and ripped the page to shreds.

THIRTY-FIVE

13 July 1584

T hree days after Audrey disappeared from Priory House, Rosamond rode into Liskeard. She was accompanied by her usual escorts – Charles, Luke, and John – and by Jacob Littleton. Since it was Monday, the day of the weekly market, their arrival went unnoticed by most of the townspeople. Liskeard was second only to Bodmin as a market town and drew both buyers and sellers in droves, including many strangers.

After a long morning on horseback, Rosamond was out of sorts and in no frame of mind to be distracted by the high, rocky terrain. Even so, she could not help but notice that the local castle, located on a prominence north of the town, was naught but a ruin. It appeared to be in use as a cattle pound.

The conduit in the center of town, although it must once have been impressive, had seen better days, but St Martin's Church was a fine, large building atop a hill to the south. Rosamond considered the structure in light of the intelligence Jacob had gathered. Much of it came from Sir Walter's carefully kept lists of those individuals suspected of being secret Catholics. The vicar of St Martin's had provided him with the names of several parishioners alleged to practice forbidden Catholic rites in the privacy of their homes. He believed that the widow of the head of a minor branch of the Mohun family was the chief offender. There had never been enough proof to arrest her, but she was suspected of harboring a Jesuit priest.

The Mohun manor lay just beyond the town. The stables were large and the number of outbuildings – everything from a brewhouse to a dovecote – suggested a goodly number of servants might once have been employed in the household. That did not seem to be the case any longer. Everything looked a trifle run down and the only person who appeared to greet them was a young serving maid.

Rosamond's brusque manner and unstoppable forward momentum forced the girl to scurry backward or be run over. She felt no sympathy for the terrified maid but rather addressed her in a tone of voice that brooked no disobedience. 'Fetch Mistress Gravitt. Mistress Jaffrey would speak with her.'

Mouth hanging open, eyes fixed on Rosamond as if she expected her to grow horns, the maidservant sidled along the screens passage until she reached an opening. Then she was gone. Rosamond could hear her sturdy leather shoes pounding across a stone-flagged floor.

At a more leisurely pace, leaving the four men who had accompanied her to Liskeard in the passage, Rosamond followed in the girl's wake, striding boldly into the great hall that was the house's principal room. It was dominated by two features, a huge fireplace and a staircase leading to the upper regions of the house.

As this was summer, there was no fire in the hearth, but the rushes on the floor were fresh and the scent of fleabane rose up with every step Rosamond took. She advanced to the center of the room and surveyed her surroundings, wondering if she had startled a priest into hiding by her sudden arrival.

Quietly confident, Rosamond waited for Audrey to appear. It was possible she was wrong and the girl had fled to some other household, but this was the most likely refuge for a Catholic girl seeking her own kind. When a sound from the stairs drew her gaze in that direction, she made a small sound of satisfaction.

Audrey descended, her steps slow and reluctant, an expression of chagrin on her face. She kept her hands clasped tightly together, no doubt to keep them from trembling.

'You must not blame Mistress Mohun,' she whispered when she came to a stop in front of Rosamond. 'She has been nothing but kind to me.'

'Why did you run away, Audrey?' Rosamond asked.

The girl's chin came up at a defiant angle. 'I was willing to be humble, Mistress Jaffrey, but I am not willing to be beaten for no reason.'

Taken aback, Rosamond peered more closely at Audrey's face, for the first time noticing three-day-old bruises that had not yet faded. 'I heard that Mother boxed your ears but no more than that. You should have come to me.'

'You refused to take me into your service.'

That was not quite how Rosamond remembered it, but she did not correct the girl. Instead she went on the offensive. 'You lied to me, Audrey. You said you knew no Catholic families in Cornwall.'

'I did not.' She took a step back when faced with Rosamond's stern expression. 'Not at first.'

'And when did that situation change? On the day, mayhap, that Sir Walter died?'

Audrey paled but this time she held her ground. 'So you know.'

'That the man in the black cloak who came to Priory House that day was a priest looking for you? I did not, not for certain, until you just now confirmed it.'

Audrey hung her head. 'Was it so wrong to want to escape? I did not think I would have the courage to flee, even knowing where there was a family that would take me in, but when Lady Pendennis struck me, I was afraid for my life.'

'What of the priest?' Rosamond asked. 'Did he aid you in traveling to Liskead?'

'What if he did? He is not here now. You will never find him.'

'I have no interest in finding him unless he did more than counsel you that day. Tell me true, Audrey. Did he express any interest in Sir Walter's whereabouts? Did you tell him that Sir Walter had gone riding or where he was bound?'

'We did not speak of Sir Walter at all. Indeed, for all I knew then, he was still at Priory House.'

A new voice drifted down the stairs. 'Audrey holds you in high regard, Mistress Jaffrey. Was she mistaken in thinking you are an honorable person?'

The speaker was a little woman of middle years who was as round as she was tall. Her smile seemed genuine, but reproach underscored her words.

'Mistress Mohun, I presume?'

'Widow of Godfrey Mohun, gentleman,' she agreed, 'and lady of this manor even if I cannot call myself *Lady* Mohun. I have been taught since childhood that there is no excuse for the brutal mistreatment of young women, in service or not. For the nonce, Audrey is under my protection.'

'And later?'

'A like-minded family will take her in, one living at some distance from anyone who might recognize her and force her to return to her former mistress.'

'She is not a slave, nor even a servant bound for a year to one employer.'

'Nevertheless, I would prefer that she be safe and well cared for, both physically and spiritually.'

Rosamond's brows lifted.

The woman chuckled. 'Whatever suspicions you may have, Mistress Jaffrey, even those young Audrey may have been foolish enough to confirm, we have always been good, upstanding church-goers in this household. During a long and respected lifetime, my husband's only offense against the parish was to object to the practice of making pews available to buy, sell, or lease. He thought it appalling that parishioners should be charged anywhere from two pence to two shillings to attend worship services.'

Rosamond met Mistress Mohun's eyes with a steady gaze. 'My interest does not lie in Audrey or her beliefs and I do not care what rites are or are not practiced in this house. In truth, it is a relief to have her gone from Priory House and a certain book with her. It could have caused much trouble for my family had anyone discovered it there.'

'Why, then,' the widow Mohun asked, 'did you follow her here?'

'To assure myself that her flight had naught to do with the murder of Sir Walter Pendennis.'

Rosamond believed Audrey and the astonished look on Mistress Mohun's face only added to her conviction that the young woman was innocent. Reassured, and in a much better frame of mind, she shortly thereafter took her leave of them.

THIRTY-SIX

Liskeard boasted a goodly inn. Although it was bustling with market-day activity, Rosamond was able to bespeak a small, private room in which to dine. She felt the need for a period of quiet thought before she and her men set off on the return journey to Priory House. She told herself she was glad to eliminate both Audrey and the mysterious stranger as suspects in murder and treason, but those who remained on her list did not seem any more likely to be guilty. The thought of failing in her self-imposed mission was intolerable.

One thing seemed plain. No single person had killed all three victims. It was even possible that the villain behind the deaths had delegated others to do the dirty work in all three cases. As she ate and quenched her thirst, she considered each possibility in turn.

Her mother was dangerous and unstable, but she risked losing more than she gained by killing her husband . . . unless Sir Walter had once again discovered that she had involved herself in a treasonous plot. But *how* had she done it? She was more mobile by far than she had been in Rosamond's youth, but she was not capable of traveling any distance over rough ground on foot and if she had ridden out that day, one of the grooms would have said so when Rob questioned them.

Henry Leveson had admitted to secret visits to Cornwall. Had he been lurking near Priory House on the day Sir Walter died? Had he acted, on his own or on behalf of Sir Francis Walsingham, to eliminate a threat? What threat? There was the rub. Sir Walter had been a loyal Englishman. If Sir Francis had sworn him to silence about some secret matter, Rosamond's stepfather would have given his word and kept it, even if he had misgivings about the scheme. That Leveson had acted on his own did not make sense, either. What could he hope to gain from betraying his powerful master?

Was Leveson in league with the pirates? That did not seem reasonable, but was that only because Rosamond did not have any idea what it was that the pirates wanted? What *would* pirates want? Rich cargoes – that went without saying. A safe harbor. Boscastle, mayhap?

She was quick to dismiss that idea. Once in Boscastle's inner harbor, ships would be trapped, but Lundy Island, where Rob was bound, was said to be a pirate haven. What if there were two factions, those pardoned and sworn to fight for the queen and those who had evaded capture and had some other plan in mind?

Silently damning Sir Francis Walsingham and his penchant for keeping secrets, Rosamond rose and began to pace. She had finished her meal without tasting a single morsel.

Even a small amount of information would have been an enormous help in finding a connection between Sir Walter's death and those of Alexander Trewinard and Honor Piers. She wondered if Sir Walter had somehow threatened the pirates who used Lundy Island as a base of operations, but she did not see how he could have. From everything she'd heard, he'd had no interest in trying to control either piracy or smuggling. That he'd turned a blind eye to Trewinard's trade in contraband was proof of it.

On every circuit of the inn chamber, Rosamond passed the door. The sixth or seventh time she did so, she was dimly aware that someone had opened it and stepped inside. She paid little heed, assuming the intruder was a servant come to clear away the remains of her meal. Only when she heard quick, light footfalls behind her did she realize her danger. By then, it was too late.

Something heavy and suffocating settled over her head. In the next instant her arms were pinned to her sides and she was lifted off her feet. The world tilted as her captor slung her over his shoulder. Ignoring her muffled cries for help, as well as her attempts to kick him, he carried her swiftly along the inn's narrow corridor and into another room. Even through the thickness of wool that imprisoned her, Rosamond could hear the door thud closed and the click of a key as it was turned in a lock.

A moment later, she was deposited on her feet and released. Even before she began to fight her way out of the heavy folds draped over her, she reached for the knife in her boot. Her fingertips had scarce grazed the handle when she was shoved backward into a chair. Large, strong hands settled on her shoulders.

'I mean you no harm, Rosamond, but we must not be seen together.'

She stilled. She did not recognize the voice and she most assuredly did not trust her captor, but as long as he had hold of her, she could not reach her weapon. She heartily wished she had not removed her cloak with its hidden dagger. That garment remained draped over the back of a chair in the room where she had dined.

The man hesitated, as if trying to decide if he dared release her.

In the dark, smothering prison of heavy woolen cloth, Rosamond's breathing was ragged. Her heart raced. Then she sneezed.

After a moment of startled silence, she heard a bark of laughter.

The blanket covering her was swept up and off in one movement, leaving her free to glare at the reprobate grinning down at her. She recognized him at once, despite the many years since she had last seen him.

'I had forgotten that your father owns land in Liskeard,' she said.

Rosamond was pleased to hear that her voice was level. Diggory Pyper had too many advantages over her already. He did not need to know how frightened she was.

'And I had forgotten how stubborn you were as a child.'

'I persevere,' she corrected him, lifting her chin so that she could look down her nose at him.

He laughed again. 'I liked you in those days. You had spirit.'

Rosamond fumbled for the handkerchief in her pocket and blew her nose. That gave her time to study her childhood friend. He had a commanding presence. Not only was he a large man who radiated physical strength, but there was also an aura of authority about him. Although he was dressed in plain clothing more suited to a yeoman than a gentleman, no one would ever mistake him for a person of no consequence. Few men, she suspected, ever contradicted him.

He placed a second chair in front of the one Rosamond occupied and seated himself. He was so close that their knees were touching, much too close for her to draw the knife in her boot without him noticing. He would disarm her before she had it halfway out of its sheath.

'By what right do you abduct me?' she challenged him.

Diggory's smile vanished. His expression serious, with not even the hint of a twinkle in his bright blue eyes, he leaned toward her and took her hands in his. Even through the gloves they both wore, she could feel the heat of his grip. 'To warn you. You must stop asking questions, Rosamond.'

'Why?'

'To preserve your life. There are some who already perceive you as a threat. If you persist, you will be eliminated. Three deaths are more than enough.'

'Did you kill my stepfather?'

'I am not a murderer.'

'No – only a pirate, or so I hear.'

He shook his head. 'You always were one to tease a tiger. I am not your enemy, Rosamond. I am trying, in my own small way, to help you.'

'Why did Alexander Trewinard give Sir Walter your name?'

Her question seemed to surprise him. He pulled away, releasing her hands. She studied his face but could find no sign of anger in his expression. If anything, he looked rueful.

'I need answers,' Rosamond said.

'You are better off without them.'

Diggory did not appear to have any evil intent. Her fear of him had subsided, but Rosamond still contemplated drawing her knife and pressing it to his throat. *That* would persuade him to tell her what he knew! Instead, for the nonce, she left her weapon where it was and tried sweet reason. As a boy, he had been biddable and willing to please. If she was lucky, old habits died hard.

'It was my stepfather, Sir Walter Pendennis, who was murdered,' she reminded him. 'I cannot allow his killer to escape justice.'

'I would feel the same if it was my father who'd been slain, but there is more at stake here than one man's death.'

'Two men,' she corrected him. 'And one woman.'

'Even so.'

'What is at stake?' she demanded. 'If you are trying to protect England's enemies as they plot an invasion, you had best rethink your plans.'

'How much do you know?' He seized her upper arm in a bruising grip and gave her a little shake.

She glared at the offending hand. 'I know that there have long been rumors that the Spanish are about to attack the south coast of England. If such an invasion is real and imminent, it is your duty to warn the Lord Lieutenant.'

Diggory removed his hand and held it up, together with the other one, in a gesture of surrender. 'No lectures, I beg of you. You do not know as much as you think you do.'

'Then enlighten me.'

'I cannot.'

'You are a most annoying fellow. *Are* you, in truth, a pirate?' She was beginning to think he might be a spy instead, but for whom?

'Some might say so.' The engaging smile returned. 'Others take me for a simple merchant. In truth, there are times when little differentiates the two. I have a ship and seek to transport profitable cargo.'

'*Pirates* are executed.'

'Some are, yes.'

'And some are pardoned. Some side with England's enemies and some, despite their crimes, remain true Englishmen. Which sort are you, Diggory?'

Rosamond felt certain she knew what his answer would be. If he had been on the side of the traitors, she would already be dead.

'I am loyal to Crown and country, so long as that stand does not go against my own best interests. You can ask your friend Leveson if you do not believe me.'

Rosamond drew in a sharp breath. 'You know Henry Leveson?'

'I have met with him twice since Sir Walter's death.'

It was not news to him, then, that Trewinard had told Sir Walter to talk to him, only that Rosamond knew of it. 'When?' she asked. 'And why?'

He shook his head, but his eyes were once more alight with mischief, reminding her of the wildhead boy she'd once bested at bowls. This was all a game to him.

'When?' she insisted. 'What harm will it do for me to know that much when I can easily wheedle the truth out of Leveson himself?'

He studied her for a moment in silence, somber again. 'I

suppose there is no harm in your knowing that the first time was the day after Sir Walter's death. We met here in Liskeard.'

'And the second meeting?'

He shook his head. 'I have told you more than enough.'

'Not by half! Did Sir Walter ever find you? Were you really at sea when he questioned your father?'

'My whereabouts need not concern you.' Abruptly losing patience with her persistent questions, Diggory stood.

Still trying to assimilate the fact that he had met with Henry Leveson at all, and that Leveson had kept their meetings secret from her, Rosamond was slow to notice that Diggory was leaving. He was already at the door before she realized his intent.

'Heed my advice, Rosamond,' he said as he unlocked and opened it. 'Let matters fall out as they will while you bide safe at home.'

She surged to her feet, meaning to stop him, but the blanket he had used to subdue her had pooled on the floor beside the chair. Her boot caught in its folds and she stumbled, nearly falling flat on her face. By the time she reached the passage, Diggory Pyper was nowhere in sight.

THIRTY-SEVEN

Rosamond and her escort arrived at Priory House after dark that same evening, guided for the last few miles by a moon just past the full. The road had been nearly as brightly lit as on an overcast day, but she was glad to reach journey's end.

Diggory Pyper had not told her much, but his revelation of those meetings with Henry Leveson disturbed her peace of mind. Leveson had led her to believe he did not know the pirate captain. Had he deceived her about other matters, as well?

She did not like the way her thoughts led her, but it was a logical progression. If Leveson had been lying all along, what better reason for it than that he was behind all three murders. From that reasoning followed another conclusion – he was also involved in treason.

She could think of nothing more benign that would have prompted an otherwise honest man to kill so many people.

Despite Pyper's warning, Rosamond had little fear for her own safety. Leveson was far away . . . with Rob. She was worried about her husband. She'd had no word from him since his departure. If all had gone well, he and Leveson should be aboard the *Rosamond* and on their way to meet Captain Carleill at Lundy Island, but until Ulick Carnsey returned to Priory House, she would have no confirmation of that. She was deeply disappointed not to find Carnsey waiting when she got back from Liskeard.

The next morning, Rosamond ventured into the stables in search of Gryffyn. Sir Walter's groom was the one servant at Priory House most likely to know when Henry Leveson had visited Sir Walter. He was happy to tell her all he knew. Unfortunately, that was very little. He paid more attention to the various horses Leveson rode in on than to the man himself. Carnsey, Gryffyn told her, had spent far more time in conversation with Leveson than he had.

Resolved to ask Sir Walter's secretary about this as soon as he arrived, Rosamond returned to the house. Surely he would be back soon . . . unless Leveson had killed both Rob and Carnsey to prevent them from reaching Bristol.

With an effort, she repressed her wilder speculations. There was no sense in fretting over half-formed theories and foolish imaginings.

THIRTY-EIGHT

15 July 1584

On Wednesday, for the first time since Rosamond's return from Liskeard, her mother presided over dinner. Eleanor spoke with considerable animation to Jacob, recalling how much pleasure Sir Walter had taken in the rebuilding of Priory House. Her cheerful mood dimmed only a little when she turned to her daughter.

'I had hoped you would bring Audrey back with you,' Eleanor said.

'Did you?'

Deliberately, Rosamond picked up the crystal goblet in front of her and sipped the Rhenish wine it contained, avoiding the necessity of saying more. She did not trust her mother's high spirits. There was something not quite right about the sparkle in Eleanor's eyes.

'I was told you went to Liskeard to fetch her.'

The hard, cold note Rosamond heard beneath the words convinced her that Eleanor still held a grudge. On the surface, she looked and acted like any other gentlewoman, but Rosamond knew better. Despite appearances, Eleanor was a deeply troubled woman, one far from being in control of herself.

Rosamond's gaze shifted from her mother to Melka, standing in attendance just behind her mistress's chair. A shaft of light from the window shone on the Polish woman's face, illuminating the fresh bruise that marred her cheek. Had Rosamond not seen the effect of one of Eleanor's powders for herself, she might have given her mother the benefit of the doubt, but since she had borne witness to Eleanor's dependency on the drug and knew well how prone she was to fits of temper, she had no regrets about leaving Audrey where she was. A lie came easily to her tongue.

'Your companion was not in Liskeard.' She continued eating, although she tasted nothing of the meal.

'You're certain?' Eleanor asked.

'Even the reports that there was a recusant family living in the vicinity proved to be inaccurate. They were false rumors started by fellow parishioners jealous of a gentleman more fortunate than they.'

Jacob stared at her in slack-jawed astonishment, but he had sense enough not to challenge either statement. Later, Rosamond promised herself, she would explain to him why she felt the need to protect both Audrey and the good woman who had taken her in.

For the nonce, she held her tongue, her goal simply to survive the rest of the meal without an open quarrel with her mother. That was no easy task. Eleanor had not forgotten that Rosamond had betrayed her by purchasing Benet's wardship for herself. She managed to maintain an attitude of civility, but declared, as if the matter were already settled, that her daughter would no doubt be glad to leave her young charge behind when she returned to London.

'Nothing is settled,' Rosamond said.

'What reason have you to linger in Cornwall now that your husband has gone off adventuring?'

The barb struck home. Rosamond barely managed not to wince. 'If Benet remains here,' she said in carefully measured tones, 'it will be with supervision. Jacob received word yesterday that Sir Walter's brother Tristram is willing to act as the boy's trustee.'

'Why was I not consulted on this matter?' A dull red color crept into Eleanor's cheeks. Her hand shook as she lowered the wine she had been about to sip.

Rosamond rose from her chair. 'There was no need to consult you, Mother. You have no say in Benet's future.'

And thank God for it, she thought as she left the dining parlor. She was braced for shrieks of rage to rise up behind her but only silence followed her.

Rosamond felt sorry for her mother, but not sorry enough to trust her to change her ways. Neither would she shackle herself to Priory House solely to safeguard her half-brother from their mother's heats. She had been procrastinating, reluctant to speak with the boy about his future. She could do so no longer. Rob thought him a sensible lad. She hoped he was right.

When she reached the schoolroom, she sent both Mathy and Master Sutton away. A few minutes later, seated beside Benet on a window seat, Rosamond asked the boy what he wanted.

He looked up at her, his expression solemn. 'What choices have I?'

'Why, I suppose there are three,' Rosamond said. 'You can stay here at Priory House until it is time for you to matriculate at Cambridge. It is your inheritance, although you must wait until you are twenty-one years of age to claim it fully. Or you can come and live with me in Bermondsey for a few years. That is a village just across the River Thames from London.'

When Benet did not immediately choose one or the other, Rosamond offered up the third possibility, that he could live with Tristram Pendennis. In addition to finding Audrey for her,

Jacob had made inquiries about Tristram and had confirmed that he was an honest man who would look after his nephew's interests.

With a serious look on his face, one that belied his years, Benet stared out the window while he considered his choices. After a long silence, he spoke. 'I like Uncle Tristram, but what about Mathy?'

'Mathy Ludlow?'

Benet nodded.

Belatedly, Rosamond remembered that Rob had mentioned the friendship between the two boys. 'If you wish it, Mathy will be your companion, whatever you decide.'

'Then I should like to go to my uncle, if he will have us.'

'Be assured that he will, Benet. But what about your mother?'

Benet lowered his head. His words were so quiet that Rosamond had to strain to hear them. 'She does not like me very much, and sometimes I do not like her at all.'

Rosamond took hold of his hand and squeezed it. 'I understand. She is a difficult woman. Like you, I love her with the devotion a child owes to a parent, but I do not like her very much.'

'Will she be cared for? Someone must make certain she takes her medicine.'

With tears prickling the backs of her eyes, Rosamond embraced her brother. 'You have my promise.'

He hugged her back before he broke away, face flushed. 'May I go and tell Mathy?'

She nodded, not trusting herself to speak. He was at the door before she remembered one last matter of business. 'Benet,' she called, 'what about Master Sutton? Do you want to take him with you?'

He turned, the impish grin of a carefree boy on his face. 'Can I pension him off, now that I am lord of the manor?'

Surprised into a laugh, she grinned back at him. 'Indeed you can. Or, rather, I will do it for you and then find you a tutor who is more to your liking.'

She'd let Rob hire him, Rosamond decided when the boy had gone.

Once again, her mood shifted. Where was her husband? Why had Carnsey not yet returned to Priory House? Worry made her abrupt when she dealt with Master Sutton, but she gave him two weeks to make arrangements to leave Priory House and a generous bonus for his service.

That done, she went in search of Jacob and found him in Sir Walter's study. Although her thoughts continued to stray to Rob, she managed to report the results of her visit to the schoolroom.

'I will deliver the boys to Benet's uncle,' Jacob promised.

'You do not mind? I'd have thought that, by now, you'd be growing anxious to return to London.'

'As it happens, I have decided to stay on here at Priory House for an indefinite time.' He took off his spectacles and polished them before adding, in a mumble, 'I am concerned about Melka.'

Remembering the bruise on the tiring maid's cheek, Rosamond did not blame him. 'She will be glad of it, I think.'

'That remains to be seen.' Flustered, Jacob dropped his spectacles when he tried to remove them for another, entirely unnecessary cleaning.

'I am happy to leave you in charge here, Jacob, especially since I plan to depart on the morrow. I have had no word from Rob and the easiest way to determine if he reached Bristol safely is for me to travel to Boscastle and talk to the owner of whatever fishing boat he hired to deliver him to the *Rosamond*.'

'Did he promise to send word when he arrived?' Jacob asked.

Rosamond had to admit that he had not.

'Then it is possible he has no idea that, in the absence of news, you are worried about him.'

'Carnsey should have returned by now.'

Jacob tilted his head, hearing a new note in her voice. 'Are you concerned that something in particular has happened to Sir Walter's secretary?'

'I have concerns about Leveson,' she said, and told Jacob what she had learned from Diggory Pyper. 'I am afraid he is the one behind all our troubles.'

'But why would he commit such heinous crimes?'

'As to that, I am as bewildered as you are, but the lack of a reason does not make me any less concerned about Rob's safety. I will go mad if I do not do *something*!'

'Then by all means go to Boscastle.' Jacob patted her

shoulder. 'In addition to interrogating fishermen, you will be able to question Trewinard's widow again.'

'Morwen? Why?' But before Jacob could reply, Rosamond answered her own question. 'Of course – if Leveson lied to us about meeting Pyper, then he most likely lied about other matters, too. Now that I think about it, he was most anxious that he be the one to go to Boscastle while Rob and I traveled to Padstow.'

THIRTY-NINE

15 July 1584 – 16 July 1584

'Try a little ginger to settle your stomach,' Rob suggested. He'd heard an infusion of ginger and rosewater was most effective in forestalling seasickness.

Leveson sent a baleful look in his direction and kept the latrine bucket close. 'Aqua vitae would suit me better.'

'You'll only spew it back up.' Insisting Leveson eat some of the cook's oatmeal pottage with parsnips had not been one of Rob's better ideas.

Since the two men and Ulick Carnsey shared one small cabin aboard the *Rosamond*, Rob prayed his companion would soon adjust to the steady rolling motion. He held out little hope of it if the weather worsened, and those in the crew who were experienced in judging such things were predicting a squall that would last a day or two. Such a storm would wreak havoc with the ships at anchor in the roadstead on the southeast side of Lundy Island, where outward bound vessels found shelter and those that were inward bound took on pilots and provisions.

'I can have you rowed ashore,' Rob offered.

The southern part of the island was cultivated. The rest was pasture. From the deck of the *Rosamond*, Rob had glimpsed farmhouses and tenements and the ruins of a castle high on a bluff. The landing place was a little north of the castle, while to the south a low green hummock jutted up from the gradual descent of the castle bluff – a landmark with the unprepossessing name of Rat Isle.

'Leveson?' Rob prompted the sick man when he got no reply. 'Do you want to be put on land? Carleill can find you there as easily as on board the *Rosamond*.'

Eyes closed, Leveson waved him off.

Rob frowned at the negative response. The other man had been sick as a dog and likely would be again. It made no sense that he continued to torture himself by remaining aboard. 'Is there someone on Lundy Island who would recognize you as Walsingham's man?'

'Let it be, Jaffrey.' Moaning, Leveson rolled over on the narrow box bed, turning his face to the bulkhead into which it had been built.

Rob left him to his misery, venturing out on deck to survey the activity of the crew. With the storm fast approaching, the captain had already given the order to extinguish all fires, from the charcoal braziers to the brick firebox amidships in which the cook prepared their meals. The large copper cauldrons had gone into storage for the nonce, leaving them with provisions that did not need to be cooked: ship's biscuit, cheese, beer, and heavily salted dried beef and stock fish. They were fortunate that supplies taken aboard in London were still plentiful. The biscuit was free of weevils and there were chickens in the hold to provide fresh eggs.

As he strode to the rail to study the shore of Lundy Island, Rob was pleased to note that he had regained his sea legs. For all the discomforts of life on shipboard, he relished the sense of anticipation that came with sailing to new places. The New World, despite what he had told Rosamond, called to him, much as Muscovy had a few years earlier.

Even Lundy Island qualified as an exotic locale. Situated all alone at the point where the Severn Sea met the Atlantic Ocean, it rose up, cliffs and coves, splendid in its shapes and colors. It had as wild and alien a look as any foreign shore, especially when it was shrouded in mists, as it was at the moment. They parted just often enough to give him a glimpse of particolored rock and soaring seabirds. The rest of the time, the disembodied cries and screeches of gulls and guillemots and razorbills lent an air of eerie unreality to the scene.

Lundy was a haven for sea rovers, a place closer to England

than Ireland where ships could be refitted and victualed. The prizes taken by men-of-war, as the pirates called their vessels, no matter the size, yielded plunder of great diversity and variety in value – canvas and cloth, ordnance, wax, alum, and even exotic pets like the parrot Captain Piers had captured. A ship taken en route from Lübeck to Spain had been loaded with timber and copper. Another's cargo had been one hundred chests of sugar. Here on Lundy Island, some of the booty was traded for provisions, in particular beef, mutton, wine, and bread.

Rob had met with Captain Carleill the previous day, without Leveson. Their exchange had been brief and unsatisfying, only long enough for Carleill to inform him that their mission was to capture and recruit more sea rovers. For this purpose, he had assembled a small fleet. In addition, Carleill had with him a pardon for the notorious pirate William Arnwood. Walsingham had arranged for Arnwood's release from gaol. Carleill was to meet him and his crew in Cork. Two more pirates Walsingham had freed were also to join Carleill when he got to Ireland.

'How can you trust them?' Rob had asked the captain.

Carleill had avoided answering, but he had looked uneasy.

As Rob stood on the deck, staring up at the ruins of the castle, he admitted the truth to himself. The man he admired had a weakness. Carleill would blindly follow any order that came from his stepfather.

With a sigh, he turned away from the waist-high rail. Twilight had descended while he'd been lost in thought. The wind had picked up, as well, coming from the southwest. As the first drops of rain struck his upturned face, barefoot seamen in coarse white linen trousers scurried to finish battening down the hatches before the full force of the storm hit. The crew would sleep on pallets below deck with the cargo this night, rather than on deck under the aftercastle.

It was time to seek shelter himself. He turned toward the cabin with considerable reluctance. It would stink of sickness and there would be little room to move about, especially after Carnsey joined them. It was a blessing that Sir Walter's secretary spent most of his time in the chartroom, apparently fascinated by the maps and charts and the way the steersman controlled the whipstaff and rudder.

Rob stepped inside, barely remembering in time to stoop a little so he would not bump his head. A taller man would not have been able to stand upright anywhere in the cabin. A single window let in enough light to find his way to the small table nailed to the floor and light the candle in the lantern that hung above it. With the horn slats adjusted, it was safe enough for the nonce, but if the coming storm was a bad one, he would have to extinguish the flame.

He glanced toward the trunk in which they'd stored their clothing and personal items. Heavy as it was, it would be bounced about by the waves, presenting a danger to life and limb. His mouth kicked up in a wry smile. Odd how he had managed to forget the many things he had *not* cared for about life at sea. Wet bedding and festering bilges were the least of it.

Thinking to empty Leveson's latrine bucket before conditions on deck grew any worse, he turned toward the bunk. He blinked, thinking at first that the dim light was playing tricks on him. It was not. Leveson was not there.

'Damned fool,' Rob muttered, moving toward the hatch. He had chosen a poor moment to go outside to relieve himself.

Even at anchor, the *Rosamond* was in constant motion. Now she shifted in unexpected ways, throwing Rob off balance more than once before he located Leveson on deck. Timbers groaned and water smacked repeatedly against the sides of the ship as he made his way closer. Only when he had reduced the distance between them to a few feet did Rob realize that the other man held a small lantern in one hand. In a methodical manner, he opened and closed the slats, stopping every few seconds to renew his death grip on the rail.

Rob had to shout to be heard above the roar of the wind and the crash of the waves. 'No one will be on deck to see your signal!'

Leveson turned at the sound of his voice, nearly losing his balance. The lantern fell from his hand and bounced once on the deck. The candle inside winked out.

It was no good trying to talk. Rob lurched to Leveson's side, grabbed hold of his sleeve, and hauled him toward the cabin. They might not have made it had Carnsey not appeared, seemingly out of nowhere, to help them manage the last few steps.

Inside, out of the wind and the wet, Rob shoved Leveson onto the bunk and loomed over him. Carnsey sank down on the stool.

'Time for honesty,' Rob said. 'Who were you trying to signal?'

'Pirates, most like.' Carnsey made no attempt to hide his contempt.

'On the contrary.' Leveson held his head in his hands, but his voice was steady. 'I was trying to send my report.'

'To Carleill?' When Rob had informed the captain that Leveson was indisposed, Carleill had shown no interest in rushing to the sick man's side to confer with him.

'To . . . a confederate.' Leveson moaned as the ship rose up and dropped again.

The movement was so sudden and so violent that it knocked Rob clear off his feet. His elbow struck the side of the table as he fell, causing his entire arm to go numb. He rubbed it as he scrambled upright again. The sensation would come back, but he would be left with considerable soreness and, no doubt, an enormous bruise. Using the other hand, he seized Leveson by the throat and shoved him back against the bulkhead.

'Talk!'

'I cannot,' Leveson gasped.

'He cannot, in truth.' Carnsey sounded amused. 'Not when you are choking him.'

Rob eased his grip as the ship pitched yet again, but he did not let go. 'What have you been keeping back?'

'Release me and I'll tell you.'

With great reluctance, Rob did so. He braced himself with one hand against the beam overhead to counter the constant side-to-side roll of the ship.

Leveson rubbed his neck, cleared his throat, and sat up a little straighter on the bunk. 'Yes, I know more than I have said, but you are already aware of most of it. I was sent to Cornwall to gather information for Walsingham. To that end, I had several meetings with pirates, including Diggory Pyper. Some can be trusted but most cannot. There is treason afoot.'

'You have said all that before. What treason? Who is involved?'

'We sail to Ireland, do we not?'

'It appears so, after Carleill makes contact with several more pirate vessels known to be heading for Lundy Island.'

'It is Ireland where the trouble lies.'

'Go on,' Rob said. He was aware of Carnsey's elevated interest but he kept his eyes on Leveson.

Walsingham's man shook his head and winced when the movement caused him pain. 'I am under orders to report to Captain Carleill and no other.'

'Who did you attempt to signal, then?' Carnsey wanted to know.

'Someone Walsingham trusts to keep an eye on his stepson.'

'Another spy? They are as untrustworthy as pirates!' Carnsey's lips twisted into an expression of extreme distaste. 'Do you think any pirate can be counted upon to stand with England? Why, if they had their way, they would throw the English out of Ireland entirely, thus making the whole of the country a safe haven for their captured prizes.'

'Not so,' Leveson argued. 'Many pirates are loyal Englishmen and only a small minority are actively involved in treason. The trouble is, they can count upon the others to sail away rather than fight for either side. That leaves the English forces at a disadvantage.'

Before Carnsey could argue further, a swell sent the sea chest sliding into his stool. Toppling off, he sprawled on his back like a landed fish. He swore creatively while he righted himself.

Leveson laughed. 'Struck down for speaking false words, I have no doubt of it.'

'But why should we believe *you*?' Rob asked, addressing Leveson but reaching down to yank Carnsey to his feet.

Leveson grinned at him. 'Because you have no choice. Kill me and no one will ever know what I have to report.'

'As soon as the storm passes, we will have ourselves rowed to Carleill's ship.'

'Agreed. Now, with your permission, I will rest my uneasy stomach and pounding head.' He turned his back on the others to curl into a ball on the bunk and nurse his misery.

'I do not trust him,' Carnsey muttered. 'What if he gives false information to the captain?'

Rob had his own doubts about Leveson. The fellow's earlier sickness had been real enough, but now? He was skilled at deception. According to Rosamond, who had seen him perform both on and off the stage, he could even be convincing in the role of a woman.

Aloud, he said only, 'Close questioning will bring the truth to light.'

Although Rob spoke with more confidence than he felt, Carnsey seemed willing to accept his opinion.

'Best get some food, and then some rest,' Rob added. 'None of us will be leaving the *Rosamond* tonight.'

Early on, sleep proved elusive. It was only after the waves subsided and the ship resumed a gentler, steadier roll that Rob drifted into slumber. He woke to pale daylight that suggested the time was not much past dawn. Despite the early hour, he was alone in the cabin.

Slowly, his mind muddled by a far from easy night, he staggered to his feet. Leveson's whereabouts concerned him. If he was a traitor, he might be trying to escape. He had barely reached the half deck when the early morning stillness was shattered by an ear-splitting shriek.

It was followed a moment later by a shout of 'Man overboard!'

FORTY

The horses were being saddled for the journey to Boscastle and Rosamond was on her way out of the guest lodgings when she caught sight of the gatekeeper's wife in the bake-house, collecting her daily allotment of bread. She had time, she decided, to unravel one of the small puzzles she and Rob had uncovered in the course of questioning the household.

Peter Ludlow had all but accused his wife of cuckolding him with Carnsey. Since Rosamond still did not understand the secretary's failure to return, it behooved her to discover if Tamsyn knew more about him than she'd admitted.

Rosamond intercepted her quarry in the herb garden where Audrey had been playing with the kitten. Off to one side was a small pleasure garden, complete with a rose arbor, where two people could sit on a stone bench and be all but invisible to anyone passing by on the footpath. Tamsyn did not object when Rosamond caught her arm and steered her that way, but resentment simmered in her eyes at finding herself trapped.

'I do not have time for aught but blunt questions,' Rosamond said. 'Is Ulick Carnsey your lover?'

Color flooded Tamsyn's cheeks, but when she denied it, Rosamond believed her.

'Tell me about his visits to the gatehouse, then. He must have been seen there or your husband would not be so wroth with you.'

Tamsyn allowed that Carnsey had visited her now and again, in particular when her husband was not at home, but she insisted that they'd done naught but talk. Rosamond gained the impression that the gatekeeper's wife had been trying to make him jealous and thus more attentive to her, but she did not understand why Carnsey had gone along with the ruse.

'What do you talk about?' she asked.

Tamsyn clutched her loaves of bread so tightly that her fingers left little pockmarks in the crusts. Her answer, when it came, was in Cornish.

Rosamond translated it into English: 'He is wont to tell me about his travels with Sir Walter. Went everywhere with him, he did, when Sir Walter went about doing his duty as Justice of the Peace.'

'Did he talk of their visits to Boscastle?' Rosamond asked.

'No more than any other place. I heard what happened there. It is a terrible thing, murder.'

'What about pirates? Did he talk of piracy or smuggling or contraband?'

This, Tamsyn flatly denied.

'What about kin? Did he ever tell you about his family. I know he has a distant cousin, William Carnsey, at Bokelly. Are his parents yet living?'

'Both dead,' Tamsyn confided, 'and a very sad tale that is, too. His father died when he was nine and he was but ten years old when he lost his mother. Poor woman. Like my own dear mother, she was a stranger in these parts and found life difficult after she was widowed.'

Rosamond probed more deeply, but learned only that Tamsyn's mother had been born in Wales and had never truly found a welcome in Cornwall.

'Who took Carnsey in after his parents died?'

'He told me he was raised for a bit by his grandfather, but then the old man died, too, and he was sent to school in London.'

That he had been well educated was obvious, else Sir Walter would never have employed him as a secretary. Rosamond plucked a rose and toyed with it, inhaling the faint, pleasant scent as she tried to think what to ask next. 'Did anyone ever come here asking for him?'

Tamsyn had no answer for that question, but when Rosamond inquired about messages Carnsey had received, she responded with a vigorous nod. He had, indeed, collected a goodly number of letters at the gatehouse. If he was there when a packet arrived for Sir Walter, he had taken charge of it. Otherwise, Mathy or Tamsyn's next oldest child would have had to deliver it to Sir Walter.

The rose, unnoticed, tumbled from Rosamond's lap. 'Did that happen often – letters arriving for Sir Walter while Carnsey was in the gatehouse?'

Tamsyn gave a rueful chuckle. It seemed that they had been interrupted by the arrival of a messenger almost every time Carnsey visited her.

'These letters for Sir Walter, the ones Carnsey took charge of, do you know who sent them?'

'And how would I know that, Mistress Jaffrey, when I cannot read?'

'The seal might have told you. Signet rings are distinctive. Did you notice any particular design?' Her own signet left the impression of an apple pierced by an arrow, the Appleton crest.

At the sharp note in Rosamond's voice, Tamsyn's resentment returned. She switched from Cornish to the local version of English, the better to put an uppity gentlewoman in her place. 'I never seed 'n. 'E give it to 'e, didn'a?'

Had Carnsey given the letters to Sir Walter? Rosamond supposed collecting them might be one of his duties. It would not be unusual for all messages that came to Priory House for Sir Walter to go to his secretary first. On the other hand, Carnsey

himself had told her that Sir Walter dealt with some correspondence personally – letters in code, if naught else. Rosamond's
stepfather would not have wanted his secretary to read those. By
intercepting such messages, Carnsey might have deciphered
them before Sir Walter saw them. It would not have been difficult
for him to work out that the *Book of Martyrs* was the key.

What if Carnsey had done *more* than decipher the letters?
What if he had withheld some of them? Sir Walter would never
have realized a message was missing unless a later one made
some reference to its contents. Even then, he would suppose that
the earlier letter had been lost.

A secretary was in the perfect position to control what his
master did and did not see.

Tamsyn abruptly stood. 'I know nothing else,' she said, 'and I
cannot waste any more time answering foolish questions.'

Tossing her head, she stalked off without a backward glance.

In another household, such disrespect might have cost her
husband his post, but in this one the mistress's dislike of
her daughter was well known among the servants. Tamsyn had
been cooperative enough to have no fear of reprisal.

Rosamond, too, had no more time to waste. She hurried to the
stableyard and her waiting henchmen, but her mind was racing
even faster.

Rob had briefly suspected the tutor of treason because he had
so many correspondents. No one else had appeared to write many
letters, save for Sir Walter himself. But in many cases, it would
have been Carnsey who acted as scribe, thus giving him a perfect
way to conceal the exchange of clandestine messages. Sir Walter's
secretary had not only been in a position to intercept letters from
Sir Francis Walsingham, he had been ideally situated to carry on
a secret correspondence with fellow conspirators.

Had he done so? Or was she making something out of nothing?
Rosamond could think of no reason why he would betray his
country, or resort to murder, but his failure to return to Priory
House in a timely manner aroused her darkest suspicions.

She rode toward Boscastle in a deeply troubled state of mind.

FORTY-ONE

Morwen Trewinard was not pleased by Rosamond's return to her establishment. She thumped the jug of ale down on the table so hard that some of the brew sloshed over the rim and into Charles's lap. Luke and John prudently shifted away from the puddle. Rosamond ignored it.

Once again, the alehouse was crowded. Outside, rain pelted down, drenching everything. For the last few miles of their journey, the road had been a sea of mud. The safeguard Rosamond wore to protect her skirt was caked with the stuff.

'We need to speak in private,' Rosamond said.

Morwen's lip curled into a sneer. 'I have no time for idle chatter.'

'There is a reward in it, if you find the time, and the possibility of being taken up as a land pirate if you do not.'

'You have not the authority.'

'I can get it.' Rosamond clung to her temper by a thread. 'Do not thwart me in this, Morwen. I have far more powerful friends than anyone who may have warned you to hold your tongue.'

The alehouse keeper stalked away, carrying her jug to the other table, but when she had seen to the needs of the local men seated there, she returned. 'Speak your piece and begone.'

Rosamond shook her head. 'It is you, Morwen, who must speak to me.'

After ordering her henchmen to leave, Rosamond gestured for the other woman to take a seat. Grudgingly, Morwen complied.

'First, I would have word of my husband. Master Jaffrey, Master Leveson, and Master Carnsey should have arrived in Boscastle six days ago seeking transportation to Bristol. Did they lodge with you overnight?'

Morwen shook her head. For a moment, Rosamond's heart stuttered. Her voice shook when she asked her next question. 'Did they reach here at all?'

'They came, but they did not stay here. Master Hender

entertained them at the mansion house.' A downward twist of Morwen's lips told Rosamond what she thought of the hospitality offered by the local gentry.

'Did they find a boat to hire?'

'I pay such things no heed,' Morwen said.

Rosamond waited, certain the other woman was lying. No matter where they had spent the night, everyone in the village would have known of it if they had hired a local fisherman to transport them. Added to that, any fisherman who had taken Rob to Bristol would have returned far richer than when he'd left. She had not the slightest doubt that he would have spent some of that largesse at the local alehouse.

After a lengthy pause, Morwen jerked her head toward a group of rough-looking fellows seated on a bench. 'Ask them.'

They were instantly recognizable as men who earned their living from the sea. In addition to shaggy thrum caps, they wore sea gowns – loose, knee-length, long-sleeved garments of tightly-woven canvas designed to protect them from wind and water.

Standing, Rosamond squared her shoulders. 'Remain where you are, Morwen. I have not finished with you.'

She made her way to the bench, pasted a friendly smile on her face, and asked which one of them had taken her husband and his friends to Bristol. Her question garnered nothing but blank stares until repeated in Cornish.

Speaking in the same language, a gray-bearded ancient doffed his cap and admitted that he had been hired to transport three gentlemen to the anchorage called King Road.

'Were they in good health when last you saw them?' Rosamond asked.

'Standing on the deck of a fine, new-painted bark they were,' the old man reported, still speaking in his native tongue, 'when my boy and I left them to make our way home again.'

'All three of them?' Rosamond frowned. Had Carnsey meant to go with Rob all along? He'd said nothing of such a plan before they left Priory House. 'Did anything seem amiss?'

'What could be wrong, mistress?' Unexpectedly, he winked at her. 'Though the one fellow did look a bit green about the gills. Not a good sailor, that one, I warrant.'

Certain he was not talking about Rob, and therefore given no cause to worry, Rosamond rewarded the fisherman with a silver half crown that left him slack-jawed at her generosity. She returned to Morwen just in time to stop the other woman from slipping away. It required clamping one hand on her forearm to keep her in place.

'You are hurting me!' Morwen whined.

'I will see you in gaol if you do not stop trying to thwart me.' She waited until Morwen met her eyes, then seated herself to pursue the other matter that had brought her back to Boscastle. 'Just prior to the last time I was here, Master Leveson questioned you. He told me that you refused to cooperate with him. Is that true?'

A slow smile overspread Morwen's flushed face. 'Is that what he said?'

'Do not toy with me, Morwen. Given that you have lost both a husband and a kinswoman to a vile, murdering scoundrel, I should think that you would want to see him brought to justice.'

'Answering questions did not do either of them much good.'

Rosamond shook her head and at the same time released her hold on Morwen's arm. 'You are laboring under a misconception. They did *not* share what they knew. That is what led to their deaths. Had they been more forthcoming, it might have been possible to protect them.'

Morwen worried her lower lip, as if she was trying to decide how much it was safe to reveal. When the silence stretched past the breaking point, Rosamond added an incentive.

'The man you are afraid of is on board a ship with my husband.' That might even be true. 'He cannot hurt you, or give orders to anyone else to dispose of you. It will never be safer for you to talk to me than it is now, and by doing so you will doubtless save other lives.'

'I do not know why my husband was killed.' Morwen's face wore a mulish look.

'But you know something. What did you tell Master Leveson?'

'Nothing.' She looked down at her hands where they were knotted together in her lap.

'Do you know who killed your husband?'

She shook her head.

'You must have suspicions. Tell me.'

Morwen lowered her voice to a whisper. 'Why did my cousin Honor come here, mistress?' A hint of desperation underscored the words.

'You do not know?'

'I can only guess that she thought she would be safe with me. Poor fool!'

'How would she travel if she wished to keep her journey secret? Did she have a horse? A boat?'

'Her father owned a skiff. I thought, when her body was found, that she attempted the journey alone and been unequal to the task. I thought she drowned by accident . . .' Her voice trailed off and she shook her head.

Alert for every nuance, Rosamond pounced on the way Morwen phrased her answer. 'What is it?' She put one gloved hand on Morwen's forearm. 'What have you discovered that makes you think she was murdered?'

'The skiff has not been found.'

There was more. Rosamond felt certain of it, but she warned herself to be patient and let Morwen reveal it at her own pace. The wait seemed endless, but at last she burst into speech.

'It was on the day that Master Leveson and Master Carnsey were to take my cousin's body to Padstow to be buried. You and your husband had already left for Priory House. Master Leveson was arranging for a cart, and I was about to start my brewing. Just as Ulick Carnsey passed by, I stepped out of the brewhouse to visit the privy in the garden. There was something odd in his manner. I cannot say why it made me uneasy, but when he started up the path toward Willapark, I followed him.' She drew in a deep breath before she blurted out the rest. 'He met two men, both armed with cudgels. One of them had been injured. He wore a bandage on his arm. Here.' She touched her upper arm in the same spot that Rosamond's knife had struck when she'd wounded one of the attackers at Tintagel.

'Were you near enough to overhear what they said?'

'I did not dare go that close, but I could tell they were quarreling. It was only after one of the men raised his cudgel in a threatening manner that Master Carnsey gave him a purse full of money. Fair bulging with coins it was. After the men had it, they left, and I fled before anyone caught sight of me.'

Rosamond felt a chill seep into her bones. She took a deep, slow breath. Carnsey. He could not have killed Trewinard. At the time the alehouse keeper was murdered, he was riding toward Boscastle. But he knew that Trewinard had talked to Sir Walter. He had been outside the window on the ale bench that day. Had it been because of Carnsey's presence that Trewinard had kept a wary eye on the opening?

But why? Neither treason nor murder were acts to be undertaken lightly. She wished now that she had taken the opportunity to ask Carnsey's cousin at Bokelly about his kinsman's past.

Since Ulick Carnsey spoke Cornish, she had assumed he was Cornwall born and bred, but was he? Hadn't Tamsyn said that Carnsey's mother was a foreigner. They'd had that in common, she'd confided, because Tamsyn's mother had been born in Wales.

Carnsey's mother could have been born almost anywhere. Local people would brand someone a foreigner if he hailed from Exeter. For all Rosamond knew, she might have come from as far distant a place as France or Spain.

A man with *Spanish* blood in his veins might think he had good reason to involve himself in treason . . . and with plans to invade England. But murder? Even if all her suppositions were true, Rosamond did not understand why so many deaths had been necessary. For that reason alone, she was increasingly worried about Rob's safety.

When last seen, Carnsey had been aboard the *Rosamond*.

FORTY-TWO

17 July 1584

Dawn found Rosamond standing where she had been when Honor Piers's body was discovered. Once again the scene was peaceful, the storm having passed in the night, but she felt anything but calm. The previous evening, one setback had followed another in rapid succession when she'd tried to hire someone to take her to Lundy Island.

She'd approached the old fisherman first. It should have been a simple matter to find the *Rosamond*, go on board, and tell her husband what Morwen had seen. Together they would then force Carnsey to tell them the truth.

In a kindly but firm manner, the old man had explained that no one could set out to sea with night coming on, let alone in the middle of a storm. She would have to wait for morning to embark. Rosamond had seen the sense in that, but as soon as she named her destination, she came up against a more formidable problem. Not one of Boscastle's fishermen was willing to take her to Lundy Island, not even for ready money.

'Dangerous currents,' one said.

'Too far,' said another.

'Women do not belong on boats,' someone else muttered, but he was careful not to say so to her face.

It was the fisherman whose boat Rob had hired who gave her the real reason. 'The haunt of pirates, that place is.' The old man shook his shaggy white head at her foolishness in wanting to go there.

And so it had gone. Even with Morwen's help, when Rosamond's command of the Cornish tongue faltered, she had been unable to find anyone who would agree to take her to Lundy Island. She wondered now if she should have hired one of the men to take her to Bristol instead. Mayhap there she could have found a ship already planning to sail past the island.

A gull cried overhead. Somewhere nearby, a cow lowed and a dog barked. Rosamond kicked a stone out of her way, sending it flying into the water to land with a loud plop. Her situation was intolerable, but if she tried to explain how much was really at stake, she'd likely be locked up as a madwoman.

The sound of a soft footfall on the path behind her had her reaching inside her cloak for her knife. Holding it at the ready, but still concealed in woolen folds, she swung around to face whatever new threat might be approaching.

A man stopped a few feet away from her and held both hands up in front of him, palms out. 'I mean thee no harm, Mistress Jaffrey.'

'How do you know my name?'

He choked back a laugh. 'It do seem to I there idden many do not.'

Rosamond frowned. There was something familiar about that laugh. She scrutinized the stranger's appearance, trying to think where she had seen him before. He was tall and lanky, and his dress made it seem likely that he was a sea captain. Not for him the common sailor's sea gown or thrum cap. Instead, to protect himself from wind and spray, he wore a heavy leather doublet and leather hose.

Aside from his clothing, the stranger's most distinguishing feature was a bulbous, red-veined nose. Was he friend or foe? Someone she had passed in a marketplace or on the road? Or had she encountered him in London?

'I be Otis Towne,' he said, doffing a hat decorated with an ostentatious plume. 'Captain of the *Red Dragon* and once mate to Captain John Piers.'

The memory Rosamond had been searching for abruptly popped to the surface. She *had* seen Otis Towne before . . . in Padstow. 'You laughed when my husband said the vicar would like to own a parrot.'

He acknowledged this with a slight bow.

She hesitated. She was without her usual escort, all alone with a man who, more than likely, was a pirate. She ought to flee as fast as her feet would carry her. He was not in her way. She could outrun him if she caught him off guard and made straight for the alehouse.

But he had a ship. And if he had sailed with Captain Piers, he must have known the captain's sister.

'Did you follow us to Honor Piers's cottage, and afterward back to the inn?'

'Aye.'

The next question burst out of her before she thought better of asking it. 'Did you kill her?'

Towne's face contorted. He denied the charge with a blistering burst of Cornish.

'Then why take such an interest?' She switched to Cornish herself, finding it easier to translate what he said in that tongue than to understand his English when it was garbled by the local dialect.

Although there were now other people out and about in Boscastle, including some of the fishermen she had approached the previous evening, Rosamond was still wary. Nevertheless, she stood her ground, hands on her hips, glaring at Otis Towne while she waited for him to answer.

'I heard there were strangers asking questions,' he admitted. 'I was curious.'

There was more to it than that, Rosamond felt certain. 'And now? Why approach me?'

'Word is, you seek passage to Lundy Island.'

'My husband is there with Captain Carleill.'

He nodded as if this confirmed something he already suspected. 'Well, then, I am the one to take you to him.' He gestured toward the harbor. 'Behold the *Red Dragon*.'

Rosamond looked at the ship and felt herself blanch. It was small, the paint was peeling, and the men in his crew, what she could see of them at this distance, were a disreputable-looking lot.

'Do not judge her by her appearance, mistress,' Towne said. 'She's built of stout timbers and is well caulked.'

Rosamond had no idea what that meant, but if she wanted to reach Rob she had little choice but to put her faith in Towne's honesty and the seaworthiness of the *Red Dragon*. At least she would not be alone. Wherever she went, her three strong henchmen would be with her.

'What do you want in return?' she asked.

'Revenge.' He began to walk toward the alehouse with a rolling gait, fully expecting her to accompany him to collect her belongings and her escort.

She stopped short, staring at his back. 'For Honor Piers's death?' When he did not even pause, she scurried to overtake him. 'What do you know that I do not?'

'Come inside, mistress. Tale-telling is thirsty business and I have not yet broken my fast.'

'The alehouse is not open.'

'Morwen will serve us. She knows me of old.'

'Through her cousin? Or because of her husband's . . . business?'

He chuckled. 'Both.'

A short time later, Rosamond sat at one of the alehouse's tables. Charles, Luke, and John had joined her and were keeping a wary eye on Towne. Morwen, as he had predicted, had voiced no objection to letting him come in, or to feeding him. For Towne's benefit, she even repeated what she'd told Rosamond.

'So Carnsey met with two cudgel-carrying strangers here in Boscastle,' Towne mused. 'No doubt they were part of the band of ruffians I saw him conspiring with in Padstow.'

Rosamond froze with her ale cup halfway to her mouth. 'When was this?'

'After you and your husband returned to the inn. I was on my way back to the *Red Dragon* when I recognized him as the man I'd seen with you two earlier.'

'How many ruffians were there? Did you know them?'

'A half dozen that I saw, and I knew them for vagabonds and masterless men, although not their names. It was not difficult to guess that your friend was negotiating with them. Such men are always for hire.'

Rosamond was glad they continued to converse in Cornish. In English, she'd have been fortunate to be told more than 'I seed they'. In her turn, she gave Towne an account of the attack at Tintagel. By the time she was done, he was nodding his head. It was not unheard of to pay to have murder done, he agreed, and added that if Carnsey had hired them, they'd have made certain not to hurt him too badly.

'Did they also kill Honor Piers?' she asked.

Once again, his face twisted. He blamed himself for not staying at her cottage to keep an eye on her. He had thought her greatest danger came from the vicar, who had been trying to persuade her to marry him. For all his fine talk and false piety, Archer believed that Honor knew where her brother had buried pirate treasure.

'If her'd a-married en,' he added in English, shaking his head, 'e woulden have got e's gold. Her dooth not have more than the cottage.'

'It sounds as if you knew her well,' Rosamond said. 'I am sorry for your loss.'

Morwen offered crusty brown bread and honey instead of sympathy.

'If there's aught in the house, I shan't clam.' Towne smiled at the alehouse keeper before devoting all his attention to breaking his fast.

'Clam?' Rosamond asked, momentarily distracted.

'Starve,' Morwen supplied.

A little silence fell, broken only by the sound of munching. Rosamond helped herself to some of the bread. She still had no idea why Carnsey thought it necessary to order the deaths of so many people, but with his guilt now even more firmly established, it only remained to capture the villain. Despite her natural misgivings about dealing with a pirate, especially one who had sailed with the bloodthirsty Captain Piers, Rosamond had made her decision. She would trust Otis Towne to take her to Lundy Island.

FORTY-THREE

As soon as the tide turned in their favor, the *Red Dragon* was towed from Boscastle Harbor into open water. The wind was favorable. The day was fair. With luck, Rosamond would be aboard the ship Rob had named for her in a few hours. According to Towne, the distance from the mainland to Lundy Island was no greater than that from Dover to Calais.

At Towne's insistence, Rosamond and her men retired to the ship's tiny cabin to be out of the way of the crew. It was a noisome hole, stinking of pitch and fish and other smells she did not care to identify. She tried and failed to open the one small window to let in fresher air. Instead of glass, it was covered with oiled paper, making it impossible to see through.

Resigned to discomfort and boredom, she was heartened when Charles produced a deck of cards. To pass the time, she persuaded her henchmen to teach her how to play Put, a game looked down upon in gentry households but passing popular in alehouses. She caught on quickly, even though it seemed odd to her that the three and the two were valued higher than the Ace, King, and Queen.

Engaged in this pastime, unable to see what was happening beyond the walls of the cabin, Rosamond was caught off guard by an ear-splitting boom. She sprang to her feet, but fell back again when the entire ship gave a lurch and a shudder. Her three henchmen reached the door ahead of her, rushing out on deck to the accompaniment of thunderous crashes and the ominous sound of splintering wood.

Once the opening was clear, she could hear cries of pain, shouts, and curses, along with continuing bombardment. Her heart in her throat, she crept closer to the door. Once there, she stared in disbelief at the scene before her.

A second ship was no more than a hundred yards distant, smoke billowing from her gun ports. Closer at hand, she saw that one of the *Red Dragon*'s yards had been severed. Instead of catching the wind to propel the ship onward, a square brown sail hung twisted and limp. When Rosamond shifted her gaze to the deck, she was horrified at the destruction wrought by only a few minutes of cannon fire. At least one man lay dead. A half dozen more were injured and bleeding. Splintered wood littered every surface.

When the cannons fired again, Rosamond yelped and grabbed hold of the doorframe to steady herself. Were the men on that other ship mad? Why were they attacking the *Red Dragon*?

At a shout from one of Towne's sailors, she turned to see a second vessel approaching the scene of battle. Rosamond had not decided if she was friend or foe before the first ship fired again, this time using smaller cannons mounted on the rails. They showered the *Red Dragon* with scrap – jagged bits of metal, musket balls, and ordinary rocks – that did an enormous amount of damage by slicing into the rigging, slashing sails, and shattering one of the flag halyards.

Another of Towne's men passed in front of her, this one armed with a musket. A moment later he screamed in agony. Blood blossomed at the center of his chest. As Rosamond watched, stunned and helpless, he collapsed and died only inches away from her.

She was still staring at the body when Towne himself, armed with a cutlass, materialized at her side. Without apology, he shoved her inside the cabin. 'Stay here,' he ordered in Cornish. 'They are firing langrage to drive everyone from the upper deck so that they can board us.'

She did not know the word, but supposed 'langrage' referred to the scraps of metal and other deadly projectiles still being shot from the smaller cannons. That was frightening enough, but the prospect of being boarded terrified her. If she allowed herself to be captured, she would be at the mercy of a band of ruthless pirates.

With shaking hands, she retrieved both of her daggers. She would not be easy to capture. She had already proven her mettle in the fight at Tintagel. This would be no different, except that this time she would make certain she aimed to kill.

She stepped out on deck, one knife in each hand, just as the newly arrived ship fired its guns. The *Red Dragon* shuddered and Rosamond's question had an answer. They now faced two enemy vessels.

Towne's crew had traded muskets for pikes and stood ready to repel boarders. Rosamond spared a glance for the musket the dead man had dropped on the deck but left it where it had fallen. Had it been a pistol, she might have taken it up, but any kind of gun had a drawback. It could only fire one shot before it had to be reloaded.

Her lips twisted into a grim smile. Some would say a woman should use that one shot to take her own life rather than be captured and violated. Such a course was unthinkable to her. She preferred to go down fighting.

Another tremendous crash made the *Red Dragon* rock so violently that Rosamond was flung against the side of the cabin. Her head struck solid wood with enough force to make her see stars. Her knives flew out of her hands to land with a clatter on the deck.

Discordant sounds reached her as she fought to stay conscious. There were shouts and screams. Steel rang against steel. Pike clashed with sword. Cutlass met cutlass.

Despite the waves of dizziness washing over her, Rosamond held on to one thought. She had to find her knives. On hands and knees, she crawled along a deck littered with debris and slick with blood. Her stomach heaved in unison with the *Red Dragon*'s erratic motion.

One of the knives was caught in a coil of rope. Her movements slow and painful, she inched toward it. She was nearly there when a booted foot appeared in front of her. Squinting against the smoke-hazed sunlight, her head throbbing with the effort,

Rosamond gazed up at the man blocking her way. In that first moment of confusion, all she could see was the vicious-looking sword in his hand.

'You never did pay attention to good advice,' Diggory Pyper said, returning the weapon to its scabbard and offering her his hand.

Rosamond grasped it, but she glowered at her childhood friend as he helped her to her feet. He ignored the look to scoop up the knife she had been reaching for. A moment later, he located the second dagger.

'Yours, I presume?' He returned both, surprising her yet again.

Swaying slightly, she replaced the dagger that belonged in her boot sheath. She could not return the other to its proper place. She had left her cloak in the cabin. Just as well, she decided. She felt safer keeping hold of a weapon. When a man she had never seen before approached them, she hid it in the folds of her skirt.

'A woman?' The newcomer's contemptuous gaze raked over her in a most offensive manner. 'What was Towne doing with a woman aboard?'

'Rosamond, may I make known to you Captain Lewes. It was his bark, the *Roe*, that launched the attack on the *Red Dragon*. Lewes, this is Mistress Rosamond Jaffrey. I would consider it a great favor if you would permit me to take her aboard the *Sweepstake*.'

Lewes was a villainous-looking individual with an overgrown beard and a cast in one eye. He sneered at the suggestion. 'The prize is mine. I did not need your help to take her.'

Diggory affected boredom. 'You'd have lost half your crew if not for my assistance.'

'Crew can be replaced. A comely piece like this one, though, she's worth money.'

'You mean to hold her for ransom?'

'That, or sell her into slavery.' Lewes grinned, showing stained yellow teeth. 'Though I'll likely use her for my own pleasure first.'

Rosamond readied herself to strike. She'd kill Lewes before she let him touch her.

Diggory showed no reaction, only clapped a hand on the other man's shoulder and drew him aside. They spoke in whispers, preventing Rosamond from hearing what they said, but the exchange was tense.

She was distracted by the sight of a body being dragged past and thrown overboard. Revulsion filled her, but her determination to defend herself never wavered. If death in battle was to be her fate, so be it. Her only regret was that she would never see Rob again.

She returned her attention to the two pirate captains in time to see Diggory slip a heavy gold ring off his finger and give it to Lewes.

'Best we leave in some haste,' he said when he returned to Rosamond's side, 'before he changes his mind. Are your belongings in the cabin?' He did not wait for an answer but pulled her in after him. While she put on her cloak, he collected the capcase that contained a change of linen and her toiletries.

'I cannot leave without my men,' she protested when they were back on deck. 'I had three servants with me. They are not part of Towne's crew.'

'The same fellows who were with you in Liskeard?'

Rosamond nodded, wincing when pain shot through her head. She felt gingerly for a lump.

'They will not be harmed,' Diggory promised.

While grappling hooks still held all three vessels together, he helped her to cross a plank that led from the *Red Dragon* to the *Sweepstake*. Once on the other side, she looked back. All the other captives were being hustled onto the *Roe*.

'Where are my men?' Rosamond would have returned to the *Red Dragon* had Diggory not grabbed hold of her arm.

'Do you wish to trade your freedom for theirs?'

'I must be certain they are safe.' Anxiety made her voice shrill.

'They are already aboard the *Roe*. I saw them taken there with my own eyes. Unlike most of Towne's crew, they had the good sense to surrender.'

'Are they unharmed?'

'They appeared to be.'

She was thankful for that, at least. 'What will happen to them?'

He released her when the last of the grappling hooks was retrieved and the *Sweepstake* disengaged from the *Red Dragon*. Towne's ship was still attached to the *Roe*.

'They will be given a choice – join Lewes's crew or remain in chains until they can be set ashore.'

'Was that the point of Lewes's attack? To recruit more men for his crew?'

'That and seizing Towne's ship and cargo.'

'But the *Red Dragon* is sinking.'

He shook his head. 'Despite appearances, there is not that much damage. It will not take long for an experienced crew to set the rig to rights again. She can sail with one yard shot through.'

Rosamond had to take his word for it. As the distance between ships grew, she saw boxes and barrels being brought up from the hold and taken aboard the victorious vessel. Towne was on deck, gesticulating and likely swearing.

Diggory left her alone while he went off to give orders to his crew. All around her, men swarmed into the rigging, adjusting the sails until they billowed out and the *Sweepstake* began to pick up speed. Soon they could no longer see the *Roe* or her prize.

Rosamond was no expert at determining direction, but a glance at the sun suggested that the *Sweepstake* was moving steadily westward. She frowned. Lundy Island lay north of Boscastle.

She found Diggory in the chartroom.

'Where are you taking me?' she demanded.

'Ireland.'

She felt her eyes widen. 'But I must go to Lundy Island. My husband's ship lies at anchor in Lundy Roads.'

'Lundy is the last place I can take you. Would you have me sail into a trap?'

Rosamond stared at him. 'What do you mean?'

He sighed. 'You'll give me no peace until I explain, will you, my dear? Come along. We will be more comfortable in my cabin, and less of a distraction to my men.'

In the hope of answers, she went with him. The *Sweepstake* was a much larger and finer vessel than the *Red Dragon*. The captain's cabin was as well furnished as any chamber in a gentleman's house.

Rosamond looked down at her bedraggled garments, then regarded his form with an assessing gaze. 'Your clothes are too

large by far to fit me. Is there a member of your crew small
enough to provide clean, dry garments for me to wear?'

'You have not spent much time at sea if you expect to stay dry.'

'I will have you know that I once sailed all the way to Muscovy
and back!'

'And survived the journey without all the comforts of home?
I am impressed.'

His tone said otherwise, and of a sudden he reminded her so
much of the boy he had been that she was tempted to stick her
tongue out at him. 'Never mind the clothes. I can manage. But
I must send a message to my husband. He is in mortal danger
from someone he believes to be an ally.'

Diggory's gaze sharpened. He gestured toward a comfortably
padded chair. 'Sit, Rosamond. Tell me what you know.'

It would be childish, she supposed, to refuse to cooperate until
he revealed his secrets. Besides, once she told him why she was
so worried, he would surely agree to her request that they sail
to Lundy Island.

'I cannot prove it, but I believe that it was Ulick Carnsey who
killed Sir Walter and ordered the deaths of Alexander Trewinard
and Honor Piers as well as a murderous attack on me and mine
that did not succeed.'

'Why?' He settled atop the sea chest opposite her chair.

'He is involved in treason. I do not know the details but Henry
Leveson insists that the plot involves an invasion.' She saw
enlightenment dawn on Diggory's face and narrowed her eyes.
'Tell me what *you* know.'

'In a moment. First explain why your husband went to Lundy
Island.'

'Captain Christopher Carleill sent for him, and for Leveson.
Carleill—'

Diggory's sudden burst of laughter silenced her, but not for
long.

'I am glad you find this amusing!'

'It seems that we have been working at cross-purposes. I do
not know why I am surprised. When it comes to intelligence
gathering, one hand rarely knows what the other is doing.'

'Never tell me you are working for Sir Francis Walsingham?'

'On the contrary. I report directly to Sir John Perrot, the newly arrived Lord Deputy of Ireland, although to any but your good self, fair Rosamond, I will swear I am bound for a safe port on the Irish coast so that I can unload my illicit cargo and take on supplies.'

'A safe port?'

'All Irish ports are safe for pirates except Youghal, Cork, and Waterford. But in truth, I am bound for Cork. I carry news to Perrot of a coming invasion of Ulster by Scots from the Western Isles of Scotland.'

'Scots? Invading Ireland?' That was a far less alarming prospect than an armada of Spanish ships attacking the southern coast of England. 'Is that what Leveson uncovered?'

'I doubt Leveson knows the half of it, or your friend Carleill, either, for all that he has been sent here to hunt pirates. Why should Cornish sea rovers talk to foreigners?'

The ache in Rosamond's head had settled into a dull throb, but she still had trouble making sense of Diggory's revelations. 'What have sea rovers to do with a Scottish invasion of Ireland? And why is that secret worth killing for?' Before he could answer, she gasped. 'Did you *know* Carnsey killed Sir Walter?'

'I did not. I do not know that for a fact even now. Carnsey has never, to my knowledge, been on the account.' At her questioning look, he translated. 'When a man says he's "on the account" it means he is engaged in piracy.'

'Pirate or not, he's a danger to Rob.'

'Why? Aboard a ship, there is little privacy. Carnsey would be seen if he attacked another man and he'd have no way to escape afterward. If he has been cunning enough to avoid suspicion all this while, surely he will continue to bide his time and do nothing to arouse suspicion. In truth, given what I know, his purpose in going to Lundy Island is most likely to create dissention among the pirates recruited by the Crown and most of them will not need much encouragement to foreswear their allegiance.'

'I wish I knew why Carnsey has been so determined to keep this invasion secret. If you could learn of it so easily—'

'Not easily.' For a moment, Diggory looked decades older than he was. Then his expression cleared and he got to his feet. 'If the wind holds, we will be in Cork before you know it. In the meantime, I will have food sent to you. The door will be kept locked for your own protection.'

'A luxurious prison,' she grumbled, 'but I suppose I must thank you for rescuing me.'

'So gracious!'

Rosamond snorted. 'At least promise me that I can send a message as soon as we reach Cork – to Captain Carleill if not to Rob himself.'

He rolled his eyes heavenward, as if asking for strength. 'I will do what I can to aid you, but all such decisions are in the hands of the Lord Deputy.'

FORTY-FOUR

20 July 1584

'**W**hat happened?' Leveson's voice was hoarse and he slurred his words.

'That is what I hoped you would tell me,' Rob said. 'To the best of my knowledge, you fell overboard, striking your head on the hull before you hit the water. You've been raving, on and off, ever since we pulled you back on board.'

Landed him on the deck like a fish was a more apt description. Rob had been in little better condition, having jumped into the choppy waters of the Severn Sea to save the other man from drowning. He had been one of the few men aboard the *Rosamond* who knew how to swim. Most mariners thought it tempted fate to know how to save themselves in the event of a shipwreck.

'How long ago?' Leveson asked.

'Three days. You were feverish a good part of that time, to the point where I began to despair of your recovery.' In his delirium, Leveson had once or twice cried out that he had been pushed.

Leveson touched the bandages wrapped around his head and winced. 'I cannot remember anything about what happened.'

'You were out on deck in the early morning. Were you attempting to signal someone again?'

'I tell you I cannot remember!'

'Do you know where you are?'

That question produced a bleak smile. 'Still aboard the *Rosamond*, I presume. Are we yet anchored in Lundy Roads?'

Rob nodded. 'Carleill went in search of pirates to capture and delegated me to keep watch in the anchorage.'

'Be glad of it. This ship is not equipped for battle.'

'I've guns to defend us.' But he knew Leveson was right. In truth, he had been relieved when Carleill left him behind.

'Is there any possibility that I was pushed overboard?'

'There is a chance of it. Have you enemies aboard?'

'None that I recognize,' Leveson said, 'but it would be in keeping with the other deaths that someone thinks I know more than I do and tried to get rid of me.'

The two men regarded each other with solemn expressions. If Leveson had been pushed by the same person already responsible for three deaths, that narrowed the field of suspects. Since the crew had sailed from London with the ship, there was only one person, besides themselves, who had come on board after she reached the West Country.

'Why?' Rob asked.

'How?' Leveson countered. 'Sir Walter, yes. Carnsey had the opportunity to stage his accident, but he was with us when Trewinard was killed. And how could he have known that Honor Piers would come to Boscastle?'

'Shall we ask him?'

'Not until my head stops spinning. He's not likely to escape, is he? Where would he go?'

'To friends on Lundy Island? This must be tied, somehow, to piracy.'

Leveson started to reply, but his answer was cut short by a shout from the lookout. Captain Carleill's ship had been sighted and he was bringing back a prize.

Rob took the precaution of loading a pistol and giving it to Walsingham's man before he left the cabin.

From the deck, he had a clear view of Carleill's ship, a pinnace of 150 tons, as it dropped anchor nearby. Moments later, a boat was lowered to take a single passenger ashore.

When Carnsey came up beside him, Rob instinctively tightened his grip on the rail, but in no other way did he give away his newly formed suspicions of the other man. 'Any idea who that is?' He gestured toward the small watercraft slowly making its way toward the landing area.

'He's dressed too fine for a common seaman.'

'The captain of the captured vessel, then. I'd best have myself rowed over to Carleill's ship. I've nothing to report, but I admit to being curious.' Rob gave the order, then forced a smile. 'Come with me, Carnsey. You've not yet met Captain Carleill.'

It did not occur to him until they were halfway there that his companion might present a danger to the captain. Still pondering that, and wondering if he should order Carnsey clapped in irons as a precaution, Rob heaved himself over the rail and came face to face with one of the last people he expected to find aboard Carleill's vessel.

'Charles? What in God's name are you doing here?'

Being mute, Charles did not answer.

'So you do know him?' Carleill himself pushed through the milling mariners. 'These two as well?'

'Luke and John.' For a moment, Rob's throat closed up. If they were here . . .? Frantic to locate Rosamond, for these three men would never willingly have abandoned her, he scanned the other faces on the deck. It was soon obvious that hers was not among them. 'Where is my wife?'

'By all accounts, she is safe enough,' Carleill said. 'Safer than if she had stayed aboard the *Roe* with Captain Lewes. He is an unrepentant scoundrel with an evil reputation when it comes to women. After these two men denied being pirates and claimed to be in the employ of your wife, along with the mute there, Lewes confessed that Mistress Jaffrey is on her way to a port on the southeast coast of Ireland aboard a ship belonging to one of his confederates.'

Despite Carleill's attempt to reassure him, Rob did not like the sound of that. Rosamond was being held prisoner by a pirate. He could only hope the brigand would see the advantage in treating her well while he waited for a ransom to be paid. 'Who is this confederate?'

'A fellow called Diggory Pyper.' Carleill's jaw dropped. 'Good God, Jaffrey. You've gone white as a sheet.'

FORTY-FIVE

Although the queen's Lord Deputy in Ireland, Sir John Perrot, had made them wait aboard the *Sweepstake* for a day and a half for an audience at his headquarters in the governor's house, he greeted Diggory Pyper with warmth and enthusiasm. Rosamond hoped that boded well. Diggory had explained that she would have to petition Perrot for permission if she wished to hire a ship to take her to Lundy Island. She could not even send a letter to Rob without his approval.

She'd seen little of Cork since they'd docked at the quay inside the walled city. Even Diggory, until now, had gone no farther from his ship than the custom house. When he had given the officials there a list of the goods he carried, he'd returned to the *Sweepstake*. These days, he'd explained, Cork's merchants took extreme precautions to protect themselves from their neighbors in the adjoining countryside.

A series of drawbridges and the portcullis at the Watergate denied or granted entrance to the prosperous settlement. Rosamond knew when people were allowed in. Every time a drawbridge or the portcullis was raised or lowered, it filled the air with noisy creaks and screeches.

She supposed she could not blame the citizens of Cork for being cautious. Until the previous year, rebellion had been rife in the vicinity. Thousands of people had fled their farms to pour into Cork, seeking the protection of those thick city walls. Unfortunately, they had brought sickness with them. It was to keep out the plague, as much as to protect against potential enemies, that the rules were so strict.

Perrot was a big, rawboned man with an impressive beard. After listening to his agent's low-voiced report, he gestured for Rosamond to approach, watching her with heavy-lidded eyes. His intense stare made her nervous, the more so when he licked his lips and pronounced her a 'tasty morsel'.

'A respectable married woman, I assure you, Sir John.' Diggory kept his voice light, but Rosamond could see the tension in his shoulders.

Would he fight for her honor against the most powerful man in Ireland? Somehow, she doubted it. Her fingers itched to draw one of her knives, but she resisted the impulse. Defending herself was the last resort. She tried sweet reason first. Pretending to be unaware of his lascivious regard, she affected a simper.

'Has Captain Pyper presented my request, my lord? I am most anxious to rejoin my husband and I feel certain, if you can but send word to him, that Sir Francis Walsingham will urge you to grant my humble petition.'

It was the wrong thing to say. Perrot's eyes narrowed.

'Walsingham?' He turned to Diggory. 'What is she to Walsingham?'

Rosamond spoke up – she had nothing to lose by telling the truth. 'I was able to do him a small service in the matter of negotiations with Muscovy.'

The Lord Deputy's face darkened, suggesting that he knew something of that affair, although surely not her part in it. Her misgivings increased when he ordered her out of the audience chamber. Diggory remained behind.

Seated on a hard wooden bench under the watchful eye of Perrot's guards, Rosamond had no choice but to wait and worry. She had money secreted on her person, although not a great deal of it, but without help it would be both difficult and dangerous to try to hire someone to take her to Lundy Island. Trust the wrong person and she'd find herself robbed of all she possessed and most likely dead in a ditch.

After what seemed like a year, Diggory came to fetch her. He escorted her out of the governor's house and into the market square. A garrison for soldiers was located nearby, as was a goodly church. Keeping one hand on her arm, he walked east, toward a three-story, castle-like house situated close to the North Gate Drawbridge.

'You are to be billeted with a local family.'

'What about Rob? Am I permitted to send a message to him?'

'That will not be necessary. Carleill's fleet has received orders to come here to meet Perrot. They should arrive by the end of the month.'

'But what if—?'

'Perrot will not allow you to leave.' Diggory did not slow his steps. 'I doubt he would have in any case, but your mention of Walsingham assured it. Perrot cannot abide the fellow. He'll give Carleill a hard time, too, for no other reason than Carleill's family connection to the queen's principal secretary.'

Rosamond swore under her breath, then asked, 'Where are you taking me?'

'To the house of a merchant named Edmond Tirry. You will be treated as an honored guest, but you will not be allowed to leave Cork. Perrot has already sent a message to Tirry to make his wishes known.'

'What do you know of this man? Has he a wife?'

'He does. And children. You will be safe and comfortable in his keeping.' He stopped in front of the impressive tower house. 'Tirry is one of the wealthiest men in Cork. Not only does he own this place, but he has another in Youghal, a mill, and over six hundred acres of land. Do you recall that we passed two small islands when we sailed into Lower Cork Harbor? The ruins of a church rose from the first. Sheep grazed on the second.'

Rosamond nodded, but her gaze remained on the impressive structure that would be her home until Rob arrived. There were no bars on the windows, but it was a prison all the same.

'The first is called Inis Pic and is owned by the Ronans of Kinsale. The other, Inis Sionnach, is the property of your host.' He chuckled. 'Those sheep must have a care. Inis Sionnach means Island of the Fox.'

'You seem to know a good deal about Ireland,' she murmured, still studying the building before them.

'I have done much . . . business here during the last few years. It only made sense to study the language and customs. If naught else, such knowledge cuts down on the likelihood of being cheated.'

Rosamond turned to him, struck by a thought. 'Diggory, is Ulick a common Cornish name?'

'I do not believe it is common anywhere, but it is more often found here in Ireland than in Cornwall. Ulick is the English version of Uilleag.' He thought a moment before adding, 'It means playful.' The door of the house opened before he could ask why she wanted to know.

Diggory introduced Rosamond to her jailers, pleasant people and English in their ways. So, it turned out, were most of the merchants of Cork. In short order, Rosamond was installed in a pleasant chamber and provided with a maid. Edmond's wife, Margaret, a woman of about Rosamond's size, offered her own clothing from a selection of many fine garments. She seemed delighted to have a guest, even an uninvited one, and Rosamond spent her first full day in the household doing needlework with Margaret and her maids and listening to her hostess talk about her children.

Rosamond found Edmond Tirry's father, David, who lived with him, far more interesting than the womenfolk. He had been a customer of Cork for nigh onto fifteen years. Holding that post meant he had dealt with the cargo of every ship that entered the port. She bided her time. When the moment seemed right, she approached the older man.

He suffered from gout. One heavily bandaged foot was propped up on a stool. Despite this painful condition, he had all his wits about him and he loved nothing more than a game of pass-dice. As Rosamond had hoped, he invited her to play with him.

'Have you ever heard of a man named Ulich Carnsey?' she asked as she made her first cast, throwing a two and a three. They would take turns until the same number appeared on both dice.

'Carnsey? That is not an Irish name.' Tirry took his turn and also failed to come up doubles.

'His father was Cornish, but I believe his mother may have come from Ireland. This Carnsey is perhaps thirty years old.' Her second cast produced two fours, but to win she needed a score higher than ten.

The old man smiled at her and reclaimed the dice. 'Why would you think I know this fellow?'

'From what I hear, you know everything about everyone going back for decades.'

'In Cork, mayhap.'

She smiled at him. 'But Cork is one of the largest cities in Ireland with one of the largest natural harbors anywhere, and loyal to England besides. Would this not be the most likely place for an Englishman with Irish kin to visit?'

He regarded her with rheumy eyes that saw far more than she'd expected them to. 'I am thinking there is more to it than that.'

Rosamond considered as she made her next cast. One of the ivory dice tumbled off the small table between them and fell to the floor. By the time she retrieved it, she had come to a decision. What difference did it make if she told him what she suspected? Diggory had made his report to Sir John Perrot. If rumors of an invasion were not already flying in Cork, they soon would be.

Tirry listened, his expression grave, as she related her tale.

'You are a grand storyteller, lass, but you have no proof of any of this, nor do you know of a reason why this fellow Carnsey would do such terrible things.'

'What if the reason lies here in Ireland?' she asked. 'I have been told that his English father died when he was a lad of nine and his mother a year later. If she was Irish, might she not have returned here with her son?'

Tirry ceased rolling the dice over and over in one hand and frowned. 'If the man is thirty now, you speak of a time some twenty years in the past. That is a considerable time ago, lass.'

'I have heard that the Irish have prodigious memories.'

He chuckled.

'Wherever Carnsey went, he lived for a few more years with a grandfather, long enough, especially at that age, to develop strong loyalties to his mother's homeland, and mayhap a deep hatred for the English, too, if he was indeed in Ireland.'

A short bark of laughter confirmed the likelihood of her surmise. 'Some would say it does not take long at all to learn to resent English overlords.'

She flushed. 'I expect your son resents having me thrust upon him, but it was not my choice to be billeted here.'

'We had even less say about taking you in, even though we have been loyal subjects of the English Crown for generations. In many areas of the English Pale, and outside it, too, English soldiers settle in an area and take what they want. There is supposed to be compensation, but it is rarely paid. Why do you think there are so many riots and rebellions?'

They resumed play, and Rosamond thought that was the end

of the matter, but two days later, David Tirry drew Rosamond aside after supper and bade her sit beside him on a window seat.

'I have a story to tell you, lass,' the old man said. 'I have been asking questions. Something you said about that boy, young Carnsey, sparked a memory.'

Leaning eagerly toward him, Rosamond hung on every word.

'There was an incident some years back. It did not take place here, but rather in Dublin, but it was talked of everywhere. With the help of a few friends, I have pieced together the tale.'

'You have discovered that Ulick Carnsey *was* in Ireland?'

'An English boy of the right age surely was, a boy brought here by his mother after his father died. When she died, he was left in the care of his Irish grandfather. Until he was fourteen, he lived with the old man just outside the Pale.'

'Sixteen years ago,' Rosamond calculated.

'Aye. That was when Sir Henry Sidney was Lord Deputy.'

When she drew in a sharp breath, Tirry looked a question at her. She shook her head, reluctant to admit to even a slight acquaintance with Sir Henry. She had a feeling that he was the villain of this story.

'Troops lodged with the grandfather spoiled his tenants of goods to the value of two hundred pounds and took away enough cattle to keep them supplied with beef for two months,' Tirry continued. 'That will come as no surprise to any Irishman. Why, I have heard that in a mere six months, Sidney's butcher slaughtered over 10,000 animals for the use of his household alone.'

Rosamond wanted to defend her countrymen, but she held her tongue. Such excesses were all too common and so was the habit of taking advantage of those who were not in a position to object.

'The grandfather, mayhap your Carnsey's grandfather, demanded compensation. All might have been well if the old man had not had a temper, but in his frustration he confronted the captain who was the worst offender. This captain cheated his own men as well as the Irish they stole from, providing them with naught but thin bread and watered beer.' Tirry paused to shake his head at such short-sightedness. 'A good leader puts the welfare of his men above all else.'

'What happened when the grandfather came face-to-face with the captain?'

'He accosted him and the captain fell and struck his head. He died of his injuries, to the joy of many, but because an Irishman struck the fatal blow, he was put on trial and convicted of murdering an Englishman. He was executed and all his possessions seized.'

'And the boy? What happened to him?'

'Despite the fact that he still had kin here, Sir Henry Sidney sent the lad back to England and placed him in a school where he'd be sure to have the rebellion beaten out of him.'

Ulick Carnsey, Rosamond thought. All the facts seemed to fit, and what had happened to his grandfather certainly provided a powerful reason for him to hate England and the English. 'Is there any way to confirm that the boy was Carnsey?' she asked aloud.

Tirry promised to continue asking questions.

When Rosamond repeated the story to Diggory a few days later, he offered to pursue the matter with certain Englishmen who had lived in Dublin for many years.

'In Dublin?' Rosamond asked in surprise. 'I am delighted, but I thought you intended to stay here in Cork.'

He shook his head. 'I depart for Dublin on the morrow to deliver messages from Perrot. He will be leaving soon himself, but for Limerick. Since shortly after he arrived in the English Pale at Dublin on the twenty-first of June, to take up his post as Lord Deputy, he has been on progress, visiting all the Anglo-Irish strongholds, both within the Pale and without.'

'Shouldn't he be mustering troops for the defense of Ireland?'

'He is considering what to do about the invasion. The Mull of Kintyre is only twelve miles from Rathlin Island off the north coast of Ulster. Then again, raids on Ireland by the Scots have been going on for hundreds of years. Perrot thinks it unlikely there is any real cause for concern.'

'At least three people have died to keep this particular invasion secret.' She could scarce keep the outrage out of her voice.

Diggory shrugged. 'I am not Perrot's only intelligence gatherer. No doubt he knows more about the invasion than I do.'

'I do not understand how you can be so calm about this. What else *do* you know?'

'It is complicated.'

'My poor feeble female brain will not explode if you try to explain.'

He drew her deeper into a window alcove and took her hands in his. She jerked them out of his grasp.

'What do you know?' she repeated, glaring at him.

He had the audacity to smile. 'Is it a history lesson you're wanting, then? Well, why not? Do you know the word Gallow-glasses? It is what the English call Scots who live in Ireland as mercenaries. It is a hereditary occupation and, in Ulster, a distinct class akin to that of bard. These mercenaries are already in Ireland and have been for generations. Perrot's land troops are fully capable of dealing with them.'

'And the invasion?'

'That is a secondary threat, a force of Scottish mercenaries who will sail from Scotland in galleys and land at a place called Lough Foyle. It was to stop them before they reached Ireland that Walsingham recruited his fleet of pardoned pirates.'

That meant Walsingham had known of the threat of invasion for more than a year. And that Carnsey, in attempting to keep the plans secret, had killed three times for nothing. Sick at heart, Rosamond had only one more question to ask, the same one she had put to Diggory every time he visited her in the Tirry house, 'Is there any news of Carleill's fleet?'

'They will be here in good time,' he assured her, as he always did. And once again he departed, leaving her to wait and worry and pray that the *Rosamond* would soon sail safely into port.

FORTY-SIX

3 August 1584

J uly turned into August with no sign of Carleill's fleet. Although Rosamond had been assured that contrary winds were to blame for the delay, she lived in constant fear that Carnsey would strike again.

She had been a prisoner in Cork for two full weeks when

Diggory sent word that he'd confirmed the identity of the boy in David Tirry's story. After that, there was no longer any doubt in her mind that Carnsey had murdered Sir Walter Pendennis. She fretted, and daily petitioned the Lord Deputy, who had not yet left the city, to send word of her whereabouts to her husband the moment the *Rosamond* anchored in Lower Cork Harbor.

When at long last Carleill's fleet arrived, she demanded to be taken to the governor's house, where the captain would go to meet with the Lord Deputy. Edmond Tirry was polite but firm. She must not leave his house.

'Then you had best go, Edmond,' David Tirry said, 'and find the lad and bring him here. Mistress Jaffrey will give us no peace otherwise.'

An hour passed, then two. Rosamond paced. She swore. And then the door opened and Rob walked in. His face lit up as though he had just received the finest of New Years' gifts when Rosamond flung herself into his arms. She was laughing and crying at the same time. Several minutes passed before she had sufficient self-control to manage coherent speech. By then, the Tirrys had tactfully left the room.

'I feared you were dead,' she whispered. 'I was afraid I would never see you again.'

'And I thought you were lost to me forever when I heard that Pyper had made off with you.' With gentle fingers, he touched her face, wiping away the tears.

Rosamond drew Rob down onto a settle, keeping his hand in hers. It was only after they were seated that his words sank in. 'You knew I was with Diggory?'

'I learned of it after Carleill captured the *Roe*.'

'Charles and the others? They are unharmed?' In her concern for Rob's safety, she had nearly forgotten to worry about her men. After all, Diggory had assured her that they would not be harmed.

'A few bruises. No more. They will be most relieved to return to your service. I do not think Charles likes the life of a sailor.'

She had to smile at that, but her expression turned to a frown an instant later. 'Is Ulick Carnsey still aboard the *Rosamond*?'

'He is, and being closely watched. Leveson will make certain he does not escape.'

'Then you know already that he is the one who killed Sir Walter?'

'I had my suspicions, especially after someone pushed Leveson overboard.'

Instead of relief, Rob's revelation left Rosamond feeling curiously deflated, but his next words gave her hope that what she had learned might still prove useful.

'We have no proof of anything,' he said. 'There were no witnesses. What have you discovered?'

'No witness to any of his crimes, but a good deal of evidence that points to his guilt. Am I free to go with you to the *Rosamond*?'

'I should like to see anyone stop us.'

'Perrot—'

'Perrot is not my master.'

'Carleill must apply to him for munitions and victuals.'

'True, and he needs the Lord Deputy's permission to chase four pirates whose ships lie some dozen miles off shore, but Carleill has already agreed to let the *Rosamond* set sail for home. She has but two culverins and two sakers to defend herself. She adds little to Carleill's fleet.'

'Does he know about the Scots?'

Rob looked at her as if she were speaking in tongues.

Rosamond supposed she should not be surprised. For all that Walsingham's spies were well organized, they were not the only intelligence gatherers at work. 'It is a pity old rivalries keep men from cooperating. If Perrot has any sense, he will even now be sharing what he knows with Carleill. The rumors of an invasion Leveson heard are true, but it is to be of Ireland, not England. *That* is what Carnsey has been so desperate to keep secret.'

'How did you learn of this?'

'From Diggory. He is Perrot's agent, even as Leveson is Walsingham's man.'

'Diggory.' The way Rob growled as he said the name and the grim expression on his face had Rosamond kissing him most thoroughly before she revealed what else she knew about the Scottish plot.

'My stepfather must have learned something more about it after talking to Trewinard, or else he was about to,' she concluded. 'He was murdered to prevent him from sending another coded message to Walsingham. It was a senseless killing in every way. From what I can gather, Walsingham already knew about Scotland's role in the endeavor.'

'But why did Carnsey turn traitor?' Rob asked. 'He is neither Irish nor Scots, and I do much doubt he is a secret Catholic.'

'In that you are mistaken.'

'He is a papist?'

'He is half Irish.'

She told him the rest of the story.

'I have learned a little of Irish history during my stay here,' she added. 'The Anglo-Irish who have lived in Ireland for centuries often betray newer English settlers to the Irish. Some spin Catholic plots at the *tuaths*, public meetings of the septs held in the hills, far from the control of the Council in Dublin. This entire island is rife with betrayals and deceits, and because the Earl of Desmond recently rebelled against the English presence in Munster, the Crown confiscated all the Desmond estates and allocated those lands, and others, to wealthy Englishmen. They plan to import new tenants from England to farm the land. The new towns that spring up throughout this plantation will provide men to defend English rule throughout this part of Ireland. Is it any wonder the native Irish grow desperate to drive us out?'

'And yet, if the invasion succeeds and mercenaries overrun the English pale, the Anglo-English who attempt to defend the land they have owned for generations will be slaughtered.'

'Now that Perrot has been forewarned, he will prevent that.'

'With a force of *pirates*?'

'No doubt it seemed a good idea at the time. Does this change things, Rob? Must you sail with Carleill's fleet?'

Deep furrows appeared in Rob's brow as he pondered his dilemma. 'I owe him my allegiance.'

'And you owe Sir Walter justice.' Rosamond's voice shook, but she pressed on. 'We can best serve that cause by taking Carnsey back to Cornwall to face the hangman.'

Clearly torn, Rob considered for a moment longer before rising from the settle. His back to Rosamond, he gave a curt, decisive nod. For good or ill, he had settled his internal argument. When he turned so that she could see his face and offered her his hand, she almost cried with relief.

FORTY-SEVEN

I t was mid-afternoon by the time Rosamond and Rob were rowed out to the *Rosamond*. Leveson leaned over the rail, watching them as they climbed aboard. It disconcerted Rosamond to see Carnsey standing right behind him.

'It is glad I am to see you safe and unharmed, Mistress Rosamond,' said the traitorous murderer.

She fought an urge to slap that crooked smile off his face.

'Will you accompany us into the cabin?' Rob asked, addressing both men. 'We needs must make plans.'

It was not until Rob closed and barred the door behind them that Sir Walter's secretary began to suspect something was wrong. His gaze darted from Rosamond to Rob and back again. 'Is aught amiss?'

'It must have been difficult,' Rosamond said, 'leaving Cornwall as a boy to live in Ireland.'

Carnsey's face lost all expression. 'What would you know about that, mistress?'

'Quite a lot, as it happens. I am persistent when it comes to asking questions and the good people of Ireland have not forgotten what happened to your grandfather.'

His right eye twitched. 'The English killed him.' His voice was flat and hard.

'They executed him, yes, and you swore to avenge him, even as I promised to bring my stepfather's killer to justice.'

Carnsey managed only a single step toward the door before Leveson grabbed him by the arm and slung him into the cabin's only chair. He held him there while Rob relieved Carnsey of his sword and dagger. Once that was accomplished, they took up positions on either side of him. Rob nodded to Rosamond to continue her questioning.

She was prepared to badger him until he confessed, but before she could resume the inquisition, a defiant gleam came into Carnsey's eyes.

'It is too late. The invasion cannot be stopped. Before the Lord Deputy can gather sufficient forces to repel them, two thousand Scots will have landed in Ireland.'

'There you are wrong,' Rosamond said. 'Perrot has known about the invasion for weeks. Walsingham has been aware of your plans even longer and has gathered forces to repel the Scottish galleys.'

'With pirates?' Carnsey laughed. 'Do you truly believe they will fight? At the first sign of trouble, they will sail in the opposite direction.'

That, Rosamond thought, annoyed by Carnsey's cocksure attitude, might depend more upon which way the wind blew than upon loyalty to a cause, but the coming battle was not her concern. There was nothing she could do that would either help or hinder Perrot's defense of the English settlers in Ireland.

'Why did you kill Sir Walter?'

'Mayhap he reminded me of the English authorities who sentenced my grandfather to death.'

'How did you kill him?' Although she was careful to keep her distance, she leaned in his direction, letting him see how much she despised him for what he had done.

'Do you wish to hear every detail?' He laughed again. 'So be it. I left Priory House in secret, walked cross-country, and used a shepherd's sling to kill him.'

'For what reason? The real one, this time.' Rosamond did not understand why he was so willing to confess and suspected a trick or an attempt to bargain, but she was too desperate for answers to quibble about the manner of getting them.

'As you will.'

If his familiar, lopsided grin was meant to disarm her, it failed miserably. Rosamond warned herself not to let down her guard.

'From the ale bench in Boscastle, I heard a part of what Trewinard told Sir Walter,' Carnsey said. 'He kept asking questions after he came home. He had a dozen informants like Trewinard. It would not have been long before he ferreted out the truth. I could not prevent him from sending one coded message to Walsingham, but I could and did put an end to any further communication.'

'And Trewinard? Why kill him?'

'I did not.'

'You arranged it. How?'

Carnsey's eyes twinkled. 'I am torn between tormenting you by leaving your questions unanswered and reveling in my own cleverness.'

Fists clenched at her sides, Rosamond refused to give him the satisfaction of hearing her beg. Silence stretched between them until she was painfully aware of the sounds of waves lapping against the hull and the cries of sea birds beyond the cabin window. In another moment, she would have broken, but Carnsey's need to boast drove him to speak first.

'When I saw how determined you were to investigate Sir Walter's murder, I knew it was only a matter of time before you decided to visit Boscastle. I arranged to eliminate the problem.'

'You sent men to kill Trewinard just because I might speak to him?' She wanted to be certain, even if that meant some of the blame fell on her own head.

Carnsey shrugged. 'A necessary precaution. He had already revealed too much to Sir Walter. What if he told you *all* he knew?'

'What more was there? That there was to be an invasion of Ireland?'

'And that some of the sea rovers sworn to fight for the Crown were prepared to run rather than fight. I had been working to undermine Walsingham's influence over them for months.'

'And so we learned nothing, and were thwarted in every attempt to find out more. But you must have known there was no reason to attack us at Tintagel.'

'I knew nothing of the kind. You had talked to Honor Piers.'

'But *she* knew nothing.'

'She knew enough. She knew I had been talking to pardoned pirates. We used her cottage for some of those meetings.'

His casual attitude infuriated Rosamond. She took a step toward him, halting only when both Rob and Leveson tensed.

'You might at least have discovered if she told us anything before you gave the order to attack us and kill her.'

'Oh, I received her report. I paid her a visit as soon as you left her.'

Rosamond stared at him in disbelief. 'Then she must have

told you that she gave nothing away. Neither the attack on us or her death were necessary.'

Unmoved by her outrage, Carnsey kept talking. He seemed proud of his actions. 'I persuaded Honor to meet me in Boscastle in two days' time. By then, or so I fondly hoped, I would be the sole survivor of a murderous attack by a band of brigands. I had just time enough to give them their orders before I returned to the inn. That you'd decided to leave Padstow at once made no difference. The attack was already set for Tintagel on the following day.'

'Did they kill Trewinard, too, and Honor?' Rosamond asked. 'You were seen giving them a pouch filled with coins.'

He eyed her speculatively. 'Do you mean to bring them to trial, too? I wish you luck. They are a band of mindless brigands, too stupid to manage the simple task of killing you. Yes, they did beat Trewinard to death, but I killed Honor Piers with my own two hands.' He held them up in front of him, admiring their strength. 'I crept out of the alehouse in the middle of the night and met her by arrangement on the cliffs above the village. Contrary to what everyone seems to think, she was fully capable of reaching Boscastle on her own. She hid the skiff in a sea cave and walked to our meeting place.'

For the first time, Leveson spoke. 'How is it I did not hear you? We slept in the same room at the alehouse.'

'You were drugged. You all were. I brought a sleeping powder with me from Priory House.'

'It was in the ale,' Rosamond said, remembering that Carnsey had brought the jug to the table that evening, and how heavily Rob had slept. She had not because she had drunk very little.

'I threw her into the sea,' Carnsey continued. 'I did not expect her body to wash up in the inner harbor, but in the end there was no harm done.'

Rosamond felt ill. So many murders! Carnsey might have wanted the English out of Ireland to avenge his grandfather's death, but it seemed to her that he had also killed for his own satisfaction. He'd reveled in the deaths of Sir Walter and Honor Piers.

Rob circled the chair until he was face-to-face with Carnsey. 'Did you intend all along to sail with us to meet Carleill?'

Rosamond stepped back, content to let her husband take over the interrogation.

'I seized an opportunity.' Carnsey looked smug.

'As you seized the opportunity to push Leveson overboard?'

A glance at Carnsey's intended victim showed Rosamond a calm demeanor, but she suspected that Walsingham's man was seething with barely suppressed rage just beneath the surface. Her own temper was close to the boiling point. This callous fiend did not deserve to live. She'd be glad to see him hang.

'I hoped to dispose of you both,' Carnsey admitted, 'and of Carleill, as well. What a victory that would have been!'

His self-satisfied smirk was more than Leveson could stand. He went for Carnsey's throat, only to find himself grasping empty air. Weasel-fast and twisty, the prisoner slipped out of the chair and bolted for the door. Rob and Leveson both moved at once, attempting to stop him before he could lift the bar. In their haste, they collided, giving Carnsey time to escape the cabin.

Rosamond had been farthest from the door but she was the first to gain the deck. Carnsey was already at the rail, preparing to heave himself over. The boat that had brought Rosamond and Rob to the ship was still tied up below. If Carnsey dropped into it and rowed fast enough, he stood a good chance of getting away.

Rosamond did not stop to think. Instinct and long hours of practice put her boot dagger in her hand and sent it flying through the air. As Carnsey began his descent, he had to turn to face the hull. Rosamond's aim was straight and true. Her blade struck him square in the chest.

With a cry, he fell backward, landing in the water with a tremendous splash.

Feeling as though she was walking in mud flats at low tide, Rosamond made her way to the rail and looked down. Carnsey's body floated just below, face up. The sight of her dagger imbedded in his heart had her swallowing convulsively.

Rob came up beside her to slide his arm around her waist. She turned and buried her face in his doublet and burst into tears. She was not sorry Carnsey was dead, but it appalled her that she had been the one who had taken his life.

Rubbing her back, murmuring soothing words, Rob waited

out the storm. After a long time, he spoke to her in a quiet voice. 'He'd have been hanged for his crimes. Or worse.'

'I know.' She sniffled and took the handkerchief he offered.

'He wanted revenge.'

'So did I, but . . .'

Rob framed her face with his hands. He waited until she met his eyes to speak, his voice soft, comforting, and filled with his love for her. 'This is justice, Ros, not revenge.'

'Yes.' She drew in a steadying breath. 'We have done what we set out to do. Now I would very much like to go home.'

He kissed her forehead. 'How convenient, then,' he said, 'that we are not only already on board a swift ship, but are also blessed with a freshening wind.'

AUTHOR'S NOTE

A number of pirates were pardoned by the Crown in 1583 and 1584 and recruited to serve their country at sea. A band of Scottish mercenaries did invade Ireland in the summer of 1584. They were defeated, but not by the pirates, who did scatter at their first opportunity. Christopher Carleill and Sir John Perrot clashed, probably because Perrot was no friend to Sir Francis Walsingham. They worked at cross-purposes throughout Carleill's time in Ireland. Diggory Pyper was also a real person, although his whereabouts in 1584 are unknown. The rest of this story came from my imagination.

I am greatly indebted to the nautical expertise of James L. Nelson. He kindly read my seafaring chapters for accuracy. Any errors that remain are my own. I am also to blame for any mistakes in the Cornish language or in the dialect of English spoken in Cornwall in the sixteenth century. The sources I consulted on linguistics, as well as other subjects, can be found in the bibliography at www.KathyLynnEmerson.com. One book, however, deserves special mention here. Reading Ruth Goodman's *How to Be a Tudor* reminded me of dozens of small details of Tudor life that I once knew but had forgotten. She also does a magnificent job of explaining aspects of daily living that seem downright peculiar in the twenty-first century.

I would also like to thank the Historical Novel Society and David Blixt for offering a hands-on sword and dagger workshop at the North American conference in Denver in 2015. Rosamond's skill with bladed weapons improved greatly as a result.